THE CUCHILLO PLAINS

**Center Point
Large Print**

**This Large Print Book carries the
Seal of Approval of N.A.V.H.**

THE CUCHILLO PLAINS

A Western Duo

RAY HOGAN

CENTER POINT PUBLISHING
THORNDIKE, MAINE

Library of Congress Cataloging-in-Publication Data

Hogan, Ray, 1908-
  The Cuchillo Plains : a western duo / Ray Hogan.
    p. cm.
  ISBN 978-1-60285-442-0 (library binding : alk. paper)
  1. Large type books. I. Hogan, Ray, 1908- Lawless strip. II. Title.

PS3558.O3473C83 2009
813'.54--dc22

2008053183

TABLE OF CONTENTS

The Lawless Strip
7

The Cuchillo Plains
135

The Lawless Strip

I

For seven scorching days and bitter nights he had been on their trail—a hunched, persistent shape on a bay horse, dogging the three outlaws like a silent, deadly shadow. And now the chase was about to end.

In the beginning they had known of his presence and that fact, he finally realized, was defeating him. As long as he pursued, they would continue to run and never permit him to draw within striking distance. And so Sam Kyler had come to a decision; he had chosen a time and place when he was clearly visible to them and turned back.

He took no chance on the ruse failing. They would make certain he had given up before relaxing their vigilance, and to convince them he wasted ten miles of riding, cutting east through the rabbitbrush-choked arroyos and across the snakeweed-covered hills before he began to circle.

The scheme had worked. The outlaws were just below him now, moving leisurely, no more than a quarter mile distant. It would be easy to close in and capture them—or have it out with guns if they so chose. And then the long, tedious hunt would be at an end.

Kyler's mouth hardened as he looked down upon

the men. Joe Grimsby, thick shoulders slumped, was apparently asleep in the saddle. Shad Collins rode with one leg hooked over the horn as he sought to relieve his tired muscles. Ed Tilton was rolling himself a quirly, his elbows extended as he worked with paper and tobacco. Once they had been his friends—now all were deadly enemies, men he must face and possibly kill, or else be killed in the confrontation. The change had come abruptly, a little more than a week ago when they had all been working for Arch Clayborn on his A-Bar-C spread in Texas.

The four of them had been fairly close companions both on the job and off, and, when Clayborn had turned over to Kyler a wallet containing $1,000 in cash with which to pay for a small herd of cattle he had purchased from a New Mexico rancher, Sam had naturally chosen his three friends to assist him in driving back the stock. On his own since the age of fifteen, knocking about from job to job, town to town, Sam Kyler had come to know the way of the world only too well; he was aware that a desire for money could do strange and terrible things to a man's mind and character, but he never expected to have the fact driven home to him so forcibly—and by those he considered trustworthy.

It occurred on the second night out as they lay in their blankets around a dying fire. He had awakened to an unnatural sound, opened his eyes to glimpse Grimsby standing over him, arm upraised. He had tried to dodge the blow but the inner warning had come too late. The outlaw's gun barrel had smashed into his skull with a sickening force.

Near daylight Kyler had regained consciousness and struggled to his feet. Clayborn's $1,000 was gone—and with it Grimsby, Tilton, and Shad Collins. It was noon, however, before he had fully collected his scattered senses and located the tracks of the departed horses. Immediately he had begun the pursuit.

There had been no doubt in Sam Kyler's mind that he would eventually overtake the outlaws; he was that sort of individual—patient, determined, and inflexible once he had committed himself. What did concern him then was what Arch Clayborn would conclude when he discovered his foreman had dropped out of sight with the money entrusted to his care.

Clayborn had been a good man to work for, and Sam at first had intended to pause long enough in some town and send a letter to the rancher giving him full particulars as to what had happened. But as the days wore on and the trail of the outlaws led steadily north, missing all settlements of any size where he could have dispatched a note, the advisability of not getting in touch with Clayborn became more apparent. By then, he knew the rancher would have made up his mind, and closed it. No explanation would suffice. The only thing that would satisfy him would be the return of his money.

Thus Sam Kyler had chosen that course; he would recover the $1,000 stolen from him and return it to Clayborn. It would be the only means by which he could convince the rancher of his innocence. Besides, writing Clayborn could prove dangerous; likely his first move, upon learning the whereabouts of his missing foreman, would be to notify the law. Kyler did not want that. Because of his own misplaced trust he had lost Clayborn's money; by his own efforts he would recover it. Locked in a cell somewhere he would be powerless to accomplish it.

He reached down, rubbed at the bay's sweat-soaked neck, his eyes never straying from the outlaws. He had no liking for the chore that lay ahead, but he knew there was no avoiding it. During the last year of the war, while serving under the command of bearded Bill Hardee in the Carolina campaign, he had witnessed enough bloodshed to last him for an entire lifetime. But even there it had not ended. When the war was over, he had become a shotgun guard in the gold-rich country of Nevada; later, he had served a time as a deputy marshal, following that with a stint at ramrodding trail herds from Texas to the Kansas markets.

When he had signed up with Arch Clayborn as foreman, he had figured the heavy .45 in his holster and the sawed-off, ten-gauge shotgun hanging from his saddle with which he was so proficient could be put away for good insofar as his fellow man was concerned. Now he was again faced with using them.

That thought brought a stillness to his features, but after a moment he shrugged off the melancholy mood and brushed at the sweat beading his forehead. There are times when a man must accept and discharge a disagreeable duty. Pushing his hat to the back of his head, he drew his six-gun, thumbed open the loading gate, and checked the cylinder. It was ready. Leaning forward, he pulled the shotgun from its boot, made certain of its charge. Satisfied with both weapons, he touched the bay with his spurs lightly and moved out from behind the clump of cedar where he had halted.

Immediately he hauled back on the reins. A sound had reached him. A cry for help, he thought. Frowning, he sat motionlessly in the saddle, listening into the heat-filled hush. Somewhere below a jay scolded noisily. A ground squirrel chattered an angry reply. Then the cry came again.

"Help! If they's somebody up there on the trail . . . how about givin' me a hand?"

II

Sam Kyler turned, threw his glance upslope. The voice seemed to have come from that point. He could see nothing but dense brush and mounds of rock.

He looked back to the outlaws. They were drawing away steadily. Unless he moved in upon them at once, he would again fall far behind, perhaps even lose them and be forced to start the search all over again. But no decent man ignored the cries of another in desperate trouble. Jaw set, Kyler wheeled the bay, headed up the mountain. Winding in and out of the sage, the squat cedars, and piles of boulders, he climbed a short distance and broke out onto the rim of a butte.

"Careful . . . up there!"

At the warning shout he halted the bay and dismounted. Crossing to the edge of the cliff, he looked over. An old man, scratched and bleeding, was clinging to a shoulder of rock ten feet or so down on the face of the bluff. Farther down, in a maze of boulders, lay his dead horse.

The old cowpuncher managed a tight grin. "Be obliged was you to toss me a rope, mister. Afeared this here hunk of rock ain't goin' to stay put much longer."

Hurriedly Kyler returned to the bay, obtained his lariat, and retraced his steps to the rim of the butte.

Lowering a loop, he said: "Put it under your arms . . . I'll haul you up."

He waited until the cowpuncher was ready, then going back to the bay, he threw a hitch around the saddle horn and led the horse down the slope.

"That's good!" the old man sang out a moment later.

Sam halted. The cowpuncher was over the edge of the butte and on solid ground. He glanced off in the direction the outlaws had taken. They couldn't have gotten far. Gathering in his rope as he went, Kyler returned to the bluff.

The old rider was sprawled out, breathing heavily. His worn clothing was ragged and his lean face and neck were cut and scratched from the fall, but he was still able to muster a smile.

"Sure am grateful to you, friend. Had about made up my mind I'd be joinin' old Buck down there in the bottom of the cañon."

Kyler squatted beside him. "You hurt?"

"Nope . . . nothin' bad, I reckon. Got skinned up a mite and sort of twisted my leg. Expect I'll live." He extended a weathered hand. "Folks what knows me calls me Wasco."

"Glad to know you, Wasco. I'm Sam Kyler. How long you been hanging onto that rock?"

"Since daylight. Sure was gettin' right uncomfortable."

Kyler finished coiling his rope, got to his feet.

He looked again to the north, came back to Wasco. "What happened?"

Wasco swore, wagged his grizzled head. His iron gray hair was long and hung about his face, making it appear even sharper.

"Danged bobcat spooked old Buck. Went shyin' too close to the edge. Next thing I knew I was hangin' onto that there ledge and Buck was kickin' his last in all them rocks below me."

The old cowpuncher sat up, brushed at the dirt plastered to the front of his linsey-woolsey shirt. "Reckon you're a stranger to these parts. Don't recollect ever layin' eyes on you afore."

"Guess I am," Kyler replied, turning to hang his rope on the bay.

Wasco frowned, then grinned. "Ain't meanin' to be nosy, Sam. Just talkin'. Ain't every day a man gets his neck saved."

"Forget it," Kyler said in the same clipped way. "You live around here close?"

"Nope. Just ridin' through. Ain't got no real home . . . unless you figure now and then when I get myself a job somewheres."

Sam Kyler continued to work with his rope, securing it to the saddle. Wasco couldn't be left to fend for himself. Without a horse, and having an injured leg, he wouldn't last long. Unconsciously Kyler glanced once more in the direction taken by the outlaws. If he delayed to help Wasco, he would surely lose them.

"Was three, four riders by here earlier this mornin'," Wasco said. "Done a lot of hollerin' but seems they didn't hear me." He paused, his wise old eyes pulled down into slits as he studied Kyler. "They got somethin' to do with your bein' here? You maybe chasin' them?"

Kyler shrugged, said: "Think you can ride?"

The old cowpuncher chuckled. "Reckon I had that comin'. Always stickin' my nose in other people's business. Wouldn't surprise me none was you to knock it slantwise just to be teachin' me a lesson."

"I'm trailing them," Kyler said. "And I'm losing them . . . fast. How about it?"

Wasco bobbed his head, pulled himself upright. "Leg's a mite stiff," he said, taking a few experimental steps. "But I reckon I can make out, seein' as how you're in a hurry."

"Don't aim for you to walk. Asked if you could ride. The bay can carry us both."

"Sure would slow you down a powerful lot. Better just go on."

"Not that short of time. There a town anywhere near here?"

"Sure. Place called Jericho. Real stem-winder of a town. But it ain't so close. Reckon it'd be dark, time we could make it."

Kyler considered thoughtfully. "Which way?"

"North. Way you was headed. And them others?"

Sam Kyler relaxed slightly. That was welcome

news. The outlaws, on the move for over a week and now believing themselves free of him, would undoubtedly halt in the first town they reached. Perhaps his stopping to aid Wasco wouldn't prove so costly, after all.

A moment later Wasco corroborated his thoughts, and then added: "Say, you ain't no lawman, are you?"

"No . . . why?"

"Jericho ain't exactly no healthy spot for a badge toter. Lot of the wild bunch hangs out there."

That would suit Joe Grimsby and the others. They would feel right at home with their kind—and believe themselves to be safe. Sam nodded at Wasco.

"Let's move out."

The old cowpuncher flung a glance toward the bluff, clawed at the whiskers on his chin. "Well, if you ain't mindin' too much, everythin' I own in this here world's down there on Buck. Sort of like to collect it first."

Kyler said—"Sure."—and began to shake loose his rope for the second time. Securing one end to a stout juniper, he tested it briefly, then walked to the rim of the butte. "You want the whole works?"

"Sure would be obliged."

Bracing himself against the taut rope, Sam went over the edge and lowered himself to where the horse lay. He was in for another half hour's delay, he realized, but, if the outlaws stopped in Jericho, it wouldn't matter. If for some reason they did not—well, he'd just have to start all over again.

Stripping the dead animal of its gear did not take long. Fastening it to the end of the lariat, Kyler waited for Wasco to draw it up and return the rope to him.

When that was done, the old cowpuncher called down: "You want I should tie onto the bay, let him do the work?"

"Let him rest . . . I can make it," Sam answered.

He climbed out of the deep wash, going up hand over hand, digging the pointed toes of his boots into the steep side of the bluff to assist him in the ascent. When he reached level ground, breathing heavily, he paused, stared curiously at Wasco. The rider was strapping on an ancient pistol that evidently had been inside his saddlebags.

"You figure on having to use that iron when we get to Jericho?"

"If it's needful," Wasco said. "I ain't no greenhorn when it comes to handlin' a gun. Just never seen no use of packin' it around less'n there was a reason."

"And now you do?"

Wasco hawked, spat. "With what I figure you got in mind to do, you'll be needin' somebody watchin' your backside."

Kyler shook his head. "No need for you to mix in my trouble."

"Maybe, but seems I already have. Wasn't for me you'd done slipped up on them sidewinders and had them hog-tied for market. Now the job's goin' to be a heap harder. Only right I return the favor."

The belt and holster in place, Wasco made a few testing passes at drawing his old cedar-handled weapon. That he was no stranger to the six-gun was apparent. Kyler smiled at him.

"Be pleased to have you siding me," he said. "Now, climb aboard and I'll hand you up your gear."

Wasco crossed to the bay, crawled stiffly to a seat behind the cantle of Kyler's saddle. Sleeving the sweat from his jaws, he looked down at Sam. "I'm all set."

Kyler hoisted the old rider's belongings to the back of the bay, resting them partly on the man's shoulders and partly on the hindquarters of the horse, and then swung to the saddle. The bay bunched slightly at the load but he made no move to balk.

"You figure he can make it?" Wasco asked as they turned downslope.

Sam nodded. "Be slow going, but he can do it."

III

The bay made better time than expected. It was shortly before five o'clock when they broke suddenly from a cluster of round-topped hills and saw Jericho before them.

Kyler pulled up at the end of the street. The settlement was considerably larger than he had expected and he made this observation to Wasco.

"Got a reason to be," the old cowpuncher said. "Only town in this part of the Strip."

"Strip?"

"Yeah. . . . We're in the panhandle west of the Indian Territory. Maybe you've heard it called No-Man's-Land. Lots of folks call it that 'cause it ain't claimed by nobody."

Sam nodded. "See now why the outlaws like it."

He allowed his gaze to probe the town slowly. The single street was narrow and dusty. He could see a hotel, the Fargo; it was a ramshackle, sun-grayed building with a high false front. Beyond it was a general store, a livery barn and corral, an office where a doctor and a barber plied their professions. Elsewhere there was a feed store, a café, gun and harness shop, several saloons—the largest of which offered gambling and dancing as well as liquor. A white-steepled church, badly in need of paint, stood at the far end of the town and beyond it lay a scatter of residences.

There were no pedestrians in sight, but in front of the Fargo he saw a buggy and a half dozen horses drawn up to the rail. His glance drifted on, came to an abrupt halt when his eyes settled upon the three horses tethered at the side of the Palace, the largest saloon.

Kyler's mouth hardened. The mounts were those of Grimsby, Tilton, and Shad Collins. Luck was with him. They had done as expected.

"Any sign of them jaspers you're huntin'?" Wasco asked.

Kyler said: "Horses there at the Palace. The ones they were ridin'."

"Figured they'd hole up here. What's next?"

"Little talk with them," Kyler said, and put the bay in motion.

They moved on down the street. As they drew abreast the Fargo, Sam was conscious of several men filing out onto the porch, lining up to watch him pass. He gave them a brief glance. Cattlemen and several merchants, he guessed. Having some sort of a meeting.

He headed directly for the Palace, wasting no moments on preliminaries. The café, he noted as the bay walked through the ankle-deep dust, was called Mrs. Ashwick's. The doctor's name was Patton—Carl Patton, M.D. The general store bore the sign SOL WEIL in faded lettering across its front. Fred Turnbull operated the harness shop. Swinging his horse up to the Palace's hitch rack, he sat quietly while Wasco let his gear fall to the ground and dropped beside it. Only then did Kyler leave the saddle. He stood there for a moment, his face still and hard-cornered as he looked off toward the flats and then, seemingly almost regretfully, he came back to the business at hand.

Reaching down, he touched the handle of the pistol of his hip as though assuring himself of its presence. Then, half turning, he drew the short-barreled shotgun from its scabbard, slung it into the crook of his left arm. He paused, glanced at Wasco.

"Still no reason you should mix in this."

"Got a dang' good reason, far as I'm concerned," the old cowpuncher replied.

Sam Kyler shrugged, said: "All right. But it's my fight."

"Sure, sure . . . won't go hornin' in unless you need me."

Kyler nodded, moved up the steps to the gallery of the Palace, and walked slowly toward the batwing doors.

He paused there, Wasco a stride behind him. Inside, he could hear the drone of conversation, the laughter of women. A man swore in a deep voice and a chair scraped across a bare floor. Again he touched the pistol at his hip, and then moved forward, pushed into the smoke-filled room.

He rocked slightly to one side as he collided with

a cowpuncher on his way out. The man staggered, off balance, face going taut with anger.

"Watch where you're goin' . . . dammit!"

Kyler, never removing his eyes from the patrons ranged along the bar, nodded briefly. "Sorry."

"Sorry . . . nothin'!" the cowpuncher growled, and reached for Sam's arm. "I ain't takin'. . . ."

"Keep movin', son," Wasco cut in quietly, blocking the rider's way. "Sure ain't the right time to be startin' a ruckus with him."

Kyler walked deeper into the room, taking slow, easy steps, paying no more attention to the offended rider. He came to a halt a third of the distance to the bar. Abruptly his drifting glance settled on three men seated at a corner table.

The murmur of voices died gradually. In the hush Sam saw Collins and his two companions lift their heads lazily, look questioningly toward the crowd. When they saw him, they stiffened with surprise.

Men crowded through the batwings behind Kyler. He heard the thud of their boot heels, flipped his gaze to the backbar mirror, as quickly returned it to the outlaws. It was a group of townsmen and ranchers coming in for a drink. The ones he had noticed on the porch of the Fargo. He dismissed them from his mind.

Moving deliberately, watchfully, Kyler headed for the outlaws. A dozen paces short he stopped. From the tail of his eye he saw Wasco saunter up to the bar, take a position against it. He placed his direct glance on Grimsby, Ed Tilton, and the younger Collins. In the deep hush his low voice reached every corner of the room.

"I'll take the money."

Joe Grimsby forced a smile. His teeth showed whitely through the dark stubble of his beard. He nodded to Collins.

"Told you we should've done the job up right. Now we got to do it all over again."

There was a forced quality to his voice that betrayed the confidence he was attempting to display. Shad Collins made no reply. Tilton shifted nervously, careful to keep his hands in sight on the table. Out in the street a dog barked, and at Calderone's stable an anvil sang musically as a blacksmith worked at his trade.

"Stand up!"

Kyler's voice was sharp, carried the promise of violence. Collins rose at once, overturning his chair in his haste. Tilton followed. Joe Grimsby did not move. Kyler studied the man coldly for a long ten seconds, then shifted the wicked-looking shotgun to his right hand. Lazily Grimsby pulled himself upright.

"The money," Sam repeated. "Take off the belt. Lay it on the table."

Tilton flung a worried glance at Grimsby. His eyes were abnormally bright and sweat glistened on his skin. "For chrissake . . . give it to him!"

The fixed smile hung on Grimsby's lips. He

shook his head. "What's eatin' you jaspers? Three of us . . . only one of him."

"Odds don't mean nothin' to him," Shad Collins said.

Grimsby's eyes flickered with a cunning light. He shrugged. "Reckon any man's real big holdin' a crowd killer."

Sam Kyler considered the outlaw for a time. He shifted the shotgun back to his left hand, carefully laid it on a near table. Someone at the bar moved, knocked a glass to the floor. At the shattering sound the outlaws jumped. Kyler seemed not to hear.

"He ain't nothin' but a man . . . same as me," Grimsby muttered as though trying to convince himself.

"You taking off that money belt?" Kyler pressed quietly.

Joe Grimsby shook his head. "You want it . . . you take it."

Kyler's hand swept down, came up swiftly with his .45 at full cock. "You're calling the play," he said, moving forward slowly. "If you don't figure to die suddenly, stand easy."

Reaching out with his left hand, he ripped Grimsby's shirt front open. The dull glint of a buckle told him he had guessed right. The older man was carrying the money belt.

Sam flicked Tilton and the sullen-faced Collins with a calculating glance, and then released the tongue of the buckle. The belt came free. He stepped back, yanked the leather-pocketed strap from the outlaw's waist.

Grimsby yelled. He lunged to one side, clawed for his pistol. In the same instant Ed Tilton threw himself to the opposite direction, went for his gun.

Kyler fired as Grimsby went to his knees, triggering his weapon. Sam loosed one bullet at the outlaw, wheeled to Tilton. Both guns blasted— almost as one. Glass tinkled as Tilton's bullet smashed into a shelf behind the bar, destroyed a pyramid of beer mugs.

Kyler, never breaking his smooth spin, faced Collins. The young outlaw stood with his hands raised above his head.

"Not me!" he yelled frantically.

Sam Kyler's half-bent shape relaxed slightly. A hard grin pulled at his lips. "Maybe you'd like me to turn my back."

Collins shook his head. "Wasn't none of my idea . . . taking the money."

"Seems you went along with it all the same."

"Nothing I could do."

Kyler raked the outlaw with his cold glance. "You had a choice. You could've sided with me. Now, step out here . . . and keep your hands up high."

Collins moved from behind the table, circling Tilton's lifeless body. A sigh ran through the saloon as tension eased. Kyler motioned to Wasco.

"Take his gun."

The old cowpuncher limped to Shad Collins's side, pulled the man's weapon from its holster, and shoved it under his belt.

"Go get the law."

Wasco started to turn. The bartender said: "We ain't got no lawman, mister. Buried the last one about a month ago."

Kyler frowned. He glanced at the bartender, tossed the money belt to him.

"Name's Sam Kyler," he said. "These three men jumped me back in Texas, robbed me of that belt. Open it. Ought to find a thousand dollars and a letter from a man named Clayburn introducing me to another man called Blye. Was on my way to buy some stock for Clayborn when it happened."

The bartender laid the belt on the counter and opened its pockets. He removed the folds of currency and began to thumb through the bills. Finally he looked up.

"Letter's here . . . but there ain't no thousand dollars. I make it about nine hundred."

Kyler's jaw hardened. He stared at Collins. The outlaw shifted nervously. "Grimsby must've got it. He was paying for everything."

Sam pointed at the dead man. "Drag him over here."

Collins turned obediently and, taking his one-time partner by the arm, pulled him into the open.

"Dig into his pockets. I want what's left of the money he took."

Collins hesitated momentarily, then dropped to his knees, and began to rifle Grimsby's clothing. He located some loose change and a small roll of bills.

"Count it."

Shad sorted through the currency, ticked off the silver. "Twenty dollars, thereabouts."

Kyler nodded. He would have to make up the loss himself. "Give it to the bartender," he directed.

Collins crossed to the counter, laid the money before the aproned man who added it to that in the pouches. That done, Kyler picked up the belt, hung it over his shoulder.

"There a bank in this town?"

"Nope. Dalhart . . . that's the closest."

"Had one once," someone volunteered, "but the outlaws busted it . . . raidin' it all the time."

Kyler accepted the information with no change of expression. He placed his attention on Collins. "Don't aim to be bothered with you," he said. "Get off your knees and start riding . . . and don't come back. We ever cross trails again it'll be a different story."

Shad Collins stirred sullenly. He glanced at his gun tucked under Wasco's belt. "My iron?"

"Won't need it," Kyler said coldly. "Move out." He shifted his eyes to Wasco. "See that he does."

The outlaw, trailed by the old cowpuncher, started immediately for the door. Kyler picked up his shotgun, turned to watch Collins leave. At once an excited buzz of voices broke out.

A tall, graying man dressed in the everyday work clothes of a rancher detached himself from a group standing at the far end of the bar and began to work his way through the crowd. He was one of those who had come in last, Sam recalled. He glanced inquiringly at the older man who halted before him.

"Something on your mind?"

The rancher smiled. "Sure is, Mister Kyler. Name's Tolliver. We'd like to talk to you."

IV

Kyler settled slowly on his heels. Being confronted by irate citizens, indignant over some incident such as had just transpired there in the Palace, was not new to him. Tolliver, however, was smiling.

"What about?"

"A job," the rancher replied.

Out in the street there was the quick drum of a horse pulling away fast. A moment later Wasco pushed through the batwings, came back into the room.

"Took off like the heel flies was after him," he said, grinning.

Sam nodded, looked again to Tolliver. "Who said I was hunting a job?"

"Nobody. Just figured you might be interested."

"We ever meet before?"

Tolliver shook his head. "Recognized you when you rode in. Saw you down in Texas once, but you don't know me. We're willing to pay plenty for the kind of help you could give us."

"We?"

Tolliver waved carelessly toward the group of men still standing at the end of the bar. "Cattlemen's Association. Some of the merchants."

Kyler considered. Curious, he asked: "How much is plenty?"

"Well . . . we haven't time to get together, and come up with a figure, but I'd say several hundred dollars. Be about a week's work."

That kind of money could only mean squatter trouble, or rustlers, possibly a range war. Kyler shrugged. "Guess it's my gun you're figuring to hire."

Tolliver smiled frankly. "Guess you could say that. Before you make up your mind to say no, why not let us talk it over with you?"

"No harm in listening."

"Right. Just give me about thirty minutes to get the men together. We've been holding a meeting over in the Fargo Hotel. I'll call them back, see you there."

Sam said: "Fine. Gives us a chance to get a bite to eat." He paused, pointed at Wasco, added: "That offer include my partner?"

"Sure does," Tolliver said, and, wheeling, rejoined his friends.

Wasco moved in closer. "Now, what's that all about?"

"Tell you later," Kyler answered, and crossed to the bar. Reaching into his pocket, he produced a double eagle, laid it on the counter. Parting with it would leave him almost broke but he felt the obligation was his.

"This ought to cover the burying," he said to the bartender. "If it doesn't, let me know."

"Be enough," the man said. "I'll see to it."

"And there's two horses out at the side of the building. Wasco, here, wants the black. Somebody else can have the other one. Maybe you know a family who could use it."

The bartender's face brightened. "Bet I do, Mister Kyler. Folks by the name of Lindsay. Mare of theirs up and died with the colic the other day. They sure do need a horse."

"Obliged to you if you'll see they get it."

"Can have the gear offen the black, too," Wasco said.

The bartender smiled again. "They'll be mighty grateful to you both. And I expect they'll be wantin' to thank you personal. You be around?"

"Doubt it," Kyler said. "You just see they get it.

That's all the thanks we need." Turning to Wasco, he said—"Let's get something to eat."—and headed for the doorway.

They stepped out onto the porch, immediately drawing the attention of a dozen or so persons scattered along the board sidewalk. Ignoring their curious glances, they waded through the dust of the street and entered the restaurant. The place was empty and they had their choice of a half dozen tables. Selecting one near the window that afforded them a good view of the town, they sat down.

Mrs. Ashwick proved to be a young woman somewhere in her late twenties. Attractive and neat, she came from the rear of the building and advanced in quick, brisk steps and halted before them. She had brown eyes, Sam noted, and, when she spoke, her voice was low and firm.

"I expect the town has already thanked you for what you've done. Let me add mine."

Kyler looked at her in surprise. "Thanked me? For what?"

"Ridding us of those outlaws. Men like that pretty well have their own way around here now."

Kyler shifted on his chair. "Was a personal matter, ma'am. Had nothing to do with your town."

"Nevertheless, it was a big favor. Have you been approached yet about the job?"

Sam stared at her. Things certainly got around fast. He nodded. "We're meeting with Tolliver and the others in a half hour."

Mrs. Ashwick bit at her lip angrily. "Might have known the ranchers would step in first!"

Kyler shook his head helplessly. "Don't rightly know what you're talking about."

"The marshal's job. We need a good man to fill the vacancy left when our last lawman was killed. Not that he was much good. Outlaws ran wild . . . sometimes actually took over the town. Not safe around here for anyone any more."

"Sounds like you sure do need a lawman," Wasco drawled. "Maybe three or four."

"One would be enough . . . if he had the courage to stand up to the outlaws," Mrs. Ashwick said. "That's why I hoped the men had spoken . . . to. . . ." Her voice trailed off into silence.

"Maybe they intend to," Kyler said, more to relieve the awkward moment than anything else.

"Too late now. If Tom Tolliver and the ranchers have already talked to you. . . ."

"All it amounts to so far . . . talk. And we haven't done much of that. Like I said, we're meeting them later."

"You'll go to work for them," she said wearily. "The ranchers always get their way."

Sam Kyler shrugged. He didn't know what it was all about but it seemed everyone was taking a lot for granted. "Could be," he said. "But there's a little matter everybody's overlooking. I'm not wanting a job. I've got one . . . back in Texas. Leastwise, I figure I have once I get things cleared up."

Mrs. Ashwick sighed, straightened the front of her white apron. "What would you like to eat?"

"Steak and potatoes," Kyler said promptly. "Plenty of coffee. And some pie." He glanced at Wasco. "Suit you?"

"Right down to a frog's hair. Been doin' my own cookin' for so long I don't hardly know what a good meal looks like."

Mrs. Ashwick turned away, returned immediately with mugs of coffee and a plate of warm biscuits and butter. "This will tide you over until I get the meat fried," she said, and again retired.

Wasco took a deep swallow of coffee and reached for a biscuit. "What you reckon this here job is Tolliver was yappin' about?"

"Hard to say. Seems to be worth plenty to him . . . and the others."

"You goin' to be interested?"

Kyler studied his cup. "Don't know. Figure I can go back to work for Clayborn after I explain what happened. But I'm not sure I want to. Felt good traveling again."

"Gets a powerful hold on a man, all right. Ain't ever been able to shuck it myself."

"Tolliver said it would take about a week. If the job and the pay's right, you willing to sign on?"

"Ain't ag'in' it. Lot depends on what you do."

Kyler glanced at the old cowpuncher and smiled. It was good having him around. He nodded. "Soon as we eat we'll go see what it's all about."

V

Sam Kyler and Wasco halted as they entered the Fargo and turned left into a shabby, dust-covered lobby. They stood silently, glancing over the withered deer heads and faded lithographs suspended from the walls, the scratched tables and sagging chairs, the threadbare carpeting that covered the floor. An octagon-shaped clock with Roman numerals faced them from an opposite corner, its hands locked at high noon, the pendulum motionless on dead center.

Men had gathered near the back of the room, and, as Kyler touched them with his look, Tom Tolliver wheeled abruptly and came forward.

"Glad you showed up. Was thinkin' maybe you wouldn't."

"Said we'd be here," Kyler replied laconically, following the rancher back to where the others waited. He glanced about.

Tolliver said: "Reckon first thing is to introduce you two." He pointed to a squat man on the extreme left. "That's Claude Hayman. Runs the Lazy H. Next to him is Al Pritchard, of the Pitchfork outfit. Then comes Bill Denby, the Box D. Bill's wife is the schoolteacher here. This is Otto Schmidt. Calls his place the Wagon Wheel. You ever get real hungry, drop by and have a meal with him. Be the best cookin' you ever tasted."

Schmidt's broad, beet-red face broke into a wide smile. "It is welcome you are, anytime, Mister Kyler. And Mister Wasco."

Tolliver was working hard at selling him on the proposition they intended to offer, Sam realized. Again he wondered what it was all about, the men were anxious—and the pay was unusually high.

"Fellow with the gray suit there is Sol Weil, one of our local merchants. Runs the general merchandise store. That's Rufe Eggert behind him. Got a saloon down the street. Then we have Dave Simon. He's the youngest and the newest around here. He's doing fine with his D-Bar-S spread . . . unless he runs into bad luck. Man with the white hat next to him is Pete Clark. Pete's Circle Seven is down in the south corner of the Strip."

Tolliver paused when he came to the last of the group, a sharp-faced, hard-eyed man with gray hair who sat forward in his chair, both hands on the curved handle of a cane.

"This is Shinn Thompson. Owns Spade . . . the biggest ranch in the country. And the oldest."

Unlike the others Thompson did not offer his hand, merely nodded. Tolliver turned to Kyler. "Not everybody's here. Charlie Kinsman, who owns the Palace, is out of town, and there's a couple of ranchers who couldn't make it, but I guess you could say this is a pretty representative bunch."

Blunt and to the point, Thompson said: "You lookin' for a job?"

Equally blunt, Kyler shrugged. "Got a job. But I told Tolliver I'd hear you out. What's the deal?"

Tolliver motioned to a worn, leather-covered couch. "Sit down. Both of you. Be easier listenin'."

Wasco sank gratefully onto the hard cushion. Kyler settled beside him. Taking his money belt from his shoulder, he laid it across his lap, then stood the shotgun between his knees.

"Expect you know where you are," the rancher began. "Some call it the High Plains country, some say the Strip. Others call it No-Man's-Land . . . and that's just what it is in more ways than one. There's five thousand square miles of fine land here that's not claimed by any of the surrounding states or territories. Nobody wants it . . . so we're stuck out here by ourselves. Not so bad in some ways, but it's got its drawbacks, too . . . main one being the law . . . or the lack of it."

Kyler nodded. He had already discovered the town had no marshal or sheriff. He hadn't realized, however, that the entire Strip was without protection.

"Result is the country's overrun by outlaws.

Every gunslinger on the dodge heads for here because a lawman can't touch him, once he's inside the Strip. Even a U.S. marshal has no authority. You can see what sort of problems that creates."

"Kind of got an idea from the lady over in the restaurant," Kyler said.

"Marcia Ashwick? She could tell you about the town's side of it. Same as Sol or Rufe, here."

"They got us ranchers goin' and comin'," Bill Denby said.

"That's for sure," Pritchard of the Pitchfork spread added. "They just set back and get fat collecting on every head of stock we send to market. Two years ago they got it all."

Sam Kyler frowned. "How?"

"There's several gangs running loose around here. When we start the drive to market . . . Dalhart . . . two or three bunches join up and wait for us somewhere between here and the Texas line. Never the same place but they're always careful to be inside the Strip. They move in on the herd and either we pay cash . . . fifty cents a head it was last year . . . or they take enough beef to make up the amount. Road tax they call it."

"And you always fork over?" Wasco asked in a disbelieving voice.

Dave Simon stirred. "What the hell can we do? Usually fifteen or twenty of them . . . all hardcase gunmen. We've got maybe ten riders pushing the herd, none of them a match for the gunslingers. Be the same story if we had twenty riders. We couldn't buck them."

"Be damn' fools if we tried," Denby said.

"And that isn't all," Shinn Thompson said. "Year before last they ambushed the crew on the way back from Dalhart. Wasn't the same gang, so the boys said. Robbed them of the money we got for the herd. Tried it last year but the boys outrun 'em."

"Sure to try again this year," Pete Clark said gloomily. "If they do, they'll flat bust me."

"Includes all of us," Denby said. "Ain't got over my losses from that deal two years ago yet. Same goes for the town. We go broke, the town goes broke."

"Got the idea you've had a lawman around."

"Tried, but we've never found the right man," Tolliver said, and hesitated. "I'll be honest with you, Kyler. These gangs are tough . . . toughest you've ever come up against, I expect. The worst men from all over the country have drifted in here."

"You ever think of calling in the Army?"

"Half a dozen times. They ignore us. We heard in a roundabout way the government was afraid the soldiers would rile the Indians . . . us being just west of Indian Territory. Politicians, therefore, only look the other way when we holler . . . make out like we wasn't even here."

Sam Kyler rubbed at the round ends of the shotgun's barrel. "So I take from what you're telling me, you want to hire Wasco and me to get your herd through to Dalhart without paying off . . . and then get your money back safe to you."

Tolliver nodded. "We figure, if it can be done, you're the man who can do it."

Shinn Thompson snorted. "It's a damn' fool idea! One man and a helper ain't goin' to get the job done . . . no matter who or what he is."

Kyler shifted his eyes to the old rancher. "You mean I . . . we do it alone?"

"How else? Sure you'll have our drovers with you. Ordinary ranch hands . . . but they're a hell of a long ways from being gunfighters. Wouldn't be no use to you in a shoot-out. Only get themselves killed."

Sam glanced at Wasco, turned to Tolliver. "How many ranches on the Strip?"

"Nine."

"Two men from each, we. . . ."

"Mace Buckman's place ain't workin' right now," Pete Clark said. "Got to figure on eight."

"Buckman's in the pen," Thompson broke in. "For murderin' my son."

"Kyler's not interested in that," Tolliver said quickly, closing what was evidently a sore subject before it could get started. "Sure, we can spare you two men from each of our spreads . . . sixteen riders. But like Shinn said, they won't be of any help when it comes to gun play. They're just cowhands."

"How about you men?"

Simon, his eyes snapping, said: "Count me in, by God!"

Tolliver wagged his head. "Don't be a fool, Dave. You're in the same wagon as the rest of us. We can all shoot a gun but we'd be in 'way over our heads taking on those outlaws. Smart thing for us to do is leave it to a professional . . . like Kyler."

Silence fell over the lobby. Sam continued to rub at the shotgun's muzzle, his eyes half closed. Finally he said: "Be quite a chore. Ever think of hiring outriders in Dalhart?"

"Tried to," Shinn Thompson said. "Nobody willing to take on the gangs."

"How long before the herd's ready to move?"

"Time's run out. Gather's begun and the stock's due at the loading pens by the end of this week."

Kyler nodded. "One thing more. What kind of money you willing to pay?"

Tolliver rose to his feet. "Talked it over while we were waiting. We'll ante up five hundred for you . . . two-fifty for your friend there. In gold. We've got to make it this year, or, like Pete Clark said, we're all broke."

"But we're only payin' off if you get the stock through without turnin' over part of it to the outlaws . . . and get back with the money," Shinn Thompson warned.

Kyler signified his understanding. Five hundred dollars in gold. It was a lot of money. He would still have plenty left after making up the shortage in Arch Clayburn's money belt. But it would be one hell of a job. He turned to Wasco. "What do you think?"

The old cowpuncher rubbed at his chin. "Well, I sure ain't buckin' for no real estate in a graveyard, but, if you say so, I reckon I'm willin'."

Sam Kyler looked up at Tolliver. "All right. You've got yourself a deal."

VI

Otto Schmidt heaved a deep sigh. Shinn Thompson shook his head. Bill Denby came to his feet, extended his hand to Kyler.

"Want you to know how much this means to us . . . all of us."

"Not over with yet," Sam said.

"He's right," Thompson broke in. "I still figure it's a fool deal. You're bankin' everything on the reputation of one man . . . and I ain't yet seen a reputation stop a bullet."

Tolliver said: "That's so . . . but at least we've found a man who's willing to try."

"Tryin' ain't doin'," Thompson countered stubbornly. "Better save your back pattin' until later."

Kyler grinned wryly. The old rancher was right. The job was a long way from being accomplished—and the odds for success were poor. But in the back of his mind a plan was shaping up. If he could split the gang. . . . "Couple of things I want to get straight," he said.

Tolliver nodded. "Shoot."

"You told me the outlaws took cattle in payment. How do they get rid of them?"

"Sell them at Dalhart or some other railhead."

"How can they get away with that? The beef's stolen."

"They force us to give them a bill of sale. We always carry a few blanks so we can list the right tally once the drive's over."

"Sure a brassy bunch," Wasco commented.

"Can afford to be," Denby said. "They got it all their way."

"Know anything about the gang . . . who they are, I mean?"

"Not always the same bunch, except for the head man. Name's Eli Hurd. He's plenty smart and knows all the angles. Ever hear of him?"

Kyler shook his head. "It's settled then. We can figure on each of you furnishing us with two riders . . . all good cowpunchers who can handle a herd."

"Count me in, too," Dave Simon said. "And Pritchard's willing."

"No," Kyler broke in. "I'd as soon you owners would stay out of it. Give me your best hands . . . that's all I need."

A sudden silence descended over the room. Shinn Thompson finally said: "Now, why the hell don't you want . . . ?"

"If I'm to ramrod this drive, I want it done my way. Don't figure to have somebody second-guessing me if I make up my mind to do something."

Claude Hayman, quiet up to that point, said: "Makes sense. We're saddlin' the man with one hell of a chore. Let him do it the way he wants."

Tolliver glanced around the circle of men. "Agreed?"

They all nodded. Sam Kyler said: "Then have your riders and your herd at the gathering place . . . ?"

"Skull Cañon."

"At Skull Cañon ready to move out by sundown tomorrow. Won't actually start the drive until the next morning, but I want everything set. That possible?"

Tolliver said: "No trouble. About all the cattle's there now. Think Denby's stuff is still due."

"Boys are driving my herd in now. Expect they'll have them bedded down by dark," Denby said.

"How long will it take to reach Dalhart?"

"Three days, more or less. Easy going . . . mostly flat land and shallow draws, route we follow."

"Any water?"

"Rifle Creek. You'll hit it just before you come to the Texas line."

"How about extra horses and a chuck wagon?"

"All taken care of."

"Good. No need for us to bother about details."

"Nope. We'll see to everything. All you got to worry about is getting through . . . and back."

"Which won't be no picnic," Shinn Thompson said, and pointed with his cane at the window. "Wolves are already beginnin' to gather."

Kyler rose, looked through the dust-streaked glass fronting the Fargo's lobby. Six riders were moving slowly down the street. All were tough, gun-belted men.

"Headed for your place, Rufe," Denby said.

Eggert, somewhat aside and in conversation with Tom Tolliver, moved quickly to Kyler's side. He gave the men a close speculation. "Strangers to me," he said after a moment. "Reckon I'd better be gettin' over there."

Wheeling abruptly, he crossed to the door and entered the street. Shinn Thompson hawked, spat at a brass cuspidor. "Be some hell around here tonight."

Kyler looked back around. None of the six men was familiar to him—but he recognized the stamp. They would be the sort he would be up against on the drive. "There only one trail out of here to Dalhart?"

Tolliver said: "Only one that's practical. You swing east or west, you hit bad country . . . outlaws would head you off anyway."

44

"Never heard nobody mention it," Wasco said. "Just how big a herd you movin'?"

"Three thousand head."

The old cowpuncher whistled softly. "Handlin' them alone's a sight of a chore without worryin' about them fancy rustlers!"

"That bunch didn't stay long at Rufe's," Denby remarked, peering through the window. "Headin' into Marcia's place now."

Kyler wheeled, placed his glance on the swaggering figures entering the restaurant. As he watched, one of the men paused, raised his foot, and deliberately kicked one of the tables, sent it skittering into the others. Suddenly angry, Sam Kyler turned to Wasco. "Let's go get a cup of coffee," he said, and started for the door.

"Hold on a minute," Claude Hayman cut in as the old cowpuncher got to his feet. "Let the widow look out for herself. You're workin' for us."

"Way I see it," Kyler replied coolly, "is we're working for everybody around here . . . and right now's a good time to start."

VII

When they reached the entrance to Marcia Ashwick's restaurant, Kyler halted, motioned to Wasco for silence. Inside, the outlaws had taken over, were sprawled about on chairs scattered throughout the room. One, a squat, dark man with a pockmarked face, had placed one booted foot against the short counter and was rocking it back and forth. Dishes were rattling noisily and a sugar bowl had already crashed to the floor, spilled its contents.

Marcia Ashwick stood defiantly before the outlaw. "Get out!" she said in a firm voice. "I won't serve you!"

"You sure better, lady," the scarred man replied, "unless you want me and the boys to just help ourselves." He glanced around at the grinning features of his friends. "Reckon I ought to tell you, howsomever, we ain't so handy in a place like this. Doubt if it'd look like much once we was through."

Marcia shook her head in helpless anger. "Do what you like . . . I can't stop you! But I won't serve you. Last time you were in here you refused to pay. I . . . I'd rather be out of business than put up with. . . ."

"Guess that means we got to help ourselves," the outlaw cut in, and gave the counter a final, hard shove. It went over backward, spilling dishes all over its surface, dumping various supplies from its shelves.

Sam Kyler stepped through the doorway. Wasco followed, halted just outside, long arms folded across his chest. Kyler moved straight to the pockmarked outlaw, seized him by the collar. The man yelled, jerked free, and whirled.

"Who the hell you think you are?"

"I'm the man who's going to make you pay for all this damage," Sam replied in a tight voice. "Shell out!"

"Nobody's makin' me do. . . ."

Kyler lashed out with the shotgun. The barrel caught the outlaw across the side of his head, sent him staggering against the wall. The others leaped to their feet. Wasco's flat, nasal voice froze them in their tracks.

"Just stand easy, boys . . . and don't go reachin' for them hog-legs unless'n you want daylight shinin' through your hides."

The squat outlaw rubbed at the side of his head, glared at Kyler. For a brief moment he considered going for his gun, then thought better of it.

"You ain't got no call. . . ."

"Dig out your money," Kyler snapped. He shifted his glance to Marcia Ashwick. White-faced, she had drawn back against the partition that separated the kitchen from the dining area. "Twenty dollars cover it?"

She nodded hurriedly. Sam swung back to the outlaw. "Fork it over!"

The scarred men shook his head. "I ain't got twenty dollars. . . ."

"Then call on your friends."

The outlaw looked expectantly toward his companions. All reached for their pockets.

"Watch them hands!" Wasco shouted. He was

holding two guns, his own ancient weapon and the one taken from Shad Collins. "Sure hate to kill a man just 'cause he made a mistake!"

When the necessary amount had been accumulated and turned over to Marcia Ashwick, Kyler stepped back to the side of the old cowpuncher. He motioned with the shotgun. "Now we'll straighten things up a bit. Set that counter up the way it belongs. And put those tables and chairs back like you found them."

Grumbling, the outlaws did as they were ordered. Finished, they moved toward the door. Kyler halted them.

"One thing more. If you ever come in here again and pull a stunt like that . . . or refuse to pay for your meal . . . I'll run you down and blow your head off. That's a promise."

The pockmarked outlaw stared. "For one lousy four-bit meal?"

"For just one cup of coffee . . . all the same. Now get out . . . and, if you'd like to talk about this some more, you'll find us around."

The men trooped out into the street. Halfway across they slowed, looked back, and then continued on in the direction of Rufe Eggert's.

Marcia Ashwick's eyes were shining. She came forward. "I . . . I don't know how to thank you."

"No need," Kyler said.

"No need!" she echoed. "We've been needing someone around here for a long time to handle men like those . . . somebody to put them in their place. You're the first to even try."

"Had plenty of help," Kyler said, grinning at Wasco. "Don't think anybody's going to argue with him and all that hardware he's packin'."

"When the town hears this. . . ."

"No point in mentioning it. Besides, we'll be gone."

"Good! Then you are going to work for the cattlemen."

Kyler nodded. "Driving a herd through to Dalhart."

"And fighting off twenty or thirty outlaws doing so. Oh . . . I knew they would talk you into it."

"We're getting paid. Plenty."

"But you'll never live to spend it. Not if you do what they want you to. Tell them you've changed your mind. Stay here . . . take the marshal's job. At least the odds for keeping alive are better."

Kyler smiled. "Man stops to figure the odds, he never gets anything done. We'll make it. Don't worry about it."

Marcia Ashwick sighed resignedly. "I knew it was too much to hope for." She drew herself up, smiled. "At least you can let me serve you a fine supper for what you've done for me."

Sam glanced at Wasco. "Appreciate the invitation. We need to clean up a mite. Offer hold good a couple hours from now?"

"Of course."

"Then we'll check in at the hotel and come back later."

"Is that a promise?"

"You can bet on it," Kyler said, and started for the door.

VIII

The afternoon of the next day, Kyler and Wasco, after getting directions from Sol Weil, rode into the broad, steep-walled defile known as Skull Cañon. A heavy pall of yellow dust hung over the area and the air was filled with the sounds of bawling cattle and shouting men.

They drew to a halt on the northern lip of the natural corral and looked for signs of the camp. Riders were wheeling in and out of the confusion, but it was several minutes before they finally spotted the canvas-topped chuck wagon halted at the far end of the cañon where dust was at a minimum.

As they moved on, riding down a long slope, Wasco twisted about on his saddle. "We ain't done much palaverin' about this here fandango . . . and, way it stacks up, appears we bit ourselves off quite a chaw. You got some special ideas how we can do it?"

Kyler shook his head. "Start the drive . . . see what happens. Little hard to make any plans yet."

"Reckon you ain't forgot that, if it comes down

to shootin', it'll be just you and me. Them cow nurses ain't goin' to be no help."

"Big reason why we've got to dodge a showdown, if we can."

"Yeah . . . if we can," Wasco said morosely. "I figure them owlhoots'll have plenty to say about that."

They found most of the ranchers at the wagon, hunched on their heels, drinking black coffee from tin cups as they watched the final activities of the gather. When they rode in, Dave Simon greeted them.

"Step down. Plenty java there on the fire."

Kyler and Wasco anchored their horses to the picket line and returned to the wagon.

"About set," Pritchard said, smiling at Sam.

Kyler nodded, poured coffee for Wasco and himself. A man came from the interior of the wagon where he was arranging supplies, grinned. "Howdy. Name's Turkey. I'm your cook."

Kyler pressed the oldster's horny hand, turned to the ranchers. Shinn Thompson and Schmidt were absent, he noticed.

"Like we figure . . . right at three thousand head," Tolliver said, thrusting a sheaf of papers upon which he had been figuring back into his pocket. "Biggest tally we ever had." He hesitated, frowned. "Maybe that ain't so good. We could only scare up twelve riders for you."

A thread of impatience stirred through Kyler as

he studied the mass of shifting bodies. He would be short-handed—and that wasn't good.

"Getting this stock through is pretty important to you. Seems you could find the men somewhere."

Pritchard swore softly. "Everything's wrong this year. And you've got to understand none of us is very big as ranchers go. Exceptin' Thompson, pulling two men off leaves a big hole. On top of that there's two or three down sick, and one of Clark's boys got throwed yesterday and broke his arm."

Bill Denby nodded. "Something else you maybe won't be likin'. I got only two hired hands. Can't spare either one so it'll be me riding from my outfit."

Sam raised his cup to his lips, slowly drained its contents. They would be starting the drive short of drovers—and with one of the owners along. They would be lucky to maintain control of the herd, if anything went wrong, much less do anything about the outlaws. From behind him, Wasco's laconic voice broke the quiet.

"Was we smart, we'd forget this here jackscrew deal 'fore we even start."

Tolliver's leathery face showed instant alarm. "Now, hold on a minute! We know you laid down your conditions, hard and fast, and we figured you had your reasons. But we just couldn't do it exactly like you wanted. You got to see our side of it, too."

"It's your beef," Sam reminded the rancher.

"Realize that, but there ain't none of us in shape to just turn loose all hands. We got our ranches to look after, too. Don't mean selling our cattle's not important, just that there's other things we got to look out for."

"And if it's me comin' along that's botherin' you," Denby said, "I ain't doin' it because I want to. It's because I have to. It's either me from my place . . . or nobody."

"Bill's given us his word he won't be any trouble," Claude Hayman said.

Denby nodded vigorously. "You're the trail boss, Kyler. Whatever you say goes."

Sam considered thoughtfully, finally shrugged. "All right, we'll do the best we can," he said, and then added to Denby: "I'll hold you to your word. You're just one of the drovers until we get back. Went on a drive once with the owner of the stock hanging around my neck. Don't aim to let it happen again."

"You've got my hand on it," Denby said, his face serious.

Tolliver's features showed his relief. He took a leather fold from his pocket, drew Kyler aside beyond hearing of the other men.

"Here's your papers . . . bills of sale and such. May have to change the tally sheet when you get to the pens, depending on the kind of luck you have."

"Won't lose any stock unless we're so short of men we can't hold them," Sam answered.

"That happens, you won't be responsible. We'll understand. One other thing. Coming back with the money, you might try swinging west, keeping off the main trail. Rough country, no good for driving cattle but a man on horseback can manage it easy. Could be a way to dodge the outlaws. Chances are they'll be layin' their ambush on the regular route."

"Good idea," Kyler said. "Where do I hit it?"

"About five miles west. Trail follows along a line of red bluffs. Can't miss it. Expect you'd like to meet the rest of the boys now."

"No need," Sam replied. "Do my getting acquainted once we're moving." He crossed to the bay, unbuckled the left saddlebag, and thrust the fold of papers into the pouch.

From his place near the wagon, Dave Simon said: "When you pullin' out?"

"Daylight," Kyler said. "Let the cattle rest here for the night. Be in good shape tomorrow."

"Just what I was thinkin'," Bill Denby said, and then, catching Kyler's quiet glance, grinned and added: "Was just agreein' with you."

Wasco was probably right, Sam thought. It would be smart to forget the whole deal. Everything was starting off wrong. But he did need money—and quick. The sooner he got Arch Clayborn's $1,000 on its way back, the better. And this would be a quick way to raise the necessary amount. Tightening the straps of the saddlebags, he turned, glanced at the lowering sun, then to the back of the wagon.

"Turkey."

The cook appeared at once. "Yes, sir, Mister Kyler."

"I'm holding the herd here for the night. Figure to feed the crew about dark. You set up to handle it?"

"Sure am."

"And breakfast comes at four a.m. Want the herd on the move an hour later."

"I'll be ready . . . never you worry none," the old man said.

Kyler swung onto his horse, motioned to Wasco. He looked then at the ranchers. "See you gentlemen when we get back. Right now got to get busy setting up the night watch."

"Won't need it . . . not here in the cañon," Bill Denby said hastily. "Just ain't no reason. . . ." His words trailed off as Kyler's jaw hardened perceptibly. "I only meant we never had. . . ."

"Probably a good idea," Dave Simon said, breaking the awkward moment. "Looks like the wind's gettin' up."

Sam nodded to Wasco, and, side-by-side, they turned off toward the herd. The old cowpuncher grunted, spat into the dust. "Havin' two trail bosses is like havin' a horse with two heads. Reckon it ain't only the outlaws that are goin' to be givin' us trouble."

"Denby's a good man," Kyler said quietly. "But he's got some learning to do."

IX

The moaning of the wind awoke Sam Kyler. He sat up in the half darkness, flinched as sand blasted against his face, stung his eyes. He and Wasco had chosen a place just beyond the chuck wagon to spread their bedrolls and they were now lying unprotected against the gusts. A loud slapping sound drew his attention. He turned about, saw the angular shape of Turkey struggling to tie down the canvas top of his vehicle before it could be whirled away.

Kyler scrambled to his feet, prodding Wasco awake in the process. Hanging tightly to his blankets, he made his way to the comparative calm behind the wagon, the old cowpuncher muttering curses and spitting sand a step to his left.

"For chrissake . . . somebody . . . give me a hand here!"

Turkey's strained voice carried faintly to them and, throwing their bedrolls into the wagon, both turned to where the cook was clinging desperately to a corner of the wildly flapping fabric. Sam grabbed a loose rope, poked it through the metal eye at the end of the wagon bed, cinched it down as Wasco gave his support to Turkey.

"Obliged!" the cook shouted above the howl of the storm. "Dang' thing come loose somehow! Sure is a bad one!"

Kyler nodded, yelled to Wasco: "Turn the crew out! Tell them to meet me at the herd!"

The old cowpuncher bobbed his head as Kyler wheeled and moved to the picket line. He saddled the bay, taking time to check the other horses, and then swung back for the center of the cañon where the cattle were gathered. Darkness and swirling sand and dust made it impossible to see any distance, and he heard the sounds of the restless brutes several moments before he was upon them.

The windstorm had aroused them and they were beginning to shift nervously. Sam, riding in close, saw the shadowy outlines of the men delegated to night watch moving slowly along the fringe of the herd, doing what they could to quiet the stock. A cowpuncher loomed up before him. It was one of Pritchard's men. He pulled up short when he saw Kyler, a startled look on his face. He brushed the grit from his mouth, rode in close.

"Won't take much to spook these critters!" he yelled. A fresh blast of sand struck him. He swore, again sleeved his lips.

Kyler glanced to the east. Through the heavy pall he could see the first gray hint of daylight. He spurred the bay nearer to the rider.

"They start milling, get in behind and start pushing them south . . . I'll pass the word!"

Pritchard's man wheeled away and was swallowed immediately by the dust. Sam moved forward, halted again as Wasco, leading the balance of the crew, loped up. He repeated his orders.

"If you don't watch close, the herd will start drifting with the storm . . . north . . . soon as it's light! Got to keep them from it! One of you double back and tell Turkey to pull out! Have to eat later . . . when we get a chance!"

The riders loped off. Wasco fought his horse in closer to Kyler. "Anythin' special you want me doin'?"

Sam shook his head. "Just keep them from breaking loose and heading north!"

Wasco angled off into the murk, and Kyler rode in nearer to the stirring cattle, seeking the remainder of the crew. Unless they maintained a close watch, the herd would soon start breaking up, forming into small bunches that would be difficult to contain. In the blinding storm they would scatter to all directions.

He found most of the riders patrolling close to the nervous cattle, doing their utmost to keep the calm. But as the light grew stronger, the herd became increasingly hard to handle. Finally, with the land about them distinct, the cattle began to move. Here and there a steer would break from the main body, plunge off into the brush. A cowpuncher would immediately swing out after him, haze him back with his rope.

Bill Denby, his face strained, his mouth and eyes rimmed with sand, rode up. "Ain't goin' to hold them much longer!" he shouted above the whining wind.

"No need!" Sam yelled his reply. "Head 'em out . . . down the draw!"

Denby nodded, and whirled away, motioning to the drovers as he loped by. Wasco appeared and Kyler pointed toward the south. The old cowpuncher waved and cut back into the dust.

In only moments the herd began to move, shifting uncertainly back and forth at first but finally, after a fair-size jag of the stock had moved into the wide, shallow wash at the south end of the cañon, all fell into a heaving, bawling procession.

Kyler, circling the flowing mass, kept his drovers in tight. Once the herd was well under way, the job would not be so difficult; it would be only a matter of keeping it pointed in the right direction.

In the draw they were partly shielded from the blustering wind, and for an hour the cattle plodded along with little urging. Then, when they broke out onto a high flat and once more were heading straight into the teeth of the storm, trouble immediately developed. The drive began to stall. Cattle started milling, sought to turn, put their hindquarters to the stinging gusts. Kyler, aided by Wasco and the drovers, hammered at them ceaselessly, but progress came almost to a standstill.

Dawn broke over a swirling, choked world and Sam's hope for a cessation of the fierce wind at the arrival of daylight faded. He considered calling a halt, decided against it. Keeping the herd intact, once stopped, would be too difficult, better to keep it moving, however slowly.

They overtook the chuck wagon a short time later. Turkey had coffee and fried meat ready and the men took turns, two at a time, to have a quick, if gritty meal.

The morning wore on with no let-up in the storm or the hard labor. The riders changed horses and Kyler forsook his worn bay for a chunky little buckskin that had no liking for him or the storm, either, and continually fought the bit.

Around noon the wind began to decrease. The herd became less difficult to manage but Kyler knew this was only temporary. The driving storm had dried out the stock, turned them thirsty well before time. They would soon turn impatient for water—and Rifle Creek was still a day or more distant.

Plagued with this new problem, Sam pulled away from his position in front of the herd and drew off to one side. Wasco and Denby were riding point while the remainder of the crew were scattered along at swing and drag positions. Dust hovered above the slow-moving herd in a vast cloud and he could see neither the far side nor the rear.

Hailing the first drover who appeared in the dry boil, Kyler beckoned to him. The man was an oldster, one of Shinn Thompson's hands. His brows were thick with sand, and, when he pulled down the bandanna he had drawn across the lower half of his face, it looked as though he wore a mask.

He grinned at Sam. "One hell of a lot of real estate on the move around here!"

Kyler smiled back. "For a fact . . . any water closer than Rifle Creek?"

The cowpuncher scratched at his ear, thought for a moment. "Nope, not unless you swing east . . . reckon it'd be about twenty miles."

Sam considered that. A full day's drive. There was no point in forsaking the regular trail; they would reach Rifle Creek and the usual water stop sooner if they continued on.

"Thinkin' about changin'?"

Kyler shook his head. "Be nothing gained."

The rider signified his agreement, commented again on the storm, and dropped back to his position with the herd. They pushed on, the cattle growing more recalcitrant with the tedious miles, and, when darkness finally came, Kyler welcomed the halt. He chose a broad depression between three low-lying hills for night camp. It wasn't the best place to bed down 3,030 beeves, but he had earlier scouted ahead with Wasco and found nothing more suitable.

Taking no chances, he assigned half the crew to stand watch and sent the rest in for their evening meal. When they had finished, they relieved the others who ate, then settled back for a few hours' rest. At midnight they would spell the first night hawks.

Kyler was finishing off his second cup of coffee when Bill Denby, haggard and scoured raw by sand, came in. It was the first Sam had seen of the rancher, except for fleeting glimpses, since the storm began. Denby accepted his plate of meat and biscuits from the cook and squatted on his heels.

"We're in for hell if that wind gets up again tonight," he said wearily.

"For sure," Kyler replied. "One thing in our favor. Cattle are dead beat. They won't be so anxious to run. How far are we from Rifle Creek?"

Denby stared off across the darkening flats to a scatter of hills in the south. "Ought to reach it by tomorrow noon, figurin' we don't have trouble."

"Something we've got to walk around. If they get stirred up again, do what we did this morning . . . head them south and let 'em go."

"Temper they're in now, it maybe won't work."

Kyler rose, helped himself to more coffee. "We'll make it work. If that herd ever busts up, we'll be all summer rounding up the strays."

Denby shrugged gloomily. "Seems to me like this was a hard-luck drive right from the start."

But the night passed without incident and at daylight the herd was again on the move, rested although pushed by thirst. Where, that previous day it had been the wind and slashing sand that had made them difficult to handle, the need for water was now the threatening factor.

The crew, under the supervision of trail-wise old Wasco, handled them well, however, and the stock moved steadily southward at a fair pace. Around midday Bill Denby caught up with Kyler. He wheeled in alongside, pointed to a fall of land a mile or so on ahead.

"Creek's there," he said. "Cattle are gettin' wind of it now. They're startin' to perk up."

Kyler breathed a sigh. Maybe the worst of the drive would be over once the herd slaked its thirst. He rode out with Denby, leaving behind the herd that had now broken into a shambling trot. The two men reached the last, gradual slope, topped out the rise, and dropped over into the opposing side. The bright sparkle of a broad stream cutting a path along the floor of the valley greeted them. And there was something else—outlaws.

X

Denby pulled to a quick halt. "Just like before," he said in a taut voice. "Settin' and waitin' for us."

Sam Kyler's eyes were on the outlaws. There were fifteen in the gang. They had drawn up in a line at the foot of the slope with Rifle Creek a few yards behind them.

"What're you aimin' to do?" Denby asked.

Kyler shook his head. There was the quick drumming of a running horse back of him and a moment later Wasco pulled up at his side. The old cowpuncher whistled softly. "Looks like they're getting' ready for a cavalry charge."

"What are we goin' to do?" Denby asked again.

Kyler shifted his glance to the rancher. "We take things as they come. Whatever . . . stay out of it. Leave it to me."

Denby said: "Sure . . . sure."

Kyler touched the bay with his spurs and, with Wasco to his left, the rancher on his right, rode in close to the waiting men. Faint surprise ran through him when he saw Shad Collins near the end of the line. The young outlaw eyed him narrowly, equally startled.

"This the same bunch that jumped you last year?"

"Don't know," Denby replied. "Wasn't along, but it probably is. Same head man . . . one in the middle there with the checked vest. That's Eli Hurd."

Sam moved forward a few more paces, studying the outlaw chief. The man's dark, hard-cornered face struck no chords in his memory. A few of his followers did, however. They returned his stare sullenly. Near enough, Kyler again halted.

Before he could speak, Hurd said: "You the ramrod of this outfit?"

"That's me," Sam answered.

From down the line Shad Collins volunteered: "He's Sam Kyler, Eli. Reckon you've heard of him."

Hurd's eyes flared slightly. After a moment, he said: "Shotgun Sam Kyler. Yeah, I've heard of him." Then: "We're here for our cut. Expect you know about it."

"I know one thing," Sam replied coolly. "You better get the hell away from the front of that creek. There's a herd of beef coming over that ridge in about five minutes . . . all in a hurry to get a drink."

Eli Hurd opened his mouth to make some sort of answer, then paused as the low thunder of hoofs reached him. Not waiting to see what the outlaws would do, Kyler wheeled, and with Wasco and Denby close behind, loped off to one side.

The outlaws followed hastily, some with drawn weapons, as though suspecting trickery, others interested only in getting out of the way. The fore-runners of the herd broke over the rim at that moment, started down the slope, bawling loudly. Seconds later the remainder of the cattle appeared and a solid wave of brown, white, and black surged over the crest, flowed down to the stream, and began to split and spread out along the water.

The crew, bringing up the rear, halted on the

ridge. After a moment they cut diagonally across the slope and took up positions in a half circle behind Kyler.

Eli Hurd moved out a stride in front of his men. All of the outlaws had pulled their weapons upon the arrival of the crew and now watched intently. Kyler gave them a swift but thorough study, calculating his chances. It was as he had been told; all were tough, hardened gunmen. He understood better why the ranchers were unwilling to fight. Pitting ordinary cowhands against such killers would mean nothing short of wholesale slaughter.

"Let's get this over with," Hurd said. "You got your papers?"

Anger stirred through Kyler. The thought of being forced to knuckle under and accede to the outlaw's demands rankled him. "What are you talking about?"

Eli Hurd spat. "Don't give me that. You've been told. The pay off in cash or cattle?"

"We don't carry any cash," Bill Denby said.

The outlaw considered the rancher coldly. "All right, I'll take cattle."

"How many?" Kyler asked, slanting a warning look at Denby.

"Dollar a head."

"A dollar!" Denby shouted. "Last year it was only fifty cents! By God . . . I'll see you in hell. . . ."

"Taxes has gone up," Hurd cut in quietly. The half smile faded from his lips. "Now, if you're aimin' to argue about it . . . I got me some real good collectors along."

"He's not running this drive," Kyler broke in quickly. "You're dealing with me."

He watched the men beyond Hurd settle back gently, breathed deeper. It had been a dangerous moment. One false move on the part of the drovers and violence would have erupted.

"Then do the talkin'," Hurd said. "How many head you driving?"

"Three thousand."

Hurd twisted about in his saddle, directed himself to one of his men. "Engle, Mister Kyler says he's got three thousand head. That what you make it?"

The outlaw wheeled about, rode a short distance toward the herd, and stopped. He surveyed the watering stock for a long minute, then rejoined the line.

"What I figure," he said.

Hurd nodded. "Engle used to be a cattleman," he said. "Knows his critters. Never knew him to miss a tally more'n a dozen or so."

Kyler said nothing, leaving it up to the outlaw to make the next move. To fight was out of the question, and he was giving that course of action no consideration. A vague plan had occurred to him that seemed best, and to accomplish it he should simply lay back, let Eli Hurd have his way for the time being. His biggest worry was that Denby, or

67

one of the drovers, would lose his head, do something foolish.

"Three thousand . . . ," Hurd said, frowning. "Means my cut'll be two hundred head. Hear they're paying fifteen dollars for prime steers in Dalhart. That how you calculate it, Mister Kyler?"

"That's what it figures."

Sam reached own, unbuckled his left-hand saddlebag, procured the leather fold of papers. A low muttering arose among the drovers. Denby swore. Kyler gave them a warning look, passed a blank bill of sale to the rancher.

"Fill it out," he ordered. "And don't try anything stupid."

XI

Denby snatched the sheet from Kyler's fingers. There was a sudden stir among the drovers. Sam turned sharply. Andy, one of the younger riders, pushed forward, his hand resting on the butt of his pistol. The boy's face was taut and his eyes blazed.

"I figure it's about time we done somethin' about this," he muttered.

"Back up!" Kyler snapped.

He glanced over his shoulder at the line of outlaws. They were watching, waiting quietly, alert for any opposition.

Wasco reached out, laid his hand on the boy's shoulder. "Simmer down, youngster."

Andy shrugged off the old cowpuncher. "Was a mistake hirin' him. Could be this is all a put-up job."

Anger rolled through Kyler. Wasco glanced up hurriedly, wagged his head. "Reckon he didn't mean that, Sam. Just shootin' off his mouth. Got to remember he's still a mite wet-eared."

"You ain't talkin' for me," the boy shot back.

"Dry up, Andy," one of the drovers cut in. "Maybe none of us goes along with this here doin's, but Kyler's runnin' it. Let him do what he wants . . . he's the one that's got to do the explainin' when we get home."

"Here," Bill Denby said abruptly, holding out the sheet of paper to Kyler. "Here's your damned bill of sale."

Kyler accepted it, glanced briefly at the writing, then rode toward Eli Hurd. Several of the outlaws came to attention at his approach. Hurd laughed.

"Ease off, boys . . . Mister Kyler ain't no hero."

Sam, his mouth a hard line, halted before the outlaw leader and passed over the paper.

"We'll cut 'em out," Hurd said, thrusting the bill of sale into his vest pocket. "Be taking them off the end."

"Two hundred head," Kyler said. "No more."

Again Hurd laughed. "Sure. This here's a business deal . . . pure business. I don't aim to cheat nobody."

Under his breath Bill Denby said: "Hell of a lot of good it done to hire this Kyler. We could've just forked over the stock without him."

"Reckon he's doin' what's best," Wasco replied.

"Doin'?" the rancher said bitterly. "He ain't doin' nothin'! And we was all hopin' he'd put an end to this rustlin'."

"Last verse of the song ain't sung yet," the old cowpuncher murmured. "Just set quiet and keep your lip buttoned. Sam ain't likin' this no more'n you, but he ain't lookin' to spill no blood."

"'Specially his," young Andy commented acidly.

Wasco turned, stared closely at the boy. "How'd you grow old as you are? Sure don't hardly seem possible."

"I can take care of myself," the cowpuncher mumbled.

"Misdoubt that," Wasco said. "Leastwise, for not much longer."

Kyler, watching Hurd and part of his men turn away while anger slowly consumed him, wheeled finally to the drovers.

"One hour and we move on," he snapped. "Want to be over the Texas line by dark."

Immediately Bill Denby frowned. "No hurry now. Besides, stock ought to water good."

"God damn it!" Kyler shouted, unable to contain his temper. "You heard me!"

Behind him the outlaws, left by Hurd, watched and waited. The promise of violence still hung over the two groups of men like a threatening cloud. Kyler realized he must end the confrontation as quickly as possible before a spark could set off an explosion.

"All right!" he barked. "You've got no time to sit there. Get over to the wagon and eat. You won't have another chance until night."

For a long minute the riders made no move to comply, and then Bill Denby pulled out of the silent men.

"Come on," he said in a stiff, angry way. "Do what he says."

The drovers turned, rode slowly by Kyler. Wasco paused, looked questioningly at Sam.

"Keep them close to camp," Kyler said. "This thing's not over yet."

The old cowpuncher nodded and followed the others on to the chuck wagon. When they had dismounted, he swung the bay about and headed for the crown of the hill fronting the creek. From that point he could look down upon the activities.

Immediately four of Hurd's men pulled out of the line, angled to where they could watch Kyler. Hurd himself wheeled around and rode down to join the party hazing his 200 steers from the main herd.

A half dozen more beeves broke from the larger body, began to follow those cut out by the outlaws. Eli Hurd paused, glanced uphill to where Kyler sat. He grinned broadly, deliberately rode in behind the small jag, and drove them into the ranks of those being taken.

Kyler's mouth twisted into a hard smile. The outlaws were holding the whip at the moment—but it wouldn't be for long.

Over at the chuck wagon one of the crew, noticing the theft, lunged to his feet, shouted: "Hey . . . you bunch of damned . . . !" In the next moment Wasco had the man by the arm and was dragging him back.

Again Eli Hurd looked toward Kyler, the smile still on his dark face. He lifted his hand in mock salutation and joined his riders, now moving their herd out of the hollow. The few men remained in the line, watching the drovers, wheeled about, loped off in pursuit. As they passed, the quartet keeping a watchful eye on Sam pulled off with them.

All rode to overtake Hurd. One paused, removing his hat and holding it aloft. "So long, Mister Shotgun!" he called in a loud voice. "Was a real pleasure to meet you!"

His companions laughed. Another shouted something additional, but the words were lost to Kyler. He shifted his gaze to the chuck wagon. The drovers were watching him closely, taking it all in—and wondering.

They expected him to do something, he realized. And he would welcome the opportunity; they couldn't know how much he would like to open up on the outlaws, wipe the smirks from their whiskered faces. But it was not the time or the place. To start something would result in massacre. He could do nothing but hold his peace regardless of what the crew thought of him.

He watched Eli Hurd and his men until they were over the ridge and out of sight. They were pointing due east where lay the rough country; evidently they planned to swing wide and enter Dalhart from that end. He considered this thoughtfully for a time, and then, glancing at the sun, now sliding toward the western horizon, he returned to the wagon.

The drovers had finished their meal, were now sprawled about in the scanty shade glumly taking their ease. Kyler touched them with his eyes, jerked a thumb toward the herd.

"Move 'em out," he said crisply.

The men rose reluctantly, made their way to the horses, and, mounting, slanted for the herd. Wasco stepped up, bringing a tin cup of coffee and a thick meat and bread sandwich.

"Reckon I best keep proddin' them," he said, and sought out his own black.

Sam nodded his thanks and turned to watch. The cattle had satisfied their thirsts; most had drifted away from the creek and were now grazing on the grass along the opposite bank. The crew had little trouble getting them started, and in a short time they were plodding up the slope leading out of the valley.

Kyler finished his lunch, went back to the saddle, and caught up with the drive. The herd gained the crest of the valley's southern slope, spilled out onto a broad plain. It was easy going and shortly before dark they crossed the Texas line and entered a long cañon. Kyler called a halt just as the sun's last rays began to fade.

When the stock had settled down and the night watches established, Sam signaled Wasco to his side.

"You're taking over," he said, handing the old cowpuncher the fold of papers. "I'll meet you in Dalhart. The Longhorn Saloon."

Wasco peered at him through bushy brows. "What're you fixin' to do?"

"Going after those two hundred steers. We don't get paid unless we deliver them all. Remember?"

"I remember. But you can't do it alone. Hell . . . they's fifteen of them. . . ."

"I figure they'll split up. Hurd won't go riding into Dalhart with that many drovers for such a small bunch of cattle. Somebody'd get suspicious."

"Maybe. That Hurd strikes me as a feller who don't much care what anybody thinks. How about lettin' Denby take over so's I can trail along with you?"

"One of us has got to stay with the herd."

The old cowpuncher sighed, shook his head. "All right. We'll do it your way."

Kyler started to pull off. Over his shoulder he said: "Be waiting for me at the Longhorn."

The old cowpuncher nodded. "We'll be there. You just be dang' sure you make it."

XII

Sam Kyler cut a diagonal course to the northeast, reasoning that if the outlaws continued in the direction they had taken, he would eventually cross their path. That they had a long lead was undeniable; it had been a full five hours since the two parties had left the hollow where the cattle had watered, and, since each had taken an opposite bearing, a considerable number of miles would now lie between them.

This fact did not worry Kyler as the bay loped easily on over the grassy plain; he would catch up. For the moment, despite the grim purpose of the ride, he was enjoying the beauty of the warm night. Overhead the stars hung, low and bright, and the faintest of breezes fanned his face. Coyotes yapped from the ridges, and now and then he heard the muted chirping of birds, disturbed by his passage.

He thought of Wasco, of Bill Denby, and the drovers. The old cowpuncher had understood the problem he had faced when confronted by Eli Hurd and his men. But Denby and the others had been sorely disappointed by the way he had handled the encounter. Perhaps he should have taken them more into his confidence, but it hadn't occurred to him. A loner all his life, Sam Kyler rarely voiced his intentions, simply went about and did what he felt must be done. One thing was certain—the crew would never realize how near to sudden death they were when young Andy decided to take matters into his own hands.

Kyler knew men—and every rider backing Eli Hurd was a gunman and a killer. None would have hesitated to open up on the drovers, blast them from their saddles likely before they could even draw their own weapons. Sam Kyler felt good when he thought of that; he had prevented it from happening—at the expense of the crew's respect for him, perhaps—but that didn't matter. They were all alive.

Near midnight he intersected the outlaws' trail. The surrounding country had been growing rougher, and he came upon the welter of hoof prints in a somewhat narrow and ragged cañon. Halting, he dismounted and studied the tracks. On foot he followed them a short distance, saw that they continued to bear east. He went back onto the bay, then rode to the top of a nearby butte for a longer view of the land.

The flat plain had died, he saw, and the country stretching out before him was a shadowy world of arroyos, deep hollows, and broken buttes. He stared out across this, wondering why Hurd and his men had not begun to veer south for Dalhart; the thought came to him that the outlaws could be driving the stock to a different railhead. But that didn't strike him as reasonable. Hurd, in his roaring confidence, would entertain no thoughts of trouble or opposition; he would seek the nearest point where he could dispose of the cattle and collect cash. Such would be Dalhart. Undoubtedly the trail would eventually change its course.

He dropped off the crest, rejoined the tracks. They continued, bearing straight ahead and easily visible in the silvery night. An hour later Kyler became aware of change; the trail was beginning to turn south. He grinned in satisfaction. Eli Hurd was going to Dalhart, as he had figured. And the camp should be nearby. The outlaws would have halted at sundown.

Locating another high butte, he climbed to the top. From there he swung his gaze to the south, hopeful of detecting the red eye of a campfire. There was nothing—only the pale flats and the dark shadows where the land fell away in the distance.

He allowed his eyes to travel back slowly, thinking perhaps the trail had not made so definite a turn. Abruptly he drew himself up on the saddle. Far ahead a solitary light winked through the night. He studied it closely. It was no campfire but a lamp shining through the window of a house.

Again satisfaction flooded over him. He had stumbled upon the hang-out of Hurd and his men.

There would be no one else on that desolate, infertile area.

He left the butte and, abandoning the cattle trail, rode in a direct line for the lonely beacon. It was a rough course through deep-sided, sandy-floored arroyos, across a broad strip of brakes, but finally he reached the edge of a field, now badly overgrown with brush and weeds. There he pulled to a stop.

Once it had been a homestead—some man's dream of independence; now a rotting rail fence surrounded the small tract, enclosed a sagging frame house and several adjacent sheds and barns, equally deteriorated. A half dozen shade trees, carefully spaced and dead from thirst, stood, bare and stark, in the night.

The light came from a room at the back of the structure, Kyler saw, and immediately began to work in nearer. Holding the bay to a walk, he approached from a corner of the house, unwilling to risk meeting one of the outlaws who might be outside or close to the door.

He didn't see the horses until he was almost upon them. Halting, he counted them. Nine—and the cattle were not to be seen. It could mean only that part of the outlaws had gone on with the herd while the remainder awaited their return here.

Eli Hurd's party was divided. It was what he had hoped for. Smiling grimly, Sam Kyler continued on for another twenty yards, and then, in a thick stand of osage orange, pulled to a stop. Dismounting, he tied the bay securely and, taking his shotgun, proceeded on foot.

Reaching the corner of the house, he paused. He could hear laughter coming from the interior of the structure, along with an occasional oath. Some of the outlaws were playing cards, he guessed. Likely others were sleeping.

He moved on, planting each step with care. The night was quiet and he realized that any unusual sound—the snapping of a dry branch, the rattle of brush—would carry through the open door and window and be heard by the outlaws.

He gained the window, stopped, peered cautiously around its splintered frame. He was looking into the kitchen of the abandoned house. Five men were gathered around a table engaged in a game of stud poker. A sixth slept in a nearby chair. The remaining three, he assumed, were in one of the adjoining rooms.

A coffee pot sat on the squat, nickel-trimmed cook stove placed at one end of the quarters. Several tin cups were stacked beside it. The outlaws, however, confined their interest to a half-empty bottle of whiskey before them on the table.

Sam watched silently as a plan built slowly in his mind. He wondered if the back door represented the only exit and entrance to the building. After a moment he doubled back, made his way to the opposite side. There was a front door but apparently never used. Drifted sand had piled up, several inches in depth, against it. Most likely it was barred on the inside.

Satisfied he could expect the men to come and go only by the rear opening, Kyler retraced his steps. Again he halted at the corner, centered his attention this time, however, on the yard. The first of the smaller buildings, a tool shed, stood directly opposite the door at a distance of fifty feet or so. It would serve his purpose ideally.

He spent most of the next hour collecting dry brush and weeds in the field and laying piles against the front and the south side of the old house. When that was done, he noted that daylight was not far off.

Taking a match, he fired the mounds of brush, and, when they were burning briskly, he crossed the yard and took up a position behind the tool shed.

XIII

The card game continued. Tensely Sam Kyler watched smoke rise above the far side of the house and, moments later, along the roof edge of the south wall. An orange tongue of flame appeared, and then a crackling sound broke the hush.

"Somethin's burnin'!" a voice inside the building shouted.

Kyler, crouched behind the shed, kept his eyes

on the sagging screen door at the rear of the structure. Abruptly it flung open. Men rushed into the yard, stumbling over one another in their haste.

"It's around the front . . . !"

"Front, hell . . . the whole works is burnin'!"

Kyler waited patiently. Six of the outlaws were in the open. There were three more to account for before he could make his move. They should make an appearance soon. Flames were now shooting above the roof of the tinder-dry building and smoke boiled about it in thick, black clouds.

The screen door banged again. The missing outlaws trotted into the yard, pulling on clothing as they shouted angry questions at their friends, now collected in a group along the fringe of the flaring firelight.

"How'd it start?"

Kyler, holding the shotgun before him, stepped from behind the tool shed.

"I started it," he said in a voice that reached above the crackling flames.

The outlaws whirled. A man near center yelled: "It's him . . . Kyler!"

"Keep your hands high!" Sam shouted his warning.

They raised their arms slowly. A heavily built man with a long scar on his face that showed whitely in the glare said something to the outlaw beside him, then came back to Kyler. "What do you want?"

"You," Kyler said in a flat, uncompromising way.

The big outlaw laughed. "Just like that, eh? You come by yourself?"

"Something you'll have to find out," Sam replied.

A moment of silence followed, and then another man said: "What are you figurin' on doin'?"

"Driving you out of the country . . . one way or another. The ranchers around here have had enough of you."

"So they hired you to do the job."

"All by yourself?"

"I've got help."

Again there was quiet broken only by the roaring flames that had now spread to the roof and were racing through the interior of the house. The heat had grown intense. Sweat glistened on the features of the outlaws but none risked moving.

"So what's the deal?"

"You've got a choice. Throw down your guns and ride out. Stay off the Strip from here on. Or else we settle it here and now."

"You ain't much on countin'," the scar-faced man said. "Nine of us to your one."

"The scatter-gun evens it up," Kyler said. "I'll get four . . . maybe five . . . of you the first blast. Rest will be easy."

"Hell . . . he's alone!" the big outlaw yelled suddenly, and clawed for his pistol.

Kyler threw himself to one side, fired off one barrel of the shotgun. The scarred outlaw heaved backward, slammed to the ground as the full charge of shot caught him. Wheeling fast, Kyler pressed off the other trigger, taking only quick aim at the group. Three of Hurd's men went down. He dropped the empty shotgun, came up with his .45.

Guns blasted through the smoke. Bullets thudded into the tool shed, sent up a shower of needle-sharp splinters. Kyler felt a slug rip at his sleeve, burn across his arm. He snapped a shot at an outlaw down on one knee and leveling at him. As the man toppled, he saw the remaining four racing for their horses. He cut down on the nearest. The outlaw paused in flight, went crashing headlong into the brush.

Sam leaped away from the shed, hoping for another try at the escaping three. The blinding smoke and thick shrubbery concealed them and he could find no target. He hesitated, jerked aside as one of the men lying in the yard threw a final, desperate shot at him, then collapsed.

Wheeling, Kyler dropped to the tool shed as the quick pound of horses rushing away reached him. Grimly he recovered the shotgun, hurriedly replaced the spent shells. He stood there for a long minute, listening, and then walked to where the outlaws lay.

Three were dead. Two others were wounded, but

they would live if they could reach a doctor and receive proper treatment.

"Go on . . . finish the job," one said as Sam looked down at him.

Kyler shook his head. "You'll make it," he replied. "Both of you. But if I ever find you in this country again, I sure as hell will finish it. Now, get up. And help your friend there."

Sam stepped back, watched the outlaw stagger to his feet. The second man, hand clamped to one shoulder, managed to get upright unassisted.

"Drop your guns," Kyler said. "Then get on your horses and ride north. Dodge isn't far."

"Dalhart's lots closer."

"You're not going there. Head north. Maybe you'll find a rancher who'll patch you up so's you can reach Dodge."

The outlaws nodded woodenly, turned toward their mounts. Kyler halted them. "I'll say this once more . . . don't come back. If you do, I'll kill you."

The pair again moved their heads, continued on. Suddenly there was the hammer of running horses coming in fast. Kyler, reacting instantly, hurled himself to the ground. Gunshots smashed through the crackling flames. Sam heard the whine of bullets, saw one of the wounded outlaws sag, go down. He rolled to his back, gun in hand. He had only the fleeting shadow of one of the riders for a target as the man thundered for the protection of the brush. He triggered the weapon, saw the outlaw fling up his arms, and start to fall. And then smoke hid him from view.

Sam remained motionless. The sound of hoof beats was a fading rhythm, moving south. He got to his feet quickly. The outlaws would have to be stopped before they could overtake Eli Hurd and the rest of his men somewhere between the burning ranch house and Dalhart. He started across the yard at a run.

The second of the wounded men, again on his feet after ducking low when his companions opened up, wheeled in fear. "I'm goin'!" he yelled.

"Be quick about it," Kyler snapped. "And keep remembering what I said about coming back."

"I sure will," the outlaw answered, looking at the bodies in the yard. "You ain't ever layin' eyes on me again!"

Sam, anxious to be in the saddle, waited impatiently until the wounded man had mounted and pulled away, and then trotted to where the bay was tethered. Climbing onto the big horse, he gave the house a final glance.

It had burned to its rock foundation and the fire was now spreading through the dry weeds and grass, beginning to lick hungrily at the nearest of the smaller structures. Before the day was over the entire homestead would be a charred ruin—never again offering a handy hide-out for men outside the law.

Wheeling the bay out of the osage orange, he

rode across the field to the crest of a hill. Pausing there, he looked to the south. There were two riders in the distance. Immediately he put the bay to a lope. He would have to move fast.

XIV

The outlaws' hide-out was about a day's ride from Dalhart, Kyler estimated, and the herd was likely somewhere near halfway by that hour. It didn't afford him much time in which to overhaul the fleeing riders.

He pushed the bay hard, holding him to the lower ground where he would not be seen by the two men should they be watching their back trail. He doubted they were. After he had downed the third member of their party when they surged in for a final try for him, they had pulled off fast, anxious to put as much ground between themselves and the old ranch as possible.

The bay was not in very good condition. He had received only a few hours' rest since leaving Skull Cañon, but, thinking it over, Sam concluded the outlaws' mounts were probably in no better shape. They would have been on the move almost continually in the past two days so he could expect them to be far from their best.

He did not realize how accurate that assumption was until an hour later when he broke out of a long, brush-studded arroyo onto a flat and saw the outlaws no more than a quarter mile distant—and directly opposite. They were taking it slow, favoring their horses, allowing them to walk in the hot sun. They saw Kyler ride into the open at the exact moment he located them. Both halted instantly, then, driving deeply into the flanks of their worn mounts, they wheeled left and rode hard for a ragged bank of buttes a short distance away.

Kyler swung in after them. He crossed a few yards of solid ground, and then was again in the broad, sandy bed of a wash. The bay began to labor in the loose footing and the outlaws, on firmer surface, drew off rapidly. Just as the bay climbed out of the arroyo, the two men gained the butte and disappeared into the heavy brush skirting its base. Kyler swore softly. Now he would have to dig them out—and that could take hours. He glanced at the sun as the bay raced on. He had hoped to be in Dalhart when Hurd arrived with the cattle. A lengthy delay here would upset that plan.

He drew his pistol, began to veer toward the right of the brush into which the outlaws had vanished. He covered only a short distance when a rifle cracked spitefully and sand spurted from beneath the bay. Kyler, ducking low, wheeled the big horse sharply toward the shelter of the bluff and leaped from the saddle. He struck the ground as the rifle barked a second time. The bullet struck a stone, ricocheted noisily off into the warm air. Kyler hurriedly crawled deeper into the tangle of weeds and creosote bushes, halting finally when he came up against the face of the butte.

He paused, listened. The outlaws were on ahead 100 yards or so, he guessed, and likely now above him hiding in one of the many narrow ravines that gashed the formation. He looked back. There was no break in the steep wall behind him that would enable him to ascend and circle around the pair. He would have to chance it from below.

Gun in hand, he resumed the slow approach, keeping in close to the bluff and making full use of the brush. Every few yards he halted, listened, hopeful of pinpointing the outlaws' exact position. He heard nothing. They were waiting him out, watching for him to expose himself.

Somewhere ahead gravel rattled hollowly. Kyler stopped again, pressed himself tightly against the rough, red surface of the butte. A horse stamped wearily—the sound so close that Kyler stiffened. He realized then he was in the same badly over-grown area in which the men had sought cover, that their hastily abandoned horses were only paces away.

The meaning of the spilling gravel came to him; the men were descending, leaving the cut in the butte where they had hidden and taken their shots at him. They were returning, still cautious, for their horses.

"I tell you . . . I got him."

The hoarse whisper came from Kyler's right and slightly overhead. More displaced shale clattered.

"Was that last shot . . . seen him go down."

"Maybe, but we ain't takin' no chances," another voice said. "I keep rememberin' what that scatter-gun did to Webb and them others. I ain't anxious to buck up again it twicet."

The voices had grown louder, the scraping of boots more pronounced.

"Reckon we're the only ones that got away?"

"Wouldn't surprise me none."

"Hurd'll raise holy hell when he finds out . . . nine of us and only one Kyler. What'll we tell him?"

"I'll tell him for you," Sam said, and stepped into the center of the draw.

Both outlaws fell back, surprise and fear blanking their faces. The older of the two tripped, fell. A yell burst from his flaring lips.

"Don't shoot!"

"Get up," Kyler said coldly. "Both of you . . . walk out here . . . hands high."

The pair moved into the small clearing, the old man complying hastily; the other, a husky redhead, took his time all the while watching Kyler with narrowed eyes. "Now what?" he asked when they had halted. "You aim to shoot us down?"

"Probably what you've got coming," Sam replied, "but I'm no judge and jury. I'll give you the same choice I offered you before . . . get out of this country and stay out, or go for your gun."

"I'm for ridin'," the oldster said instantly. "And we won't come back, neither. You got a promise."

"Maybe I can bank on that, and maybe not," Kyler said, "so I'll make you one. I give you my word I'll kill you on sight if I ever run into you again. That clear?"

"Sure is."

"Head north. I don't want you around Dalhart."

"Yes, sir . . . north," the older outlaw said readily.

Kyler settled his gaze on the redhead. "You're not talking. You agree with the old man?"

The outlaw shrugged. "He's makin' his own deal. I'll do what I figure's best for me."

Sam Kyler felt the tension grow within him. "What's best for you?" he asked softly.

The redhead moved his shoulders again. He was holding the rifle in his left hand. He raised it, broadside, toward Kyler, apparently surrendering the weapon. "This," he said in a quick, breathless way, and threw the long gun straight at Sam. In that same instant his right hand swept down, came up fast with his pistol.

Kyler, warding off the rifle with his left forearm, fired twice in rapid succession. The redhead jerked half around from the impact of the .45's bullets, went to his knees. He hung there briefly, then sprawled full length.

Sam Kyler had not removed his eyes from the older man after triggering his weapon. Abruptly his taut shape relented. The oldster had no intention of following his partner's example. He stared at the dead man, then raised his gaze to Sam.

"Was a danged fool . . . that Red," he muttered. "Anybody'd know better'n try that."

Relieved but still wary, Kyler said: "I take it you got a different idea."

"Yes, sir . . . sure have. You bein' willin', I'll just climb onto my horse and head north."

Kyler nodded. "That's what I want. Drop your gun and move out."

The outlaw lifted his pistol carefully by the butt, allowed it to fall. Sam stepped forward, kicked it off into the brush.

"This country's not for you," he said. "You got that straight?"

"Yes, sir." The old man hesitated, looked questioningly at Kyler. "It all right if I walk?"

Sam took a step to one side, permitted the outlaw to pass, then fell in behind and followed him to where the horse stood. There could be another rifle. His glance probed the saddle. There had been only one. Silently he watched the oldster mount.

"Take Red's horse," Kyler said when the outlaw was settled. "No sense leaving him here to starve."

The outlaw nodded, took up the reins of his partner's sorrel. He leaned forward, his features mirroring the relief that filled him. "Obliged to you for seein' things this way."

Kyler shook his head. "Just don't forget what I told you."

"Ain't no danger of that," the old man said, and rode off.

XV

Sam Kyler returned to the bay and immediately struck south for Dalhart. He had no hoof-marked trail to follow but he knew in which general direction the settlement lay; the rest of the outlaws, with the herd, should be somewhere in the intervening area.

Two hours later he caught sight of a small dust cloud well off to his right. He angled the tired bay toward it, again taking the precaution of keeping below the horizon as much as possible, and soon was near enough to size up the cattle and drovers.

There were only four riders with the herd; there should be six. Frowning, he considered that. He was certain it was the stolen beef, but he was reluctant to move in closer for a better look. He was still too far from Dalhart to reveal himself.

Puzzled, he cut back east into the choppy hills and circled widely to place himself ahead of the slowly moving herd. Then, in a narrow arroyo choked with rabbitbrush and Apache plume, he waited for the cattle to pass.

He had been right. The first rider he saw was Shad Collins. Eli Hurd, however, was not among the other three. Apparently he had ridden ahead with another of his crew to make necessary arrangements for the sale of the cattle.

Kyler heaved a sigh of relief. For a brief time the possibility of there being two small herds on the flats and *en route* to the settlement had plagued him, and, if he had picked the wrong bunch of steers to follow, his plan for recovering the beef would have been thrown out of kilter.

He permitted the herd to pass, and, when it was a safe distance ahead, he broke out of the arroyo and followed slowly. It would have been no great chore to close in on the four riders, overcome them, and take possession, but this he had no thought of doing. It was smarter to let them drive the stock to Dalhart than attempt to manage the unruly brutes alone.

The afternoon wore on, hot and dusty. Smoke appeared on the horizon, marking the location of the town. Sam gauged the sun. The herd should reach there an hour or so before dark, he reckoned.

He wondered then if Wasco and the crew had arrived with the main body of the drive, guessed they had, unless there had been trouble. He hoped all had gone well. If he could pull off what he had in mind for Eli Hurd, all of the beef would reach the loading pens and he and Wasco would have that much of their agreement fulfilled.

He topped out a low rise and the houses and buildings of Dalhart came into view. Almost at once a solitary rider left the scatter of structures and rode out to meet the incoming herd, now a half mile ahead. Kyler again dropped back, swept widely, and put himself ahead of the cattle. At a safe distance he watched the newcomer join Collins and the others, realized that he likely had been dispatched by Hurd to direct the crew when it reached town.

Spurring on, Kyler circled farther east and entered Dalhart from its opposite side. He had no wish to encounter Eli Hurd just yet. Keeping to the edge of the settlement, he passed behind the shacks and barns that lay along the railroad right of way and eventually came to the long string of loading pens and chutes. Most of the pens, he noted, were filled to capacity with bawling, heaving cattle. It required several minutes of persistent searching to locate Hurd. He finally spotted the outlaw in company with a well-dressed man—evidently a cattle buyer—waiting at an empty enclosure at the extreme end of the row. Pulling in behind a small shed, Kyler dismounted, anchored the bay, and once more settled down to wait.

An hour later, with the sun hovering just above the western horizon, the herd, swathed in a rolling cloud of yellow dust and complaining noisily, appeared at the edge of town and started down the lane leading to the pens. The outlaw chief and the buyer, a fold of paper in his hand, moved from the shade of the tree under which they had been standing, and crossed to the empty pen. Hurd swung back the gate, and the two men stationed themselves at one side. When the first steer entered, the tally began.

Sam Kyler, leaning against the board railing of a fence a few yards away, watched idly. When the last steer was inside and the gate closed, he straightened and, walking quietly, edged in closer.

With the securing of the cattle, two of Hurd's riders swung off at once for the center of town, anxious to find a saloon where they could wash away the dust accumulated in their throats. Kyler grinned his satisfaction. That left only three men to side Eli Hurd.

"How many you make it, Jessup?"

It was the outlaw chief's voice. Kyler paused at the corner of the pen. Hurd said something more but the noise rising from the restless, milling steers drowned his words. Sam moved in still closer.

The cattle buyer was working with his pencil. He looked up. "Two hundred seven head. . . ."

"Seven more'n I figured," Hurd said, laughing. "Must've picked up some strays."

Jessup smiled, reached into his pocket for a pad of bank drafts. "Now, if you'll turn over your bill of sale so I can jot down the brands. . . ."

"Right here," the outlaw said, taking the folded paper from his vest pocket. "You'll have to make a change in the count. Outside of that everything ought to be jake."

"Know that, Mister Hurd, but the company insists on things being just so. It all right if I make the draft out to cash?"

"Suits me fine. Now, let's see . . . you said sixteen fifty a head . . . and there's two hundred and seven. . . ."

"Comes out to three thousand four hundred and fifteen dollars . . . and fifty cents. Real nice piece of change for a small herd like yours."

The outlaw grinned. "Sure is." He slid a glance at his crew waiting slackly on their saddles.

"Got any more you'd like to sell? Market's top," Jessup said, making notes in his book. "Prime stuff is in demand. Be glad to drop back later on if you've got another bunch you'd like to dispose of."

Hurd plucked at his chin thoughtfully. "Might just take you up on that," he said. "Been my habit to sell just a small bunch every year. That way it sort of keeps the main herd from runnin' down." One of the riders laughed. The outlaw chief seemed not to hear. "But what you're sayin' makes sense. Could be I might scare up a couple hundred more."

"Fine, fine. Just leave word at the bank. They'll get in touch with me," Jessup said, snapping his book shut. "Well, guess that takes care of everything. Here's your draft."

Eli Hurd raised his arm, reached for the slip of paper.

"I'll take that," Sam Kyler said from the shadows, and drew back the twin hammers of his shotgun.

XVI

At the dry, overly loud *click* of the weapon being cocked, the outlaws froze, Jessup stared.

"Stand easy," Kyler said in a low voice. "Nobody moves . . . nobody gets hurt."

"Who the hell are you?" Hurd demanded angrily.

"The man you just made a deal for," Sam replied quietly.

He moved to the side of Jessup, plucked the draft from the man's fingers, and tucked it into his shirt pocket. Backing off, he circled around until he faced the men.

Eli Hurd stiffened. "Kyler," he muttered under his breath.

Sam placed his attention on Jessup. "You bought yourself some rustled cattle, mister. Were part of a big herd I was driving in."

"Stolen!" Jessup said in a strangled voice. "There was a bill of sale. . . ."

"He got it at gun point."

Jessup frowned, looked questioningly at the outlaw chief. Hurd's expression did not change. He continued to glare at Kyler. The rider next to

Collins shifted. Shad threw him a hurried glance.

"Forget it, Bud. He'll cut you in two with that damned scatter-gun."

"He's no cattleman," Kyler continued. "He's nothing but an outlaw . . . a rustler. Every cow he ever sold you was pirated from somebody's herd."

"First time I ever bought from him," Jessup said defensively. He turned to Hurd. "This all true?"

"Hell, no . . . it ain't true!" the outlaw said boldly. "If you got the time, I can take you to my place. North of here, about a day's ride."

"I burned it to the ground," Kyler drawled. "Your boys have pulled out . . . the ones that aren't dead."

Hurd's mouth snapped shut. Sweat stood out on his forehead in large beads. "You trailed my boys . . . ?"

"Right. Had a little talk with them. Those that were reasonable moved on . . . said they'd not be back."

"And the others?"

"Buzzard bait."

Hurd shook his head in disbelief. "I ain't swallerin' none of that," he said, and then, as his surprise at seeing Sam Kyler faded and a measure of his effrontery returned, he added: "He's feedin' you a lot of guff, Jessup. Cattle don't belong to him. He's just a damn' drifter tryin' to cash in on a good thing."

The buyer mopped his flushed face, looked at Sam. "That true? You don't own the stock?"

"Told you I was driving them through. Belong to the cattlemen in the Strip. You'll find the rest of the herd in the pens along here somewhere. Be easy enough to check the brands."

"Well . . . I don't know," Jessup said hesitantly. "Never came up against anything like this before."

"You're in the clear," Kyler said. "Money will go to the right men now. Be obliged to you if you'll go get the marshal."

"The marshal!" Eli Hurd shouted. "What for? He's got no call to go buttin' into this."

"Maybe he has. Rustling took place outside his territory . . . I know that. But the deal you were trying to pull happened right here in this town. I figure that makes it his business." Kyler paused, drifted the muzzle of the shotgun suggestively over Hurd and his riders. "Drop your hardware. Do it slow."

Shad Collins was the first to obey. He lifted his weapon with his left hand, allowed it to fall into the loose dust. The outlaw beside him, Bud, followed suit. The tall rider standing near Hurd simply stared.

"How about it?" Kyler pressed quietly.

The man hesitated a moment longer, then shrugged, reached for his pistol.

"The hell with it!" Hurd shouted abruptly, and lunged against Jessup.

Kyler leaped back, tried to get out of the way of the reeling cattle buyer. He was too slow. Jessup slammed into him and they both went down. He was aware of Hurd's voice yelling something, of the quick hammer of horses pulling away as Shad Collins and Bud made a run for it.

He jerked clear of Jessup, got to his feet. Instantly a gunshot smashed through the darkness and a bullet thudded into a cross board of the cattle pen behind him. He whirled, caught a glimpse of the tall outlaw, let him have the left barrel of the shotgun. The rider staggered back, fell.

Again Kyler heard the pound of running horses. He turned, had a glimpse of Bud and Collins, both with rifles—and the two missing members of Hurd's crew. He realized what had taken place. Shad and Bud, fleeing, had immediately run into the other outlaws as they were returning from town. They had joined forces and were coming to Eli Hurd's aid.

Sam fired at the two nearest. He saw both go off their saddles as the load of buckshot ripped into them. He dropped the shotgun, drew his revolver, and spun. He snapped a shot at the third rider— Shad Collins—missed.

From the corner of his eye he saw Hurd, running hard for the far end of the cattle pen. Sam leveled on him, checked, and ducked away as a gun roared close by and a bullet slapped into the wood behind him. He looked up, saw Shad and Bud coming in again.

He triggered a shot at Bud, saw him wilt and cut

away, almost colliding with Collins. He tried once more, this time for Shad, again missed. Through the coiling smoke he saw them both wheel sharply and disappear into the darkness beyond the brush. Sam drew in close to the cattle pen, listening hard. Jessup was a few feet away, lying flat on the ground trying desperately to keep out of the line of fire.

"My God . . . I never saw such a. . . ."

"Shut up!" Kyler hissed.

He was uncertain as to the intentions of Bud and Shad Collins. They could be moving in again. He heard hoof beats, relaxed slightly. They were heading into town. They'd had enough. He looked at the cattle buyer.

"Stay put, and you won't get hurt."

Crouching low, Kyler began to move along the side of the pen. The shadows were black in that area and he could determine very little distinctly, but he was between Eli Hurd and his horse and he was sure the outlaw was still there.

Off toward town he could hear shouting. The splatter of gunshots had attracted attention. Soon a crowd would gather—a crowd that would include not only the curious but the representatives of the law as well. Earlier he would have welcomed the town marshal's presence—but now it was different. It would be difficult to make the lawman understand his position—and the shoot-out. Best thing to do was find Hurd quickly, settle with him—and move on.

He reached the end of the pens. Still hunkered, he stopped, searched the dark pools beyond for the outlaw. He could see no sign of the man. Hurd would not have gone far; at that very moment he would be nearby in hiding, waiting for Kyler to step into the open and provide him with an easy mark.

Considering that briefly, Sam retreated a few steps, turned, and climbed over the top rail of the pen, dropping into the midst of the cattle. Shoving his way through the restless animals, he crossed to the opposite side. Removing his hat, he peered over the top board. He saw Eli Hurd. The outlaw was squatting behind a stump only paces away, his face turned toward the corner of the pen. He had been waiting just as Sam had anticipated.

Kyler drew himself upright. "Last chance, Eli. Throw down your. . . ."

Before he could finish, the outlaw leader whirled and fired. The bullet smashed into the dry timber in front of Kyler, spewed dust and stinging splinters. Sam got off two quick shots. The outlaw staggered to his feet, went back to his knees. He hung there for several moments, struggling again to lift his gun, and then fell forward.

Kyler vaulted the fence, threw a hurried glance at the approaching crowd. It was not far away. Wheeling, he ran the width of the pen, rounded the corner, and legged it to where Jessup lay.

Scooping up the shotgun, he paused beside the

cattle buyer. "When the marshal gets here . . . see that you tell the story straight," he said in a hard voice.

Jessup scrambled to his feet. He nodded vigorously. "I will . . . I sure will."

Turning, Sam Kyler trotted to where the bay waited.

XVII

Kyler hurried back along the route he had previously followed, keeping to the darkness at the rear of the buildings. He could hear shouting near the cattle pens, realized the crowd had reached that point and was having its look at what had happened there. He would be pressed for time, he knew, but with a little luck he should be able to find the bank and transact his business, and then join Wasco and the crew at the Longhorn Saloon before Dalhart's lawman got a search under way.

He came finally to what he judged to be the center of town and halted. Leaving the bay behind a small shed, he made his way along a passage that ran between two of the buildings and came out onto the main street.

He paused again, faced the blast of sound running through the clouds of spinning dust. Dalhart was bulging at the seams with drovers, just paid off and all endeavoring to spend their earnings in a single night. He studied the throng surging up and down the street, concluded he would likely go unnoticed. He had visited the town only once before, and, except for Shad Collins and Bud and perhaps someone he might accidentally bump into, he was not known.

He moved to the edge of the walk, ran his glance along the storefronts in search of the bank. He had no difficulty in locating the Longhorn Saloon—and wished then he had named a less prominent place for the meeting with Wasco and the crew. It was ablaze with light and there was a continual flow in and out of its batwing doors.

The Cattleman's Trust, he saw then, was immediately to his right. Stepping into the loose dust, Kyler shouldered his way to the structure. It was open, as were all business houses, despite the fact that the day was over. Dalhart merchants were making the most of their opportunities. Reaching the bank, he crossed the boardwalk and entered.

Two armed men sitting on opposite sides of the narrow room rose to their feet, eyed him suspiciously. Ignoring them, Kyler stepped up to the one occupied cage. He dug Jessup's draft from his pocket, shoved it under the grillwork.

"Want this cashed."

The teller, an elderly individual with steel-rimmed spectacles, nodded, studied the face of the order. "Your name?"

"Sam Kyler."

The banker shook his head. "Guess it doesn't

make any difference . . . Jessup's always making these things out to cash. How do you want it?"

"Big bills," Sam replied, and removed his money belt and laid it on the shelf before him.

He waited until the ranchers' money had been counted, then pushed it aside, and emptied the pockets of the belt. He was short a hundred dollars or so of Arch Clayborn's thousand and he considered claiming an advance from what was owed him by the Strip ranchers. There should be no objection. The worst of the trip was over; all that remained was the return, and, if he followed Tolliver's suggestion, there would be no danger of losing the ranchers' cash to outlaws. But somehow it didn't seem right to him. He handed the bills to the teller. "Like to have a draft for that. Make it out to Arch Clayborn. Burnt Springs, Texas."

The banker counted the currency and loose silver, reached for a blank check. "Even nine hundred . . . or do you want to include the odd amount, too?"

"Make it nine hundred," Kyle replied.

It wouldn't matter; he intended to send Clayton the difference as soon as he was paid. He stuffed the ranchers' money into his belt, fastened it around his waist. Picking up the cash returned to him by the teller, he thrust it into his pocket.

"Like to borrow an envelope and sheet of paper," he said. "Stamp, too, if you've got one."

The banker paused, produced the required items.

"How about a pen and some ink?" he said, his tone faintly sardonic.

Kyler grinned. "Pencil will do," he said, and obtained one from his own pocket.

He addressed the envelope to Clayborn, then wrote a short note explaining what had happened. He ended the letter with a promise to mail the missing $100 within a few days. By the time he had finished, the bank teller was ready.

"Be a dollar service charge," he said, handing over the draft.

Sam paid off, enclosed the draft with the letter, and sealed them inside the envelope. Affixing the stamp, he looked questioningly at the teller.

"Leave it with me," the man said tiredly. "I'll see it gets posted."

"Obliged," Kyler said, and, passing the letter to him, returned to the street.

He halted in the darkness just outside the door, stared off into the noisy night. Weariness and hunger were beginning to drag at him but he knew it was unsafe to remain in Dalhart. Better to look up Wasco and the others, head out, and then, when they were a reasonable distance from the town, stop for the night. Wheeling, he started from the walk for the Longhorn—suddenly drew up.

Two men had emerged from the saloon next to the bank. One was Jessup, the other was a tall, wide-shouldered man wearing a star. Sam flattened himself against the wall.

"Maybe he was in the right," the marshal was saying. "But nobody rides into my town, shoots up a half dozen men, and rides out scotfree. Can't afford to let a thing like that happen."

"They were outlaws, Marshal. Admitted it."

"Still men . . . and far as this Kyler goes, he ain't no better. Got a wanted dodger in my office for him right now. Stole a thousand dollars from some Texas rancher." The lawman paused. "Sure you got no idea where he was headed?"

"Don't recall him mentioning it. Just got on his horse and rode off. Could be putting up here for the night."

"Doubt that. Kyler's been around. He knows I'll be looking for him. You say he was working for the ranchers over in the Strip?"

"What he claimed."

"He'll be goin' back there, then. Be wanting to collect his pay."

"You aim to go after him, Gates?"

"What else? He'll have to answer to that robbery charge . . . and I sure can't let him get by with what he done here. If I did, I'd have every lousy gun toter this side of the Missouri thinking he could do the same."

"But that's unclaimed territory. There's no law."

"It'll have some when I get there," the marshal said grimly and started to turn. "Let's go take a look at that dodger. Want to be sure it's the same man."

Kyler watched them move off into the crowd. Arch Clayborn had filed charges, as he had feared the rancher would. He gave that bitter thought for a moment, then shrugged. He couldn't blame Clayborn; it did look like robbery. But it would all be cleared up when the rancher received his draft.

Meanwhile, it would be smart to keep out of the lawman's way, as he had planned. He could talk better in Jericho. For all Gates's strong words he could do nothing once he was in the Strip. Once there he could explain the Clayborn matter, persuade Gates to wait, give Arch time to withdraw the charges.

As to the lawman's other complaint, he could understand his position. Any kind of a shoot-out was bad for a town, and, while he had not fired the first bullet, there was no denying he had sought out Eli Hurd and his men for the express purpose of settling with them. He could explain that, too, back in Jericho—and he would have the Strip ranchers to stand behind him.

Kyler moved away from the wall, looked down the street. Jessup and Gates had disappeared. The next thing was to meet Wasco and the crew, pull out. He stepped off the boardwalk into the loose dirt, slanted toward the Longhorn.

"Kyler!"

At the sound of Shad Collins's voice, Sam dipped and wheeled from instinct. He saw the outlaw, flanked by Bud, standing in the entrance to

108

the building adjoining the saloon. In the next instant he looked into the orange flash of Shad's pistol, felt the shock of a bullet as it tore through the fleshy part of his leg. And then he was triggering his own weapon.

Shad Collins fired a second time but from pure spasmodic reflex. The slug splintered the door behind Kyler. Bud had leaped back out of harm's way, his good arm raised above his head. A bandage showed whitely on the other. "I ain't part of this!" he yelled.

Kyler's rigidity broke. His gun lowered. Men were shouting in the street, surging toward him. He became aware of the pain in his leg and the very thought that he had gone through two shoot-outs without serous injury, only to take a bullet there on Dalhart's crowded street as he faced one man, passed through his mind.

Recognition of danger suddenly pushed all else aside. Gates would be coming with the crowd. Limping badly, he finished his crossing and ducked into the passageway that ran alongside the Longhorn.

Reaching the corner of the bulky structure, he turned, saw a short staircase leading up to a landing. Ignoring the pain in his leg, he climbed the steps, pushed open the door. He was in a narrow hallway at the end of which a second door faced him. He moved hurriedly to it, drew it back. A wave of noise, light, smoke, and confusion struck him head on. He had entered the Longhorn from the rear.

The place was packed. Several men standing at the bar to his left glanced up at his abrupt appearance, then looked away disinterestedly. Evidently the back door was in common usage.

Sam, keeping close to the end of the counter in an effort to hide his wounded leg from the curious, worked toward the front. He saw Wasco at the same moment the old cowpuncher recognized him. Sam halted, watched his friend lean across the table where he was sitting and tap Bill Denby on the arm. Together the two men rose and made their way through the crowd to Kyler.

"Sure glad to see you!" Wasco exclaimed, then drew back. "You been shot up!"

Kyler shook his head. "No time to explain now. Got to get out of town."

Denby said: "The law?"

Sam nodded. "Out front now . . . looking for me. Get the boys together and head north. I'll meet you down the trail four or five miles."

"Ought to get that leg fixed first," the rancher said.

"No time. Going to be a chore getting to my horse."

"Don't worry about the law," Wasco said, his weathered face breaking into a grin. "Me and the boys'll keep him busy for a spell while you're gettin' started. You need anythin'?"

"Nothing . . . except to get out of Dalhart," Kyler said, and turned for the door.

"We'll sure guarantee that," Wasco promised. "See you down the line."

"One thing more!" Denby called, and, as Kyler hesitated, he added: "How about the stock . . . you get it back?"

Sam patted the money belt under his shirt. "Got the money right here."

The rancher smiled. "And Eli Hurd?"

"Taken care of," Kyler replied, and moved on.

XVIII

Kyler waited in the darkness at the rear of the Longhorn. His leg throbbed relentlessly and a dampness along his knee warned him that the wound was bleeding freely. Jerking the bandanna from around his neck, he impatiently ripped it into two strips, tied them together, and improvised a bandage. Placing it over the wound, he pulled it tight. Breathing heavily from his efforts, he leaned back against the building. That was all he could do for the injury for the present.

A wild burst of yelling, punctuated by a solitary gunshot, rose above the general hubbub of confusion in the street fronting the saloon. Kyler grinned tautly. Wasco and the drovers were creating their diversion. He delayed another few moments, allowing ample time for the crowd to collect, then crossed the open passageway and entered the shadows on the opposite side.

He could hear men running, shouting questions, but the passageway had offered only a fleeting glimpse of the street, and he could just guess at what was taking place, a fight, a staged free-for-all most likely.

Kyler kept to the rear of the buildings until he was some distance below the Longhorn, and then cut back to the sidewalk. He found he was 100 yards or so from the large crowd gathered in the glaring lights of the saloon. There were still a few persons scattered along the way, unattracted by the excitement, and he paused to give them thorough scrutiny. Town Marshal Gates was not one of them and Kyler immediately crossed over, walking leisurely so as to not draw undue attention.

He gained the opposite side of the street, stopped into the nearest passageway, and broke into a slow, painful jog. He came out below the shed where he had tied the bay, veered left through a jumble of old casks, packing boxes, and other trash.

Almost upon the shed, he pulled up short. Two men, standing beside the bay, wheeled at his sudden appearance. Alarm rocked through Kyler—and then died. Neither of the pair was Gates.

The taller of the two faced Sam. He jerked a thumb at the big horse. "Yours?"

Sam nodded, moved in closer. "Figured I ought to leave him back here," he said, giving the reins a yank to release the knot. "Hell of a commotion out there on the street."

The man shrugged. "On my property. Was about to lead him off to the pound." He shifted his glance, eyed the horse critically. "Looks mighty beat. Expect he could use a good feed."

"He'll get it," Kyler said, and swung into the saddle.

The second of the two came up sharply. "Say . . . you been shot?"

"Only a scratch," Sam replied, and started to pull away.

"Scratch, hell . . . that's a bullet hole!" The man paused, stared. "By God . . . you're the fellow the marshal's lookin' for!" he said in a breathless voice.

Kyler hauled in, came half around. His jaw was set. "Take your time telling him about it," he said in a slow, quiet way. "Don't want trouble with you."

The two men froze. Kyler favored them with a curt nod, and moved on.

Dismissing them from his mind, Sam rode due south for the full length of the town, then cut right. When he crossed the road leading up to Dalhart's main street, the racket in front of the Longhorn and elsewhere in the settlement was only a faint churning sound beneath a pale glare.

He continued his westward course until the town lay well behind him, and then again veered right.

A short time later he reached the trail that led, eventually, to Jericho and points on north, and swung onto it.

His leg was paining considerably and he held the bay to a slow lope, hopeful of minimizing the discomfort, but it helped little. Realizing, finally, that nothing would ease the leg except rest, he clamped his teeth shut and rode on.

He pulled off the trail short of the distance he had stipulated. A large outcropping of rock, well covered with brush and purple-tasseled grass, offered an inviting place to await Wasco and the crew, and he halted gratefully in the shallow coulée and dismounted.

Moving stiffly, he sat down and sank back against a ledge of sandstone as the bay began to graze eagerly. He made a brief examination of his wound. There was nothing more he could do for it until the crew arrived, which should be soon. Wasco would lose no time in pulling out of Dalhart.

His thoughts turned to Gates, the lawman. He would be passing this way, too, if he followed through with his intentions. But it was doubtful if he would begin the journey to Jericho before morning. By then Sam Kyler expected to be well on his way. He decided he had little to worry about insofar as the marshal was concerned.

A half hour later the sound of running horses reached him. He pulled himself erect, limped to the outermost point of the rocky formation, and waited. He must first be certain it was the crew before showing himself; if so, he would have to act quickly and stop them. They were expecting to meet him farther on.

He recognized Wasco well before the riders drew abreast and caught the old cowpuncher's attention by waving his hat. Immediately the crew left the trail and moments later all were gathered in the coulée.

"Got here fast as we could," Wasco said, grinning broadly. "Marshal was for juggin' the bunch of us for startin' the ruckus, but we sort've talked him out of it."

"Cost us twenty dollars . . . disturbin' the peace," Bill Denby said. "You have any trouble leavin'?"

Kyler shook his head.

Wasco looked at him with critical eyes. "How's that there leg?"

"Could use some attention. Anybody got a bottle of whiskey?"

"Me . . . I have," one of the men said.

"Bring it," Wasco directed before Kyler could speak. He squatted down and began to examine the wound. "I'll do the doctorin'. Rest of you get a fire goin' . . . boil up some coffee. And dig out the grub." He looked up at Sam. "When'd you eat last?"

Kyler shook his head. "Can't remember."

"Just what I figured," the old cowpuncher mumbled. "Shake your tails there, boys. This man ain't dyin' from a gunshot, he's dyin' from a empty belly."

An hour later Sam Kyler was feeling much better. His hunger had vanished and Wasco had done a good job on the leg, first cleaning it with hot water, then cauterizing it with the fiery liquor, after which he wrapped it with bandages made from a shirt. He was ready to move on, but the old cowpuncher would not hear of it.

"We're stayin' put . . . leastwise until daylight. You're in for a devil of a mean ride even then."

"Have to be gone by then," Kyler said, and explained about Gates.

Wasco relented. "All right, then, we'll pull out a couple hours before sunup. Ought to give us a good lead."

"Not so much that," Kyler said. "We'll be taking a different trail. Point is I want to be in Jericho when he gets there."

Bill Denby looked up from the fire. His features showed surprise. "You ain't goin' back with us?"

"Not taking any chances on losing the money," Kyler said. "Wasco and I'll be taking the road west of here, along the bluffs. You and the crew will go the usual way."

The rancher frowned. Wasco slapped his hands together. "By dang . . . I see what you're doin'! If them owlhoots aim to jump us, they'll be waitin' somewheres along the trail the boys always use. You're aimin' to decoy them while you and me's hightailin' it down another road!"

"That's the general idea," Sam said. He put his attention on Denby. "Up to you to make it look good. Keep the crew together and, when they move in on you, don't put up a fight. No need of anybody getting hurt."

"What happens when they don't find the money on us? They're goin' to be real peeved and start askin' a lot of questions."

"Tell them. By then Wasco and I will be too far ahead for them to catch up."

Denby reached for the coffee pot. "Why don't I just say we left the money in the bank at Dalhart. That'd end it for sure."

"Suit yourself. Just don't get anybody hurt."

Denby leaned forward, squinted. "Reckon this is as good a time as any to say this, Kyler. Had some wrong thoughts about you when this thing started. I'm takin' them back now."

"Forget it," Sam replied. "Expect I could have made it easier for everybody if I'd done a little talking."

Andy, the young cowpuncher who had almost precipitated serious trouble at Rifle Creek, nodded vigorously. "Same goes for me, Mister Kyler. I'm mighty sorry." He brushed his hat to one side. "That hoe-down you had at the cattle chutes sure must've been a humdinger! Folks in town was really talkin' about it. That the way you handled the rest of them outlaws?"

"They won't be around," Sam said quietly, and turned again to Denby. "Where've you got the money?"

"My saddlebags. Couldn't get it in a belt."

"Switch it to mine. Buckle it in tight." He paused, looked around. "Where's the chuck wagon?"

One of the drovers laughed. "Still in Dalhart, I expect. Ranchers' wives give old Turkey a list long as your arm for stuff to get for them. Bet he ain't home for a week."

"You want some grub to take along?" Denby said. "We brought plenty with us."

Kyler shook his head. "We can hold out until we reach Jericho. With all that cash riding with us, we won't take time to eat."

XIX

Daylight caught Sam Kyler and Wasco well on the return to Jericho. They struck the line of low, red-faced bluffs, as Tolliver had said, five miles or so west of the main trail, and now were bearing due north. So far the route had not been difficult, but looking ahead Sam could see why it was not practical for a cattle drive.

There was little forage. The ground was sandy, producing nothing other than common soap-tree yucca, prickly pear, and snakeweed. Here and there a giant cholla reached its barbed fingers toward the sun, and in the deeper arroyos and washes Apache plume and creosote bush formed scraggly barriers against the occasional torrents of water following the infrequent rainstorms.

"When you figure we'll hit town?" Wasco asked as they moved slowly on under the hot sun.

Kyler shifted himself to one side in an effort to ease the monotonous pain that claimed his leg. "About midnight . . . if we keep at it."

The old cowpuncher spat. "Which we sure can't. Horses won't last . . . and you won't, neither. That there leg of your'n is givin' you fits right now."

Sam made no reply. The wound throbbed incessantly, making it impossible to ride in any degree of comfort. But he refused to halt; with almost fifty thousand dollars in their possession, he was anxious to reach Jericho and relieve himself of the responsibility as soon as possible. Anger brushed through him.

"Ranchers are damned fools for not having a bank to deal with," he said irritably. "Carting this much money around is plain loco!"

"Expect they'd do it, had they the chance."

"They did. Let the outlaws buffalo them out of it."

Wasco sighed. "Now, you got a good look at them people. Ain't nothin' but ranchers . . . farm hands turned cowpokes. Couldn't none of them buck the likes of Eli Hurd and his bunch."

"Could if they'd get together," Kyler snapped.

Wasco gave his partner a close look. Sweat was standing out on Kyler's face in broad, shining patches, and his lips were pulled taut from pain. The old rider shifted on his saddle. "Smidgin' of shade up there ahead," he said, pointing at a clump of brush clinging to the rim of a deep gouge in the arroyo. What say we pull up and rest a spell? Old bones of mine are mighty achy."

Kyler swung his glance to Wasco, grinned knowingly. "All right . . . but you're not fooling me. And quit coddling me . . . I'll make it."

"Coddlin' . . . hell! Just plain good sense I'm usin'. You keep on the way you're doin' . . . and we never will get to Jericho!"

They halted for a half hour, then moved on, inaugurating a procedure followed thereafter throughout the day, of riding and resting periodically. It irked Sam Kyler but he was forced to admit that Wasco was right; it was far wiser to arrive in Jericho late than not at all.

Near the end of the afternoon they reached wilder country. The buttes lifted higher, forming cañons in some places, and the trail narrowed until it was little more than an indefinite path wandering along the base of steep walls and through brush-filled defiles.

"Slow goin'," Wasco remarked, casting a glance at the lowering sun. "We won't be makin' town soon if we have much of this."

Kyler, holding himself off the saddle by locking his hands on the horn and cantle, looked back. The old cowpuncher was only a few strides behind.

"Can't be much farther. According to Bill Denby, the bluffs end. . . ."

The sudden blast of a gun almost under the bay drowned Sam Kyler's words. The big horse shied violently, reared. Another pistol roared and Kyler heard Wasco yell. The thought—*hold-up!*—raced through his mind, but he could see no one—nor could he get at his weapon. The bay was plunging recklessly about in the brush, frantic with fear, trying to find stable footing so he could run.

Again guns crackled. Hanging on to the reins with one hand, the saddle horn with the other, Kyler ducked as he felt the breath of a bullet. In the same instant the bay started to fall. Kyler kicked free of the stirrups, jumped. He came down solidly on his injured leg. It gave and he pitched forward into a shelf of rock. He was briefly aware of more gunshots, and then pain and darkness engulfed him as his head smashed against the rough surface of the shelf.

It was full dark when Sam Kyler regained consciousness. He lay quietly, some inner instinct holding him motionless until he was certain all danger had passed. Hearing nothing, he stirred, endeavored to sit up. He lay face down at the base of the bluff, head lower than his feet. The bay had pitched him into a small, but deep, wash. Pain roared through him when he heaved himself around. Ignoring that, and the dull throbbing in his head, he got shakily to his feet, stared vacantly into the silence. It was full dark and he could see very little. His foggy mind began to function normally again, and with that came realization. It had been an ambush—a robbery! Wasco!

He stiffened. *Where was he . . . what had happened to him?* Moving as hurriedly as possible, Sam climbed up onto the trail, started back along its uneven course. A dozen paces on and he saw the old cowpuncher stretched full length on the sand, both arms outflung. Kyler, grim and wincing from pain, hobbled to his side and knelt down. He rolled the man to his back, peered into his face. Blood smeared the side of his head, had hardened into a crust.

"Wasco!" Kyler said in a hard, urgent way, shaking him gently. "Wasco!"

The cowpuncher stirred weakly, relapsed into stillness. Water. That would bring him around. The canteens were on their saddles. Kyler rose, looked up the narrow cañon, turned about, probed the area below. There was no sign of the two horses.

Swearing softly, he dropped back to Wasco's side, again shook him. The old man opened his eyes, stared wonderingly into Kyler's face. After a few moments he sat up, rubbed at his head gingerly.

"Somethin' sure give me a hell of a wallop," he muttered thickly.

Kyler sank back onto the sand in relief. "Bullet grazed you."

Wasco nodded. "Mite close. How 'bout you?"

"Horse threw me, hit my head on some rocks. Guess that's all that saved my hide. Whoever it was figured us both dead."

The old cowpuncher stared off into the shadows. "Got the money, too, I reckon."

"And the horses."

"The stinkin' varmints . . . leavin' a man afoot in country like this."

"Figured we wouldn't need them."

"Could've just wandered off."

"Maybe."

Sam Kyler's reply was without conscious effort. He was thinking about the hold-up—and its meaning.

"Was a mighty neat ambush," Wasco said. "What's botherin' me is how'd they know we was comin' this way? Figured it was all a big secret."

Kyler said: "Bothers me, too. Only one other man knew about it . . . the same man who suggested we take it."

Wasco leaned forward, frowned. "Who?"

"Tolliver. . . ."

The cowpuncher looked up in surprise. "The big muckity-muck of the ranchers?"

Sam nodded. "Pulled me off to one side before

we left. Told me about this trail. Said it would be a good way to fool the outlaws."

Wasco grinned. "And we walked smack dab into his trap, like a bunch of sheep." After a moment he shook his head. "Sure hard to believe. Figured that Tolliver for a square shooter."

"Had him wrong, too. Guess it worked out just the way he planned. His bunch caught us cold, got the money, and rode off leaving us for dead. When we don't show up, the ranchers will figure we kept going with the money . . . or the outlaws got us. Nobody'll ever think Tolliver was in on it."

Kyler angrily pulled himself upright. Wasco followed, slightly unsteady.

"Only thing wrong with his figuring," Sam said, "is that we're not dead. We're going to fool him . . . we're making it to Jericho, somehow."

"On that leg you ain't goin' nowhere far."

"I can manage it. Help me find a stick . . . a cane. Be slow but I. . . ."

"Just maybe you won't have to try," Wasco cut in, his head cocked to one side. "If I ain't mistook, I heard a horse."

Hope lifted within Sam Kyler. "You sure?"

"Sounded like a shoe clickin' against a rock," the old cowpuncher said. "Stay put whilst I have a look."

Wasco shambled off down the trail. Kyler settled back, shoulders to the wall of the butte. Like the old man, he was finding it hard to believe Tom

Tolliver was behind the ambush and robbery, but the facts were indisputable. It could be no one else.

"Found 'em!"

Wasco's voice echoed through the darkness in the narrow slash. Kyler rose to his feet. He could hear the cowpuncher's boots crunching in the sand, the dull thud of hoofs as he led their mounts back.

"Was down there grazin', happy as you please."

Relief coursed through Sam Kyler—relief and satisfaction, as he watched Wasco approach. Tom Tolliver was in for one hell of a surprise.

XX

They reached Jericho shortly after noon. Halting at the end of the street, Sam Kyler threw his glance along its dusty length. There were horses standing at the Fargo's rack—along with Shinn Thompson's buggy. More waited in front of the Palace and Rufe Eggert's place.

"Crew beat us home," Wasco commented idly. "That there's Denby's buckskin next to Thompson's rig. You figure Tolliver'll still be hangin' around?"

"He'll be here," Kyler replied. "He'll be waiting at the hotel with others, making it look good."

"How you aimin' to handle things?"

Kyler shrugged. "Only way I know how. Walk

right in and tell them what happened. Then throw the loop on Tolliver."

Wasco nodded approval. "Just what ought to be done."

Sam touched the tired bay with his spurs, and they moved into the street and pointed for the Fargo's hitch rack. He saw several of the merchants appear in the doorways of their establishments—one of them Marcia Ashwick—stare, and then smile quickly when they recognized him. They, too, had a surprise coming, he thought; only it would not be a pleasant one.

As he and Wasco halted at the rail, there was a sudden commotion in the hotel's entrance. Before they could dismount, a dozen ranchers and townsmen rushed out onto the porch—Tolliver among them. The big rancher, beaming, pushed forward, hand outstretched.

"Mighty happy to see you two!" he shouted. "Denby's been tellin' how you done things . . . got the cattle through and took care of Hurd and his bunch. Was a great job!"

Kyler, favoring his injured leg, came off the saddle and leaned heavily against the bay. His cold glance touched the rancher, reached beyond him. On the porch he could see Shinn Thompson, Pritchard, Dave Simon, Weil, Pete Clark—several more he had not met. He brought his attention back to Tolliver. The man was covering up well.

"Was a great job *you* done," he said finally in a

slow, distinct voice. "Plan of yours worked good."

Tolliver frowned. The men standing on the porch fell silent, struck by Kyler's quiet tone.

"Meanin' what?" the rancher asked.

Kyler pulled open his shirt. Removing the money belt, he tossed it to Tolliver. "Here's the rest of the cash. Your boys overlooked it when they ambushed us in the brakes."

Tolliver caught the belt. His jaw sagged. "What the hell you talkin' about . . . ambush . . . my boys . . . ?"

"You know what I'm talking about," Kyler snarled, coming around. He limped forward, leaned against the rack, and faced the men on the porch. "We got held up on the trail. Outlaws took your money, left us for dead."

A mutter of surprised comment ran through the crowd. Shinn Thompson elbowed his way to the edge of the gallery.

"You tellin' us the cattle money's been lost again?"

"I am. Hit us in the rough country southwest of here. Along the buttes." Kyler's hand lowered, came to rest on the butt of his pistol. "Only man to know we were coming that trail was Tolliver. Better ask him where your money is."

"Tolliver!" Thompson shouted in amazement. "You mean he . . . ?"

The rancher's mouth was still agape. He stared

at Kyler, then at the men on the porch. "That's crazy!" he cried in a strangled voice. "I . . . I never. . . ." His jaw clamped shut immediately. He stepped in close to Kyler. "You're wrong," he said in a quick way, "dead wrong . . . but I see your thinkin'. Maybe I got the answers."

"Sure goin' to take some good ones," Wasco said dryly.

The muttering on the gallery had risen. Tolliver raised his hand. His face was serious. "Think I know what this is all about. Go on back in the hotel and wait. All I want's fifteen minutes."

"So's you can get out of town?" a voice asked.

"You know me better'n that!" the rancher snapped angrily. He wheeled to Kyler. "Sure . . . I told you about that back trail . . . but it wasn't my idea."

"Then who . . . ?"

"Rufe Eggert. He mentioned it to me. And earlier this mornin' them six hardcases you tangled with over at Marcia Ashwick's rode in from that direction. They're at Rufe's now. Got a hunch they know plenty about it."

Kyler turned, pulled the shotgun from its boot. He was feeling better. He had found it difficult to believe Tom Tolliver would be involved in the crime, and it was good to realize he had been right. "Let's pay Eggert a call," he said.

Tolliver threw the money belt he was holding to Pritchard and said—"Keep everybody inside, Al.

Could be real trouble."—and headed off down the street with Kyler and Wasco.

A distance short of the saloon, Sam halted. "His place got a back door?"

Tolliver, face grim, nodded. "Sure has. Around this way."

He led them down the side of the harness shop, cut right, and paused at the rear of a low-roofed building. Pointing to a closed door, he said: "That's it."

Not hesitating, Sam Kyler stepped up to the thin panel, placed his ear against it, and listened briefly. Then, with the shotgun in his right hand, fully cocked, he pushed the door open with his left.

Rufe Eggert and a half dozen riders were grouped around a small table. Stacks of currency were before each man. Draped across the back of a nearby chair were Sam's saddlebags.

At the abrupt appearance of Kyler, closely followed by Wasco and Tolliver, the men leaped to their feet. The pockmarked outlaw Kyler had encountered at Marcia Ashwick's café yelled a curse and grabbed for his pistol. Kyler's shotgun roared, filling the small room with deafening sound and a cloud of smoke.

Through it Rufe Eggert's voice yelled: "Don't shoot! For God's sake . . . don't shoot!"

Wasco and Tolliver strode past the crouched figure of Sam Kyler. Together they disarmed the men, stepping over the body of the scarred outlaw, and herded them into a corner. There were shouts in the alley behind the building as men, attracted by the shotgun's blast, gathered hurriedly.

Dave Simon, trailed by Thompson and Pritchard, came through the doorway. Thompson stared at the outlaws—at Eggert—at the piles of currency.

"What the devil's goin' on?"

"There's our money," Tolliver said. "Was Eggert. Had the bunch ambush Kyler and Wasco. Expect it was him the other time, too."

The saloon man twisted around, shook his head in a vehement denial. "Wasn't me. Just this time."

"Makes no difference," Shinn Thompson said. "Once is enough to hang you."

"Hang?" Eggert repeated. "For just robbin' . . . ?"

"Never you mind," Tolliver said. "You'll get what you've got comin'." He began to collect the currency, paused, looked at Kyler.

"Reckon that winds things up for you two," he said. "We'll take care of these jaspers. Why don't you go over to the hotel, get yourselves some rest? I'll send Doc Patton over to patch you up. And Marcia can bring you a bite to eat."

Dave Simon nodded. "Looks like you can use it. We'll settle up with you tonight. Excepin' for that I reckon you're all through here."

"Not yet," a voice said from the doorway.

Kyler turned slowly. He didn't have to wonder at the identity of the speaker. It was Gates—the Dalhart marshal.

XXI

A hush dropped over the room. Shinn Thompson wheeled, his cane rapping against the bare floor. Coils of smoke still hung in the air and he thrust his head forward, peering through the rectangle of daylight.

"Who the hell are you?" he demanded.

"Name's Gates. Dalhart town marshal."

"Mite out of your territory, ain't you? What're you wantin' around here?"

"Kyler. I'm taking him back with me."

"You take him . . . you'll have to take the whole town."

"Forget it," Kyler broke in. "No point in you mixing up in this."

"Seems we already are," Tolliver said. "Got somethin' to do with the drive . . . them outlaws, ain't it?"

"That's part of it," Gates said. "Got a wanted dodger on him, too. Robbery."

"So you come traipsin' clear over here after him, eh?" Thompson said sarcastically. "How's it happen you never done nothin' like that before? Been plenty of outlaws come runnin' into this country, but you high-powered badge toters paid them no mind. Was out of your jurisdiction, you told us. Was No-Man's-Land."

"Little different this time, mister . . . Kyler done some killin'."

"Outlaws," Tolliver said. "You ought to be thankin' him for it. Saved you the trouble."

Sam Kyler listened. When it was again quiet, he said: "You're wasting your time, Gates. I'm not going back."

"I can take you."

"You mean you can try. If I'd done anything wrong, I'd be willing to go along. But I haven't. That robbery thing's a mistake. I got held up, but I returned the money. Few days more you'll be getting word the charges have been dropped."

Gates's expression did not change. It was evident he believed none of it.

Dave Simon said: "We know this much, Marshal. He got the money back, all right. Right here in town. Most of us saw him do it. And he figured to send it back."

"You willing to swear he did?"

"If he says he did, I'll swear he's telling the truth."

"No need," Kyler broke in wearily. "All you've got to do is check with the teller in the Cattleman's Trust. He mailed the draft for me."

Shinn Thompson laughed. "Reckon that settles it, Mister Marshal."

"Part of it . . . maybe . . . still the matter of those killin's. . . ."

"Them outlaws? What's ailin' you, Gates! You ought to be pleased he done it."

"Still men . . . and it happened in my town."

"So that makes it important. Well . . . that's a hell of a way to look at it. It was fine for them to go on stealin' us blind . . . and you couldn't do nothin' about it. Nobody could. Outside the law, we was told. Then, when we hire us a man to get rid of them, you want to jail him for it. What kind of fool figurin' is that?"

"It's law and order."

"Law and order! You sure got the wrong idea of what that means! Kyler's showed you what real law and order is. He broke up the worst gang in this part of the country . . . by hisself! He ought to be wearin' that badge, not you!"

"Reckon you could say he is a lawman . . . sort of," Tom Tolliver said. "Maybe we didn't do no swearin' in or hang a badge on him, but we could've, if we'd thought. Amounts to the same."

Gates bristled. "You've got no authority to appoint a lawman. This territory is unorganized."

"But we're livin' in it and we're runnin' it," Shinn Thompson said. "All the authority we need." He turned to Kyler. "How about you . . . you want to keep that there badge we forgot to pin on you? Goes for your deputy, too."

Sam grinned, glanced at Wasco. The old cowpuncher bobbed his head. Kyler looked at Thompson. "Be proud to," he said.

Thompson nodded to Gates. "Reckon that settles it, Mister Dalhart Marshal. Accordin' to your own thinkin', a lawman's got a right to go after outlaws that're raisin' hell in his territory. Seems that's just what ours was doin'."

"It's not legal."

"Far as we're concerned, it is . . . and iffen you don't like it, best thing you can do is write the President of the United States and bellyache to him about it. Expect he'll tell you we're within our rights."

Gates shrugged resignedly. "Let it pass," he said. After a moment he looked up. A smile crossed his stern features as he extended his hand to Kyler. "Glad to meet you, Marshal. Want to wish you a lot of luck."

Sam smiled, took the lawman's fingers into his own. "No hard feelings?"

Gates shook his head. "Nope. Just one thing. Next time you've got a problem in my town, be obliged if you'll come to me first."

"I'll do that," Kyler replied.

The Cuchillo Plains

I

Ryan, tall on his blue roan, pulled to a fiddling halt on the rim and glanced down into the shallow basin at the scatter of buildings that was Tom Strickland's S-Bar Ranch. The late afternoon sun scoured the yard and corrals and faded gray structures of the once proud spread with savage thoroughness, pointing up their weathered bleakness. And there was for Jim Ryan a man's keen regret that such sad times should come upon so fine a place. But that was the way of many things. A great ranch was born in a man's high-flung dreams. By his sweat and toil it grew and flourished and became a powerful force in a land of violence, all under the guidance of a strong hand. But a day comes when that strong hand wavers, falters uncertainly, and that dream begins to crumple and glory fade and turn commonplace. And soon there is only memory, legend to be spun around a night fire or told in the bunkhouse when day is done and moonlight streams through the streaky windows.

That was the history of the S-Bar. In his prime there was no better man than Tom Strickland, and nothing on the vast Cuchillo Plains, or for miles beyond, compared with the ranch he built and owned. But time eventually exacted its price and the saddle was finally denied him. He sat for hours in his chair on the wide porch of the rambling house or out in the yard under the shade of the trees he had planted with his own hands, a man at great odds with himself, refusing to accept defeat, challenging with bristling acrimony the bitter fact that faced him—the S-Bar was finished and the bold tracks he had made across the land were fading like the trail of a drifter crossing the windswept dunes of the desert.

For Tom Strickland had been capable of all things he had visualized—except one. He had no son and for this he cursed the gods and damned the misfortune that had given him, instead, a daughter. Not that he loved her less but in this wild and volatile land where a man carved out his share and held it by the strength of his courage, a woman had little chance. And it was not in the make-up of Strickland to lay his faith or place his trust in another man. Thus he was at one and the same time facing the inevitable, but steadfastly refusing to admit its proximity.

Ryan stirred at seeing Ann Strickland, tall and serene, come out of a back door and strike across the yard to a pen where a dozen or more chickens scuffled expectantly in the dust. A light breeze, early for evening, plucked at her dark hair and moved it gently about her face, and he felt his pulse quicken as it always did when she was near.

She emptied her pan of scraps and turned to go, and for a moment the oval of her face was uplifted toward him, but her eyes were far-seeing and she did not notice him there.

He clucked the blue roan into motion and let him pick his way down the slope. She heard him coming and paused, and he saw her brush at something on her dress and straighten the white circle of collar. When he pulled up before her, she stood with hands behind her back, her smile soft and welcoming.

Very soberly he said: "Are you the lady of the house, ma'am?"

"I am," she answered, mocking his mood.

"Do you think you could spare a meal for a poor, hungry cowboy?"

"How hungry?"

"Well, my last meal was the tops of my old boots. 'Most anything would do."

"I'm sure we can do better than that," she said, and then laughed, unable to keep up the farce longer.

Ryan stepped down from the roan, took his hat in hand, and came near her. She waited, her face calm, her lips full and curving slightly in a smile.

He said: "Ann, you don't know how much this means to me, being invited here to supper."

"It's a small thing," she replied. "We should be better neighbors. Besides," she added after a moment, "it's pleasant having company."

"For that I thank you," Ryan said. "In six months' time I have made almost as many friends on the Cuchillo Plains as I have fingers on my left hand. People here are not generous with their friendship."

"I know," she said kindly. "It takes a long time but it will come. You will see that and you must not think them all like my father."

"I wish they were," Ryan said. "I understand him. Likely I will be just the same, someday."

She touched him with her smile, showing her appreciation. Then, as if suddenly remembering something: "I'm curious. Who are those friends on your left hand?"

Ryan shrugged. "Jules Briner, for one. My foreman, Frank Sears. Your father, Ross Meldrum, perhaps."

"Four," she murmured. "No woman?"

"That is for you to answer, Ann."

"Does it need answering?" she said at once, and changed the subject. "You will find my father and George Cobb in the front yard. Join them and I will bring some lemonade."

She turned for the house and he led the roan to the corral. Tying the big horse in the shadows, he walked the short distance to the front where Tom Strickland rocked gently in his chair, beneath the deep shade of a giant cottonwood, talking with his foreman. Ryan, nodding to that man, made his salutation to Strickland: "How're you, Tom?

Looks like you might be enjoying that chair this hot day."

Strickland watched him remove his hat and wipe the sweat from his forehead and face. Ryan was lean, brown-haired, and burned dark by the prairie's constant sun. His mouth was a broad slash beneath a heavy nose and his eyes were that indeterminate color of slate, gray at one time, cold blue at another. And for a man not yet twenty-four the smooth gravity of his features was misleading, for he was a man always quick to anger and close to violence.

Strickland said: "Never gets too hot for me. As for this damned chair. . . ."

His voice trailed off and Ryan knew he was thinking of the many things that needed to be done, the many jobs that lay unfinished. A man lived a lifetime, but never got around to doing them all. Ryan knew the feeling; there was never enough time in one day. He said: "Anything I can do for my board?"

Strickland shook his head in an irritated manner. "Long as you're invited to set at my table, I'll expect no work from you."

Ryan glanced to Cobb, but the old foreman was looking off toward the windbreak of a tamarack that stretched across the north side of the yard. He was plucking absently at the straggling, yellow mustache drooping down over his mouth, his craggy profile sharp against the backdrop of green.

Strickland was in a poor mood this day and for that Ryan was sorry. He had planned again to broach the subject of buying the S-Bar.

"You moving your lower herd to the hills soon?"

At Ryan's question, Cobb swung his gaze back from the break. He started to speak, but Strickland answered first.

"George's plannin' to do just that, come mornin'."

"Need any help, let me know," Ryan said to the foreman. "I'll send a couple of the boys over to work."

Strickland pricked up angrily. "I don't need none of your help," he snapped. "Not yours or Hugh Baldwin's nor anybody else's! Don't know why everybody is so all-fired anxious to run my ranch for me!"

Ryan shrugged, ignoring the display of temper. A man took Tom Strickland as he found him and Tom Strickland responded to all things according to the status of his health at that exact moment; either he felt good or he felt bad, and his reactions to anything said or done were governed accordingly.

Cobb muttered: "Could use some help, sure enough."

"You and Dominguez can do it. Hell, man, there ain't more'n a hundred head in that bunch."

"Pretty wild," Cobb objected mildly.

"Wild!" Strickland snorted. He squirmed about in the chair, clawing at his knees. He was a small man, thin and wiry, and his eyes were black spots of sparkling fire when he got worked up. "There ain't been a wild cow on this ranch in twenty years! That stuff we got's nothin' but milkin' stock when you stack 'em up against the longhorns we used to pop out of the brush around here!"

"Maybe so," Cobb said in that same mild way, "but these here critters are tough to handle. I could use a rider or two."

Ann came out of the house and approached them, bringing a tray of lemonade. Ryan, roused from his leaning against the cottonwood's rough trunk, watched her, stirred deeply as he always was at her sight. Her dark hair was piled high now on her head and her face bore a faint flush from some activity she had been engaged in. She had intense green eyes, somewhat slanted, and the shape of her was set off by the persistent breeze that molded the light dress against her well-rounded figure.

"It's too hot for you to be getting excited, Papa," she said, lightly chiding him. "Maybe this will cool you off a bit."

She handed the three glasses around and, giving Ryan her smile, returned to the house.

"Hear you're buyin' up more stock," Strickland said after a time.

Ryan nodded. "Whiteman's herd. Killibrew's loaning me the money to pick them up. About two hundred head."

"Good buy?"

"Twelve dollars a head, range delivery."

"Good enough, if you're careful. What's Whiteman plannin' to do?"

"Move back to the States. Says he's got all this country he can swallow."

Strickland shook his head. "Never figured him for the stickin' kind. One of them flat land farmers. Had no business tryin' to raise cattle. Either a man's got it in him or he ain't." He hesitated, then: "You keep on buildin' up, you'll be big as Hugh Baldwin one of these days. Or big as the S-Bar," he added in a wistful tone.

Ryan said: "Man can't stand still. Either he goes up or he goes down. There's no staying in one place."

"That's so," Strickland agreed.

"You mentioned Baldwin. He been around?"

Strickland shook his head. "Not for a week or two. Him and that flat-eyed gunslinger rode by then."

"Dan Pike's his foreman," Ryan observed with a slow grin.

"If he's a foreman, I'm a Chinaman," Strickland said. "Doubt if that one knows what end of a steer the tail hangs off of. Only thing he knows is what that Forty-Five hangin' on his leg is for."

"Two, three his boys up on the north range yesterday," Cobb broke in. "That big feller they calls Turk and Reno Davis and another one I don't know."

"What they doin' up there?" Strickland demanded, at once suspicious.

Cobb shrugged. "Just ridin', Reno said."

"Looks to me like Hugh's hirin' a right smart lot of new help lately," Strickland said after a thoughtful pause. "Wonder what he's got on his mind." He lifted his glance suddenly to Ryan. "Reckon you got somethin' on your mind, too, lately. You been tryin' to speak it out ever since you got here. What is it?"

Ryan smiled, his thoughts all at once out in the open. He hadn't realized it showed so plainly. It wasn't a good time to broach the subject again, but then, where Strickland was concerned, it seldom was in some matters. "I was wondering if you'd given any more thought to my offer to buy the S-Bar from you, Tom?"

He stopped, letting his eyes search Strickland's face closely, seeking the reaction to his words. The old rancher said nothing, his gaze steady on Ryan. "Adding more stock is crowding my range a little and I need more room and more water. I figure Killibrew would loan me enough to make a sizable down payment and I could meet a note once a year for you, after the drive."

Strickland made no reply. He watched Ryan with a smothering closeness, his shoulder coming up a little and the points of his face turning a little white where the skin drew down tightly. Cobb cleared his throat in the silence that fell across the yard.

"I wouldn't figure on you leaving the place and I'd want George and the rest of the boys to stay on. Just add them to my crew. I'd run the herds together and make one big drive instead of two."

Ryan stopped, having no more to say, knowing he needed more but at a loss as to what it should be. He watched Strickland lay his gnarled hands on the arms of his chair and come slowly to his feet and he knew then he had said too much.

"You got it all figured out!"

George Cobb coughed again and got up. "Reckon I'd better wash up," he murmured, and stomped across the yard to the side door of the house. The screen banged loudly behind him.

"You and Hugh Baldwin been after my place for a long time!" Strickland said between clenched teeth. "You both figure I'm on my last legs and you can close me out. Well, let me tell you this, Ryan . . . this place ain't for sale, and never will be, long as I'm alive! I know that girl of mine can't run it and couldn't, if she tried, not with you hemmin' her in on one side and Baldwin on the other. You'd wipe her out like a timber wolf runnin' through sheep!"

Ryan stiffened, anger moving suddenly through him. Controlling his voice, he said: "Forget it, Tom. Forget I even mentioned it. You don't want to sell. We'll let it go at that."

"Forget it? Forget hell! You think I don't know what you're up to?"

The unreasonableness of the man plucked at Ryan and he tried to hold back the anger that kept pushing at him. "No need for all this, Tom. You don't mean what you've said and I won't listen to it."

"You'll listen to what's gospel and you'll like it!"

"There's no truth in what you're saying and you know that for a fact," Ryan snapped. "I'd never do anything that would hurt Ann."

"No, nothing except maybe swindle her out of this ranch when I'm gone!"

Ryan clung to his self-control. In a low, strained voice he said: "If anybody, besides you, said that, he would have to back it up. Being you, Tom, we'll let it pass."

"We'll let it pass because it's the truth. And what's more, you'll stay away from here and you'll stay away from my girl! I'll not have you around, schemin' like an Indian to lay your hands on this place!"

Still clinging to his temper, Ryan said: "I don't think you mean what you're saying, Tom. Cool off and forget the whole thing."

"Forget nothin'! Get off my ranch, Ryan, and stay off! I don't want to see you around here again. That clear?"

Ryan, thoroughly aroused, swept the man with a glance and nodded. "It's clear," he said, and strode stiffly by him, crossing the yard to the corral. He pulled out the roan and stepped into the saddle, coming back along the windbreak. He passed Strickland, saw him standing there rigidly, his face white and contorted with his rage, his fists clenched at his sides. Nodding briefly, he rode on, following the trail along the tamarack that led, eventually, to the main road. He had been a fool to mention buying the place from Strickland. He should have known better. He should have waited for another time, a better time. But when was there a better time?

Across the silence, a gun spurt forth its sudden, shocking racket. Ryan, startled, jerked the roan to a stop. He pulled his own weapon and turned in the saddle. Tom Strickland was weaving on his feet, clutching at the spreading stain on his chest. Ann burst through the doorway and came running into the yard, her cry breaking the silence. From the side of the house George Cobb appeared.

Strickland wilted just as Ann reached him and fell heavily to the ground, and in that moment Ryan heard the rapid pound of a running horse on the far side of the tamarack break. Throwing a glance at Strickland and seeing Cobb there now with Ann, he wheeled the roan about and drove hard for the receding sound.

II

A man does not run a horse through a tamarack windbreak. It is a little like being trapped, imprisoned in a bewildering labyrinth of crooked tree trunks and dangling, frothy curtains, and there are no direct passageways out. A half dozen lunges on the part of the roan and Ryan pulled him in, fearful of the consequences, and let him pick his own course through the maze.

The break was a full 100 yards wide, as the crow flies, more by the devious route the roan was forced to follow, and, when at last they broke out into the open, the bushwhacker was little more than a boiling dust cloud in the distance. Ryan holstered his gun and touched the roan with spurs and the big roan leaped into a stretching, ground-consuming run. They swept up the shallow valley, toward the north, keeping abreast of the buttes breaking out from the ragged bulk of the Santa Claras lying in cloud-topped silence to the west. Ryan began to gain on the escaping rider and he strained to recognize him as the gap started to close. But the man was bent low in the saddle and the horse he rode was indistinguishable, being either a buckskin or bay or perhaps a sorrel. In the dust he could not be sure.

While the roan hurried on, Ryan was searching his mind, wondering who the rider might be, and he was asking himself who would have hated the crusty old rancher enough to kill him. Off hand, he could think of no one. There were, of course, the usual number of disgruntled non-friends that any man accumulates in a lengthy lifetime of building up a big spread but it was doubtful any of those would nurse thoughts of murder. Strickland had been a stern, straight down the middle sort of man to whom black was black and white was white, and there was no room for compromise. But he had a reputation for fairness. He was never known to cheat a man (although he was a shrewd bargainer), and he never turned a hungry man from his door. In these past years, when age laid its restraint upon his activities and his S-Bar began to run down, the barb in his temper sharpened even more, but he still retained the good will of all those who lived on the Cuchillo Plains and in nearby Gunstock.

The man on the buckskin, as he was now sure, appeared to be changing his plans. Ryan saw him begin to swerve, heading for the wooded slopes and cañons of the Santa Claras in a long, swinging arc. Ryan altered the roan's course to match and, in so doing, began rapidly to lessen the intervening distance. The roan, however, immediately ran into trouble on the loose rock cropping out from the higher ground, and Ryan slacked his pace, taking no chances.

They were nearing Baldwin's Circle X south line now. Like a three-fingered hand with the heel butting up against the mountains, the ranches lay across the Cuchillo Plains. Farthest south was Ryan's own Box K. In the center was Tom Strickland's S-Bar and to the north sprawled Baldwin's huge outfit, reaching out over the prairies and low hills in limitless, blue-rimmed distances. It was said of Hugh Baldwin that only he knew where Circle X began and ended, and there were those in town who thought other things, not so complimentary about the big rancher. But such words were never voiced; Gunstock was considered Baldwin's town and a man walked on dangerous ground if he dared dissent.

Other smaller ranches spotted the country to the east and south, small, starve-out spreads that usually sold their stock to Baldwin, or at times in the past to Strickland rather than make their own drives to the railhead beyond the Santa Claras. A half dozen winter-whipped, summer-scorched squatters fought the land on the far side of the river for a bitter livelihood and these, plus those who lived in Gunstock proper, comprised the whole of the Cuchillo Plains.

Ryan lost ground in the rough country. He watched the rider curve into the first outreach of timber and vanish. But the roan, breaking at last from the rocky slope onto a grassy meadow, leveled out again and moved in fast. Ryan reached the timber and entered slightly below that point into which the bushwhacker had disappeared, pulling to a halt well within the pines. He tried to listen but the roan was breathing so deeply that he finally dismounted and walked ahead a dozen paces where he might hear better. It came to him then, standing there, that the rider could have stopped just within the grove and was at that moment laying his sights upon him.

He heard nothing and in the silence of the birds he read his answer—the man *had* stopped. He was close by. Drawing his gun, he walked back to the roan, the nerves in his neck prickling each step of the way. Taking up the leathers, he began a slow, careful advance, leading the roan closely, knowing he was a much poorer target on the ground than sitting high up on the horse. On the spongy carpet of the forest he could move quietly, and the blue roan's hoofs made no more than a soft *tunk-tunk*. Through the network of treetops he could see the full blue of the sky, but he realized that it would not be blue for long. The afternoon sun was fading fast and it soon would be fully dark. He moved slowly on, working in and out of the junipers, the thick briers, down the lanes of pine. The deathly stillness held.

Somewhere, far up through the grove, a mockingbird sang and Ryan came to a stop, considering that. The sound was distant, and he came to the eventual conclusion that the bird had not been disturbed recently by anyone passing and so he swung away, working deeper into the trees. It was then he heard the sound that again brought him up sharply. It could have been a winter-dry twig snapping under sudden weight or it could have been a dead brush stalk giving way before a heavy body. It made him immediately alert and ready, and, as the tension built in the breathless quiet, he tried to locate the point from which the noise had come. But he was unsure and, when it did not come again, he stepped to the saddle and sent the roan briskly dead ahead.

The grove was beginning to darken with shadows that grew steadily longer, and he was having difficulty in seeing. When nothing developed in the direction he had taken, he cut left again, rode for a dozen yards, and once more halted, straining into the half gloom for any sound. He was that way, leaning forward in the saddle, ears searching the silence, eyes probing the brush, when the gun crashed and the bullet came reaching for him. It missed by mere inches, thudded dully into the pine near which he waited and set echoes rolling through the grove. Instantly he swerved the roan away and laid his answering shot at the flash of orange flame almost behind him.

He kept the roan moving, feeling better now that he had located his target. He kept circling the place where the gunman had been, snapping a quick shot into the likely points. He drove in fast from the opposite side, covering his advance with two shots. One bullet left, he reached the juniper clump where the gunman had been and pulled up. He was again alone. For a time he remained quiet, listening as before but he heard nothing, and, not liking his position or the rôle of a stationary target, he drifted gently forward. It was growing increasingly darker. A few minutes of light remained for the grove. The mockingbird, stilled by the blasting echoes of the guns, took up his song, alternately trilling and challenging in his peculiar way and then, farther on to the west, another took it up.

The roan walked into a blind alley of osage orange, and Ryan wheeled him quickly around and out, not wanting to be thus caught in a box. Once clear of that, he stopped again to listen, uneasy at the necessity but knowing that it had to be. All advantage was with the other man, who could pause and listen to his approach. Ryan was relying almost completely upon his ears now, the darkness closing out sight a few feet from him.

There was only the roan's deep breathing and the mockingbird's song. He cut left again, moving eastward now, thinking he had lost the bushwhacker in the night. He let the roan have his own time and way, and, when he came to the edge of the grove and rode out onto the prairie, bathed now in the silvery fog of dusk, he did not urge the horse to greater speed. He was thinking of Ann Strickland and what lay before her. She would need him now, the strength he could lend her, the comfort he could give. The S-Bar would be hers to do with as she saw fit and that was the way it should be. He would see to that. If she wished to keep it, to try and run it as her own, he would help in every way he could. If she wanted to sell, he would make his bid along with Hugh Baldwin or anyone else interested, and the best price would prevail. That was the way it would be.

When the brilliant flash of the gun exploded, almost under the roan's long head it seemed, Ryan left the saddle instinctively in a long, low dive. He hit the ground on all fours and another bullet dug sand behind him. He half crawled, half ran for the protection of a juniper clump, trying to locate the ambusher and see where he was going at one and the same time. The gun shattered the quiet again and a bullet droned over his head. Darkness was working both ways, hiding him as it did the bushwhacker, and, when he reached the brush stand, he dropped flat and wormed his way quickly around to the opposite side.

Gun in hand, he waited for the telltale bloom of the next shot, and, when it came, digging into the heart of the juniper, he snapped his quick reply. Almost in the same breath, the gunman was after him, placing his bullets, throwing sand and trash upon Ryan's prostrate shape as he searched the brush pile. Ryan rolled away, holding his fire. He came to an abrupt halt against another juniper stand and lay there, suddenly furious and exasperated at the turn of events. He could reach no advantage; he could gain no point. At each and every turn, the bushwhacker pinned him down, helpless.

Seething, he waited impatiently, trying to pierce the black face of night and locate the gunman. He was somewhere ahead, out there on the prairie, hiding behind one of the clumps of brush or lying in the protection of a low butte. He thought he saw movement and fastened his gaze upon that spot, but after a minute it all appeared to be in motion and he shook his head to clear his vision. The time dragged by, and then he heard the distant drum of a running horse, going away from the buttes, from him, driving hard in the direction of town.

He came to his feet and started for the roan at a run. Anger still rankled through him, goading him on. The bushwhacker wasn't free yet.

III

He reached Gunstock two hours later. He came into the north end of the street and there halted, letting his gaze run the length of the short thoroughfare. The lamps were lit and a few people strolled in the evening's coolness, enjoying the change in the day's sharp heat; a cluster of horses stood before Jules Briner's Trailstop Saloon, patiently awaiting their riders. Sound and yellow lamplight and deep shadows and a thin haze of dust hung between the buildings in an ever-changing pattern.

In this ceaselessly moving picture he knew the killer of Tom Strickland was now hiding.

He drifted over to the rail in front of the Trailstop and closely examined the horses there. All were cold, apparently having been there for some time. Moving on through the thick dust, he rode the street's entire length to Steve Claunch's livery stable and there dismounted. The hostler came out of the building's gloomy interior and waited, flat-footed and silent.

"Take care of him," Ryan said, and handed the man the reins. "I'll be back later."

He stepped swiftly by the hostler into the stable, moving to the far side of the runway where the light from a single overhead lantern could not touch him.

"What's up?" the hostler demanded, at once suspicious. "What's goin' on?"

"Take care of that horse, that's all you need to know," Ryan said. The hostler stopped.

Ryan drifted silently down the wide aisle of stalls. The first three were empty but the fourth was occupied. He reached out and touched the horse's rump. It was cold. The next stall was empty and in the remaining three he found horses but they, too, had been there for hours.

At the end of that side he stopped, tension suddenly beginning to build along his nerves. In the near total darkness, rank with the strong odors of the stable, he listened, hearing the faint drop of footfalls, then a light scraping along with the vague rustle of cloth against the splintery rough surface of timber. Ryan stepped deeper into the shadows and drew his gun.

For a full minute he waited, trying to place the sound. It seemed to have come from the rear, from the end of the building where Claunch usually parked the buggies he maintained for hire. Staying close to the wall, he worked out its length, coming finally to the first vehicle. Here he paused again to listen and probe the blackness with his eyes.

After a time, he crossed the runway and made his check of the horses on that side. In the end stall he found nothing. In the next two there were horses that were warm to his touch, but likely had been in the stable for some while. He threw his glance toward the door and saw the hostler still standing there, holding the roan in close. He could not see the man's face but he knew he was watching him.

He moved up to him and was about to place his question when the quick running of a horse behind the stable caught his attention. He wheeled and ran the building's length and out into the open. Finding himself in the wagon yard, he cut left and rushed to the alley. There was nothing in sight. Whoever it had been had turned off into one of the many openings and passageways and had dropped from sight. Thinking the man might come into the street, Ryan retraced his steps, but when he reached the walk in front of Claunch's, there was no rider to be seen.

Anger and frustration again overrode Ryan. He stalked back to the hostler, grasped him by the bib of his overalls.

"Who was that?" he demanded, pulling the man up close. "Who went out the back way? Speak up, damn you, or I'll shake you loose from your boots!"

The hostler's eyes spread round and his mouth flew open. He let go of the roan and the big horse shied off down the runway.

"Nobody . . . nobody. Wasn't nobody in here."

Ryan said: "Somebody was in here. He left when I came in, going out the back. Don't tell me I'm wrong!"

The hostler shook his head and Ryan saw genuine fear on the man's face. He relaxed his grip and let him fall back a step or two.

The hostler shrugged himself, settling his clothing back onto his thin frame. "Nobody here," he said. "No matter what you're thinkin', there wasn't nobody here."

Ryan searched the man's face. He could be telling the truth, he decided. He didn't know how close he had been behind the killer when he reached town; the roan traveled fast and he could have been close. And, again, the hostler could be lying to save his own skin. Ryan said—"All right, forget it."—and turned into the street.

More lights were on now, laying their yellow squares along the boardwalk and in the dust. Keeping close to the wall of the stable, he began a slow patrol, walking softly, avoiding the bright areas where possible, his pressing glance probing the passageways between the buildings as he moved.

He reached the corner of Dunn Jackson's General Store and halted, remembering the wagon yard at the rear of the building. He made a careful inspection of the area, finding nothing there. Returning then to the street, he moved on, checking off one by one the business houses and their lots. When he reached the end of the block, he crossed over and doubled back on that side.

Killibrew's Cattlemen's Trust Bank was on the corner. Next came the two-story Kansas City Hotel, and he went carefully about that property but found no waiting horses. After that there was a row of small shops: a bakery, dressmaker, gunsmith, Coy Graham's hardware store, a saloon, and several other assorted institutions, the last of which was the combination jail and office of Marshal Ross Meldrum. The search so far had yielded nothing, and, finding himself in front of the marshal's office, the thought came to him that it would be an opportune time to bring Meldrum in on the matter. But the place was dark and the door locked.

Ryan's anger had cooled somewhat by this time and he took the moment to lean back against the jail, build himself a smoke, think over the past few hours and determine his next move. A man and a woman passed by, the man nodding. He returned the salutation, hearing the broken conversation take up a yard away: ". . . the railroad in ten years." A rider came into the street and Ryan sharply examined the man and horse, and promptly forgot them, the man's white hat answering his question. Back in the saloon he had just passed, a piano broke into tinny clatter and a woman laughed in a deep-throated way from an upstairs window of the Kansas City, the sound carrying far.

Somewhere in this town was the man he searched for, the man who had waited in ambush and killed Tom Strickland almost before his eyes, the man who had led him on a wild chase through the tamarack breaks and across the prairies, into the groves that fanned out from the Santa Claras, and finally back to the town. For the first time the oddity of that struck him. Why north to the groves and then double back to Gunstock? Why didn't the bushwhacker head straight for town when his job was done? It would have been much more logical.

Ryan flipped the cigarette into the street, watched its red coal glow brightly and die, and then crossed over to the Trailstop, the last place to be checked. He mounted the steps and pushed through the batwing doors, the crash of sound and glare of light meeting him head on. The place was crowded and smoke boiled along the beamed ceiling and voices set up a steady din within the walls.

Ryan shoved his way through the crowd to the bar, seeing no one with whom he was particularly acquainted. He called for a beer, received it, and withdrew along the curving end of the bar away from the press, where he might better see those who came and went. Jules Briner moved up, cutting through the crowd from a far corner.

" 'Evening, Ryan. Pleasure to see you here."

Briner was a thin, calm man, precise in manner and speech. He dressed well, lived moderately, and was unlike any saloon owner Ryan had ever known. Somewhere, sometime in his background he had known gentility and the flavor of that lay upon him, setting him apart from the general run of those who frequented his place of business.

Ryan nodded. "You wouldn't have noticed anyone coming in during the last hour . . . in particular, I mean?"

Briner smiled and lifted his hands in a small gesture. "They come and go. Be hard to say. I saw no one I didn't know except a drifter."

"A drifter?"

"The fellow at the blackjack table. Wearing a white hat."

Ryan shook his head. "I saw that one ride in. Not him."

"You looking for someone?" Briner asked.

Ryan said: "For a man that killed Tom Strickland late this afternoon."

Briner waited a long minute. "Killed Tom Strickland?"

Ryan nodded and related the details. "I followed him into town but he had a pretty fair start on me. I think I almost had him nailed at Steve Claunch's place but he gave me the slip."

"You've had no thoughts as to who it might be, you didn't get a look at him?"

"Hardly a glimpse."

Briner murmured: "A problem, finding him now." He voiced then the question Ryan had asked himself several times: "Who would want to kill Tom?"

"If he had any enemies, I don't know who they were."

"My guess," Briner said, "is that there is more to it than that, more than what meets the eye. Somebody had a definite purpose and reason. How's the girl taking it?"

"I didn't wait, as I said," Ryan replied. "Cobb was there and I went after the dry-gulcher when I heard him leaving. I'll ride that way now."

"Earlier in the evening there was someone here asking for Meldrum, I heard. Likely that was Cobb."

Ryan nodded. He bought a drink, and then placed his empty glass back on the bar. "I'll drop back later. Meantime, you could check around and see if anybody has heard anything or seen anything that wasn't just right."

"I'll do that," Briner said, smiled his brief smile, and wheeled away.

Ryan turned to make use of a nearby side entrance. He paused, seeing the batwings burst suddenly inward. Ross Meldrum, closely followed by George Cobb and Reno Davis, one of Baldwin's riders, entered and came to a halt. Ryan waited, thinking to make his report to Meldrum and ask Cobb about Ann when the marshal's heavy voice broke above all other noises:

"Hold it, Ryan! I want to talk to you!"

Ryan ducked his head. He settled back against the curve of the bar, little flags of danger all at once plucking at his nerves. There was something in Meldrum's manner that was off-key, not right; the same something was in the grim set of George Cobb's hawk-like face. They pushed their way up to a point in front of him and came to a stop, fanning out, shoulder to shoulder.

Ryan said: "What's on your mind, Marshal?"

"Tom Strickland." Meldrum answered at once. "I'm arresting you for his murder!"

IV

For a full minute Ryan stood, motionless, struck wholly speechless by the accusation. The crowd fell silent and Jules Briner, a few steps away, halted and came slowly around, his sharp eyes searching Ryan's face. Conversation died. The tinkling of the piano ceased, and a man's rough voice silenced a woman's high-pitched laugh.

Ryan stood completely alone, physically and literally. He recognized, in those tight moments, that he was as much a stranger as he had been that day six months ago when he had ridden into Gunstock and the Cochillo Plains country and took over the old Fergusson place. His thoughts moved quickly back, and he recalled his own words, not many hours gone, when he had enumerated for Ann Strickland his friends. A ragged smile pulled at his long lips. Friends? Were these bitter-faced accusers his friends?

Anger awoke and moved swiftly through him, bringing his temper close to the surface. In a tone sharp as a Bowie knife's blade he said: "What the hell are you talking about, Meldrum?"

Ross Meldrum was a big man, thick through the body and wide across the chest. He stood a head taller than most men and the color of his hair matched exactly the silver of his star. His broad face was square and forever flushed, as if he had been running hard, and he had a straight line for a mouth. He was a good man, an honest one, Ryan knew, and, although a bit slow-witted, no one ever questioned his integrity and courage.

Meldrum said: "You know what I'm talking about. Don't play cozy with me! I've got you dead to rights . . . witnesses and all."

Ryan's jaw sagged. "Witnesses? I never shot Tom Strickland. How can you have witnesses?"

"Well, I got them," Meldrum stated. He slanted a glance at Cobb. "Tell him, George. Tell him what you told me."

Strickland's foreman pulled himself erect and faced Ryan. "I saw you, Ryan, no use denyin' it. You was arguin' with Tom when I went to wash up, somethin' about your wantin' to buy the ranch. He ordered you offen the place and I saw you get your horse and ride out. Then I heard a shot, and, when I looked, you was settin' there, gun in your hand. That's the way it was and there ain't no use your sayin' it wasn't because I sure as hell saw you!" Cobb's eyes were snapping, his pointed chin stuck out belligerently. "Ann saw you, too," he added.

Ryan shook his head. His anger had dwindled some and reason had returned to a degree. "That's part true, but not all. Sure I had words with Tom. Who hasn't?"

"He order you off the place?" Meldrum asked.

"He did and I left. I was invited over to eat. I mentioned to Tom again that I'd like to buy his place. He got mad about it and told me to leave."

"You sayin' you didn't shoot him after that?" Cobb broke in.

"I didn't shoot him, George. You know that. You know that as well as you know your own name. I didn't shoot him."

"You was settin' there on that roan with your gun in your hand!"

Ryan swung his gaze to the marshal. "Ross, I can straighten this out. Everything's right so far as it goes, up to the point of my shooting Strickland. I left when he ordered me off the place. I rode out, taking the road along the tamarack windbreak, but just as I got to the end of that, I heard a shot. I stopped and pulled my gun. Tom was just starting to fall and George and Ann were coming out to see what it was all about."

Ryan paused, seeing the doors of the saloon swing in again. Hugh Baldwin, followed by Dan Pike, came into the hushed room and stopped, surprise at the silence covering the rancher's face. He moved in closer, Pike at his elbow like a gray shadow.

"Trouble here?" Baldwin asked, looking at Meldrum.

"Tom Strickland's been killed," the lawman replied. "Appears Ryan did the shooting."

Baldwin shifted his glance to Ryan. Once or twice before Ryan had come up against the owner of Circle X but never in anything serious. He was another big man, almost as large as Meldrum, and he took great pride in his appearance. His tastes ran to expensive broadcloths and fine woolens and the boots and hat he was then wearing probably would pay a cowpuncher's wages for a year. Ryan felt the pressure of his frankly deriding eyes and heard him say: "I figured something like this would happen. A man's ambition can ride him too hard at times. Make him do things he shouldn't."

A murmur ran through the saloon. Baldwin's words were true, just what many of them had thought. Ryan had got too big for his britches too fast. They had expected him to pull something like this one day. They should have known it would happen.

Ryan never moved his eyes from Baldwin, having his wonder at the man's definite hostility. Meldrum's voice cut through his thoughts.

"Go on, Ryan. Let's hear the rest of it."

"I heard somebody leaving on the other side of the tamaracks. When I saw Ann and George coming to help Tom, I went after him."

"But didn't catch him, I take it."

Ryan met the marshal's disbelieving gaze coolly. He shook his head. "I didn't. He hit north and went into the hills. There was a little shooting, but he gave me the slip and doubled back into town."

"And this man that was standing in the tamaracks . . . he was the one that killed Tom?"

"It was somebody in there."

Meldrum ducked his head at Reno Davis. "That the way it happened?"

The cowpuncher swaggered in a few steps, pleased at being suddenly the center of attraction. At once Hugh Baldwin said: "What you doing in town, Reno? You're supposed to be working the south range."

Ryan saw a quick glance pass between the two men and then Meldrum said: "Reno's in on this, Hugh. Witness."

"Witness?" Baldwin echoed.

The marshal nodded. To Davis he said: "Go ahead, tell them how it was."

The cowpuncher grinned at Ryan. "Well, like I told the law here, I was workin' the south pasture when I got a little thirsty. I was close to Strickland's place so I dropped by for a drink, but when I got there I heard Ryan and the old man arguin'. I pulled up, not wantin' to bust in on a private fight, when Ryan up and shoots Strickland."

Davis paused, letting the murmur that ran through the room rise and fall. He grinned at Ryan in his wicked, toothy way while small lights of triumph danced in his eyes.

"Then what, Reno?" Meldrum prompted. "Go on, go on."

" 'Bout that time Ryan spotted me there and I took off. I figured with him in a killin' mood like he was, that was no safe place for me. Like he says, he run me clean to the hills, but when dark come,

I got away and come into town lookin' for you, Marshal."

Ryan listened to the tale with prickling scalp. The baldness of the lie appalled him for the first few moments, and then anger whipped anew through him as he realized what was taking place. Reno Davis had killed Strickland. It had been that man, hiding in the tamaracks, who fired the shot and then went racing away across the prairie. And now Davis was blandly twisting the truth around to where, with the few things George Cobb had seen, it appeared he had shot Strickland. But why?

He let his eyes move from Davis to Meldrum. The marshal believed the Circle X rider, that was plain. He had all the proof he needed. On Hugh Baldwin's face he saw a smug expression, a faint smile, as if he was pleased with the way of things. Ryan had a moment's wonder if that man knew more about the affair than he claimed. Had that surprise at seeing Davis in the saloon been genuine? Talk ran around the room, gradually increasing, and in this Ryan read an open threat. He would have little chance here—or later. He was being tried and convicted at that very moment.

Ryan searched the ring of faces, and those beyond, gauging their intentions, estimating their temper and trying to calculate the next few moments. All that time his own sharp anger was whetted into a seething sort of frustration, goading him close to reckless violence. He said: "It's my word against that of Reno Davis. And my word means nothing to you . . . that right, Marshal?"

"His word and George Cobb's and Ann Strickland's," Meldrum reminded him. "That's pretty strong evidence."

"Davis is a liar," Ryan stated in spaced, distinct words that reached every corner of the room.

"Could be the other way around, Ryan. Nobody knows much about you in these parts. You blow in with a pocket full of money, buy up a ranch, and drive in a herd. And you got a hot head. That's about all we know."

Hugh Baldwin said: "Except that he's buying more cows and needs more room . . . like the Strickland place."

Ryan shrugged, an unconscious motion to stem the sudden, driving urge to reach out for Baldwin and Meldrum and all the others and bash their heads in. He let his eyes slide over the crowd and then come back to Dan Pike who was standing near Baldwin. Pike was the man to watch if he was to make a move. The little gunman's gaze was on him, his eyes flat and empty.

Ryan came back to Meldrum. A thin smile broke his lips and he stepped away from the bar in an easy, off-hand move. Outwardly he was cool, but within him the bright fires of anger blazed at white heat.

Meldrum said: "Come along, Ryan. I'm locking you up for the circuit judge."

With that same deceptive smile, Ryan said—
"No, Marshal."—and snapped a fast shot at the
lamp hanging over Meldrum's head.

The shattering of the oil lamp did not plunge the
room into darkness; a dozen more kept it well-
lighted, but the suddenness of the shot, the shower
of glass and oil, turned the crowd into a mass of
scrambling, yelling confusion.

Ryan dipped, wheeled away as he fired, and
lunged for the side door. He felt the breath of
Pike's bullet and heard it slam into the wall behind
him. Meldrum sang out his surprise, and Baldwin's
voice commanded: "Stop that man!"

Ryan placed another shot into the ceiling, jerked
the door wide, and plunged into the blackness of
the night.

V

The rectangle of yellow light followed him, and he
threw himself to one side, escaping it. Shouts lifted
behind him and a man appeared in the open
doorway. He drove the man back with a bullet that
splintered wood near his head. Behind the building
he heard a horse, frightened at the gunfire, rearing
and trying to break away from the rail, and he
raced across the intervening distance to it. More
yells were breaking into the night's solidness, and,
as he jerked free the reins and swung into the
saddle, he took another shot at the still open

doorway. He spurred the plunging horse and rushed off down the alleyway.

A querulous voice called—"What's goin' on?"—from an upper window, but Ryan paid no heed. Men had poured out of the Trailstop's front doors and were pounding toward the alley, avoiding the side door's frame of light. A gun bloomed in the blackness behind him and he realized they had located him, but the bullet was wide and he knew, also, they had not seen but had only heard him. Faintly he caught the sound of Meldrum's booming voice shouting his instructions for the calling of a posse.

He reached the wagon yard behind Dunn Jackson's and cut into the passageway that separated it from its adjoining building. He rode boldly out into the street, into full view, and a cry immediately went up from the front of the Trailstop. Tightly smiling his satisfaction at this, he spurred the pony to the opposite side, entered the passageway that ran between Graham's Hardware Store and a saloon, and eventually reached the alley proper that ran behind the structures on that side of Gunstock's one street. Following this, out he came to stop in the shadows behind the Kansas City Hotel, and from there he watched the posse gather.

In the half darkness he could see men leading up their horses. There was a babble of talk; Meldrum stood on the porch of the saloon talking with someone, and he could see Baldwin's high shape just beyond him. He stepped down and led the pony to the far corner of the hotel, pointed him due south, away from the town, and slapped him hard on the rump. The startled horse leaped away and clattered off into the night.

Almost immediately the sound of his running was heard. A man cried—"There he goes!"—and went vaulting into his saddle. Meldrum shouted something that was lost in the confusion, and then the posse got into motion.

Ryan waited no longer. He had created the diversion that would allow him to get the roan, but there was no time to lose. There was no way of knowing how far the frightened pony would lead them. He might stop soon, or the sounds of the pursuing posse could rattle him even more and cause him to lead them for miles before they would discover that he was riderless. It was a gamble Ryan had to take. He wheeled, and, staying behind the buildings in the dark alleyway, he ran the block's full length.

He came into the street on the near side of the jail and paused on the walk. The posse was out of sight, and those who had gathered to watch the proceedings were drifting back into the Trailstop and other places from which they had come. Claunch's was almost directly across from where he stood and Ryan, fighting himself to walk casually so as to attract no undue attention, leisurely covered the distance and entered the stable.

One look at the hostler's strained face told him he had made a mistake. The man stood under the lantern in the fan of yellow light, his eyes wide with their fear, his fingers restless.

From the darkness beyond, Hugh Baldwin's voice said: "Come in, Ryan. I've been waiting."

Ryan froze, cursing his own stupidity. He should have guessed they would be watching the roan. He remained silent, watching Baldwin and Dan Pike come into the spread of light. A thin smile was upon the cattleman's lips but Pike was a somber, still shadow.

"Never underestimate a man, Dan," Baldwin said with dry humor riding his tone. "Something I never do."

Pike had his own thoughts. He said: "Where'd you learn to draw iron like that, mister? You ever down around Fort Sumner or maybe Mesilla?"

Ryan made no reply. He was taking inventory of all things in his mind, sorting them out, searching for a way out of his present circumstances. He was now drawing his last breath, he knew, unless he did. A man like Hugh Baldwin played for keeps. The roan was in the first stall, and this knowledge he tucked away. The hostler stood, rooted near the wall; Baldwin was in the center of the lantern's light, and Pike was just a step aside within the fringe.

173

"Ryan," Baldwin said then, "you made a big mistake. Fact is, you made several. The first being your coming into this country. Getting in my way was the second."

Ryan shrugged, playing for time. "Meaning what?"

"Simple arithmetic. It takes twenty acres to support one cow around here. Right now I'm running three on every acre I own. Now does that make any sense to you?"

"There's room for Circle X and nobody else . . . that what you're driving at?"

Baldwin chuckled. "You're a smart man, Ryan. I said it before, I could use you. Too bad you didn't come see me at the start, instead of getting yourself all crosswise. You could have had a good job."

"Doubt if you'd had anything in my line," Ryan said dryly.

He was watching the hostler, placing his hopes on that man's throbbing fear. It showed in his eyes, in the nervous bunching of his face muscles, and in the working of his mouth. He had reached a point where the slightest, unexpected thing would send him into screaming flight. In the tense stillness Ryan listened to his rapid breathing.

"Ryan," Baldwin said then, "Dan here wants to see how fast with that gun you are. You were pretty good back there in the saloon, but Dan was hindered by the crowd. Now, he's curious to know just how good you are."

Ryan nodded. He ducked his head at the hostler. "What about him?"

Baldwin said: "What about him?"

Ryan turned to the stableman. In a perfectly level, cold voice he said: "Keep out of this or I'll kill you!"

The hostler cringed. Baldwin laughed. He drew his own gun. "What makes you think you will be in shape to kill anybody? If it turns out you're faster than Dan, I'll finish the job myself."

"And turn my body over to the marshal as a present. That the way it will be?"

"Like I said before, Ryan, you're a smart man."

Baldwin pulled away from Pike a step, coming closer to the hostler. Pike let his hands fall to his sides, his shoulders going down, his knees breaking slightly.

He said: "You never answered my question, Ryan. You from around Sumner or Mesilla? Maybe El Paso?"

"What difference does it make?" Ryan murmured.

"No difference," Pike said. "Just wondering about it."

In that fraction of time following Pike's words, Ryan made his move. In a single, blurring sweep his gun came up and he lunged into the hostler. His bullet caught Pike fully in the chest and that man went rocking backward into the shadows, never getting his own gun off. Baldwin, caught by the hostler's weight, slammed into the post at the end of the stall and reeled into the runway. His gun skittered off into the dark and Ryan closed in.

Baldwin met him with reaching hands and Ryan dodged and sent the man stumbling back with a hard right to the head. The rancher caught himself and came back, cursing between his teeth, his eyes bright with anger. Ryan stopped him with a straight left, but Baldwin recovered and came on, swinging hard. Ryan took a vicious blow in the ribs and returned it with a crackling right that landed high on Baldwin's head.

The hostler struggled out of the way of the circling pair and moved toward the doorway. Ryan hauled him up short: "Go through that door and I'll put a bullet in your back!" The stableman shrank back into the stall.

Baldwin suddenly rushed and Ryan stepped to one side, and, as the man plunged on, he staggered him with two rapid blows. Baldwin recovered quickly, wheeled, and caught Ryan with his wide-swinging fists, almost sending him down. A grin broke across Baldwin's face and he rushed in. Ryan backed away, pulling deeply for breath, and, as the big man came in close, he rocked him with a right to the jaw and a left that landed fully on the nose. Baldwin fell back and Ryan pressed his advantage, following up with two more whistling blows.

Baldwin backed into the wall and staggered forward, throwing his arms around Ryan to keep from falling and together they wrestled about the stable, locked in each other's arms, crashing into the uprights and stalls until finally Ryan broke free and stepped away. Baldwin came in after him, lashing out with knotted fists. The left drove into Ryan's ribs, throwing him off balance; the right straightened him up. Baldwin swung again and Ryan felt the solid shock of the blow go completely through him, setting lights wheeling about his head. He hung on grimly, backing away, trying to clear his head.

He felt Baldwin's knuckles skid off his mouth as the blow fell short, but it brought the warm, salty taste of blood to his lips. His senses cleared rapidly after that, and he caught Baldwin off guard by coming suddenly to life with a stiff right to the man's belly. Baldwin stopped short and Ryan came in fast, his arms working like pistons. Baldwin met him then, blow for blow, and for a full minute they stood toe to toe, slugging it out, filling the stable with the deep, meaty thudding of their hard blows.

Ryan plowed blindly on, heaving for breath, throwing all he could muster into each driving fist. Baldwin began to wilt, to give way. Ryan kept after him, keeping him moving under a hail of merciless fists. Baldwin's hands dropped and Ryan brought a long, haymaking right up from the floor. It caught Baldwin on the point of his chin, half lifting him off his feet. He went backward into a crumpled heap, crashing into the lantern post. The lantern flew from its peg and shattered against the wall.

Oil spread in a wide circle and the fire caught with an explosive flash. Ryan, hearing in that moment the sounds of running horses outside and guessing the return of the posse, shouted to the hostler.

"Drag this man outside!"

The stableman scurried to comply. He took Baldwin by the armpits and struggled toward the front door. Ryan freed the roan and fought him past the spreading flames, pointing for the rear entrance. There were shouts rising from the street and somebody was banging on the fire bell. He led the roan to the wagon yard at the side of the building and paused long enough to pull up the cinch. Smoke was rolling out into the night from the stable's doors and loft windows. The crackling of tinder-dry wood and the smell of burning stable trash filled the air.

Ryan swung to the saddle and wheeled into the alley. A rider loomed suddenly in the lurid glow directly before him, and he drew his gun and fired to turn the man aside. He saw then that it was Reno Davis, and he threw himself to one side on the roan as the Circle X rider's gun blossomed. He felt the sear of the bullet as it cut through his leg, and snapped another shot at Davis. The cowpuncher plunged away into the darkness of the alley and Ryan spurred the roan toward the hills.

VI

In the cloud-built darkness of the night, Jim Ryan rode the blue roan at headlong pace. Behind him the glow of the burning stable arched over the town in a yellow-orange pall, reminding him of the rushing events that had transpired in so few minutes. And this brought bitter thoughts to mind. He had ridden a thousand miles and more to escape the harrying press of trouble, to escape the quarrels of men. Now, again, he was suddenly and deeply enmeshed. The past was like a relentless, pursuing shadow, never very far away and always eventually catching up with a man. There was no such thing as a new life; the old one was never done.

He swung the roan from the main road and struck out across the smooth, rolling prairie. He was heading straight for the Santa Claras that lay to the west of his holdings. He was remembering a high run of buttes and sheer cliffs that Frank Sears had once taken him to. There were several natural caves along the rim of the bluffs reached only by an almost invisible trail that wound up from a short cañon that lay in the mountain's flank.

The roan began to tire. He had made two hard runs that afternoon with very little rest; once, when they had raced after the killer of Tom Strickland, and later, when they had followed him back to town. Ryan could feel the animal straining between his knees. He glanced back to see if there were any signs of the posse. It was too dark to tell but he pulled the roan down anyway. The storm that had been in the making for the past two days had the sky covered with a lead-gray blanket. There was no starlight or moon to break it at any point.

He let the roan walk slowly for a good half hour, cooling him out gradually. Afterward he set him at an easy lope. He began then to feel the pain in his leg where Reno Davis's bullet had ripped through, and he cocked himself at an angle in the saddle, absorbing as much of the shock from the roan's motion as he could in his good leg.

It was not a bad wound. This he knew. But the sticky warmness inside his breeches told him it had bled considerably and was still flowing. He mulled over the advisability of stopping long enough to bind it and thus check the loss of blood, but this he ruled out. The posse could not be far behind now, even though he could neither hear nor see anything of them. And if they should suddenly appear, the roan would be in no condition for a fast, uphill run. The leg would just have to wait until he reached the safety of the bluffs.

He was on his own range. Of this he became aware when he realized he was at a point of rocks that lay a short four miles north of his ranch buildings. He was feeling a little giddy and he had an impulse to swing down and advise Frank Sears of the night's happenings and pick up a small supply of grub and a canteen of water. And Frank could help him doctor up the leg. A moment later he dismissed the idea with a shrug. That would be gambling against high odds, for Meldrum, urged by Hugh Baldwin, would send men there at the very first. They would expect him to do something like that. It would be walking straight into a cocked snare.

Anyway, Sears would guess his hiding place when he got wind of the state of things. He would fit the facts together in that wise old way of his and show up—probably before the morning. He would bring all the necessary items: food, drink, medicine—the works. A man had to move pretty damned fast to outguess old Frank.

Ryan became conscious of swaying loosely in the saddle. He caught at the horn to steady himself, shaking his head in an effort to toss off the mist that engulfed him. That hole in his leg must be worse than he had figured. The clouds floated out of his eyes and his vision cleared. It couldn't be far to the bluffs now. He could see them, he thought, looming ahead. Great, ragged shapes of blackness deeper than the night standing in the near distance.

An owl, or some other nocturnal bird, scuttled out from under the roan's hoofs and the big horse shied violently. Pain stabbed through Ryan, coursing his entire body like a fiery streak. He clung to the saddle horn and tried to calm the roan with a few words. He rubbed at the horse's bowed neck muscles and patted him gently. The roan settled down once again, but the moments had brought the fog back and for several minutes it was a struggle to stay in the leather.

The night breeze, hurrying ahead of the storm, brought some relief and refreshment. The roan had dropped to a slow walk when he was again conscious. He had reached the first gradual slopes that fell away from the bluffs. He was wishing it would rain then, knowing that it would make him feel somewhat better.

He was depending now upon Frank Sears coming by daylight. Somehow, it had become a reality in his flagging mind, and he was not considering it could be any other way. Sears would know. He would come with grub and water. He could depend upon that. Just as you could always depend on him. He took a great deal of joy from being referred to as the foreman of the Box K. He wasn't actually; he had just come along with the land when Ryan had purchased it—same as the trees and the buildings and the Santa Claras. Ryan had taken a liking to him and they had been together many hours when work was light, just roaming across the property. A man would have thought the grizzled old rider was as much the owner as Ryan, so much pride did he take in the place.

"Don't need no payin'," Frank had said one day when Ryan brought up the matter of salary.

"Twenty-five dollars a month and found," Ryan had offered.

"What'd I do with money? Got me a place to sleep and eat. And a good horse to fork. An' I ain't figurin' on goin' no place. Reckon I got about all a man needs."

"What about smokes? What about money for boots and clothes? Man needs gear now and then."

Sears had slanted a look at Ryan from beneath his bushy eyebrows. He had a way of stroking at his mustache that he wore, full and thick. "Reckon I'll just keep on moochin' what I got to have. Howsomever, I got me an ace in the hole, ever I needs one. Got a little pocket of color back there in the hills where I can always scrape me up a little stake any time I need it."

"Gold? In these hills?"

"Yes, sir. Right in these hills." The old rider had paused. He covered Ryan with a sharp, speculative glance. "I reckon you ought to know about it, it bein' on your property. You want to see where it is?"

Ryan had grinned. "Hell, no. You know where it is, so keep it that way. It's yours."

Frank Sears had chuckled. "Figured you'd say that. I don't make no mistakes about a man that's white all the way through. Never make no mistakes about you, child."

Yes, Frank Sears would be there. He'd figure a way to get around Baldwin's men and Meldrum's recruited deputies. He would show by daylight, maybe even sooner. Nobody could outsmart old Frank.

The going had become rougher and the roan began to stumble in the darkness, partly from exhaustion and partly from the broken, uneven terrain. It was utterly dark in the shadow of the bluffs, a darkness that was broken only occasionally by a ragged flash of lightning, weakened by distance. Ryan realized he would have to stop and locate himself. He would have to find the draw up from which the trail led. He let the roan come to a halt of his own accord and for a few minutes sat quietly in the saddle, face tipped downward as weariness and the recurring giddiness took hold of him.

After a time he roused himself, the necessity for locating the cañon with its hidden trail ceaselessly hammering at his dulled mind. Shaking his head to clear it, he studied the irregular rim of the bluffs and the dark, broken face of the slopes lifting away from him. In the heavy night it was difficult to pick out anything of definite, familiar shape. A flash of lightning lifted the veil; almost directly before him was an upthrusting formation of clean granite Sears had named the Thumb. That was a clue he could use; he was close to the draw, closer than he had expected to be. It would lie a short quarter mile to his left. He stirred in the saddle and turned the tired roan in that direction, allowing him to pick his own way along the shale.

The first raindrops struck him just as he reached

the lip of the cañon. He was rational enough to be grateful for it. It would ease some of the fever that was harrying him, and it would serve another important purpose. There would be several good trackers in the posse and among Hugh Baldwin's riders, any one of whom could follow him across the prairie and up the slopes of the Santa Claras. A good rain would wash away all signs and eliminate that possibility for him.

He wound into the draw and moved across its width, gaining the opposite side. For a half mile, he bored deeper into the slash, while the sides became increasingly steep and the brush heavier. The steadily falling rain and the solid blackness were hampering him now, making it hard to see the faint trail, turning the slippery rocks into dangerous traps for the roan.

Well into the cañon's depth, he stopped the roan, fearing he had overshot the trail. He waited there patiently, hands clasped about the horn, shoulders slumped while rain slanted against him and soaked him through to the skin. He could do nothing until another flash of lightning came and broke the smothering darkness. His mind was not functioning too well, and this he could not understand, being unaware of how great the quantity of blood he had lost actually was. He grew cold and this helped some, sharpening his senses to a degree, but he could not dispel the terrible heaviness that had settled upon him.

A vivid flash of close-by lightning and the immediate crashing of thunder startled him. He saw, directly ahead, the huge boulder he was searching for. His own intuition had brought him to a halt at the right point (if only he had known it). He urged the roan forward and worked him around the mass of granite to the narrow game trail lying there. He was on barren rock and loose shale. It was already slick from the rain and the run-off of water beginning now to cascade down from the higher points. It was rough, dangerous going, and several times he hesitated, wondering if he should go on, if he should risk the roan and himself. But always he moved on. Three times in the first 100 yards the roan stumbled, almost throwing Ryan from the saddle, shooting bright flares of pain through him. But he kept on.

He gained level ground and pulled up. He dismounted. His leg was stiff from hip to ankle, and, when he placed a slight amount of weight upon it, living fire once again poured through him. He ground his teeth and held on to consciousness. He knew he could not chance any longer the possibility of the roan's falling with him. He would have to walk. Reins in hand, he started up the steep trail, bracing himself against the face of the cliff.

A sudden wave of frustration rocked through him. Damn Hugh Baldwin! Damn Pike! Damn Tom Strickland and all the rest! This fight had been no making of his. He hadn't wanted any part of it, and, now, look where he was! Look what it had brought him to. A black, wet night, struggling on the side of a mountain, a bullet through his leg; he was cold, hungry, and so tired he could scarcely breathe. Like a cornered coyote, he was scurrying for cover, looking for a place in which to hide from a marshal's posse. Worse still, a bunch of trigger-happy riders were all anxious to finish up a job on him. Why did it have to happen just as he was getting things under way?

Limping badly, Ryan gained the second level break. He paused there to rest, leaning heavily against the roan. The trail that he followed worked along a bench about halfway up the side of the cliff. It was, perhaps, six feet back from the edge. Scrub oak and twisted juniper and dove weed growing thickly in that intervening space screened it from the prairie lying far below. In places it was fairly wide but generally it was narrow, and, as they moved slowly along, there was a steady scraping noise as the roan's sides rubbed against the cliff's rough surface on one hand, the thick growth of brush on the other.

The rain had stopped. He realized this, standing there against the roan, hanging onto the saddle horn while he supported his weight on his good leg. He rested out another minute or two, and then, taking up the reins once more, he resumed the ascent. In the first dozen yards he stumbled twice and would have fallen flat had he not been clinging to the roan. But he managed to keep going, and finally he had completed the last half mile to the third leveling where there was the cave he sought.

There he dropped to his knees, not totally unconscious but filled with an exhaustion so vast it had no beginning, no end. Even breathing was an inhuman effort, and it seemed hardly worthwhile. But the tremendous vitality and determination of the man was such that it would not let him stop until he reached complete safety. He struggled to his feet and drove the roan back from the trail, deeper into the flat. A scatter of ghostly-looking trees lay in a small grove to the rear, and into this he sent the blue roan. There he could not be seen should any of the posse or Circle X riders happen to come up the trail.

After that he half walked, half crawled, to the cave that was, in actuality, a low-roofed, tunnel-like crevice at the base of a cliff hinging at right angles from the main formation. Water had drained in and stood in shallow pools on the floor but that went unnoticed. The relief in just being off his feet, clear of the trail, and out of sight was like the fulfillment of a wonderful dream.

He lay there for a full hour or more, eyes closed, senses dulled to the pain throbbing insistently through him. Weariness, a powerful anesthetic in these moments, was an ally. But the nagging pressure of necessity would not let him rest for long, and after a time he roused long enough to bind the wound crudely with a makeshift bandage.

He did not again lie down. The natural wariness of Ryan prompted him to place himself in a sitting position against the cave's back wall, facing the opening. In this way, gun in hand, he settled down to wait for Frank Sears.

VII

Ryan came awake with the sun's first warming rays. He was lying prone, having tipped sideways sometime during the night. He was cold and his leg throbbed dully but the faintness had gone and now he was only weak and hungry.

He pulled himself to the mouth of the cave, where the sun's rays were beginning to strike warmly, and looked out. The roan was cropping grass in the grove and the sky was an over-bending canopy of clearest blue. He could not see the prairie from the crevice, and for a long time he just sat there, slumped against the rough, scaly wall, gathering heat and strength. Finally, feeling up to it, he crawled through the opening. It was perhaps thirty feet to the edge of the bench but he had to see what was happening on the prairie below, and he went the entire distance on his hands and knees, favoring the injured leg all the way.

Parting the tangled growth of shrubbery, he lay flat and gazed out upon the rolling world below. It fell away from the base of the cliffs in yellow-gold waves, like a sea just before sunset. The night's rain still lay upon it and the streaming sunlight caught up the bright sparkle and capped it all with a silvery sheen. It was a beautiful world, a land he had dreamed of one day becoming a part of—and now, instead, he was an outsider. He murmured under his breath, cursing the fates that had twisted all things around for him. A man sometimes thought he owned his own soul, that he was captain of his own life; how quickly he learned otherwise!

He turned his eyes southward and saw the faint smudge of buildings that marked his own Box K ranch. He saw riders, too—an even dozen of them, spread out in a wide, slowly moving dragnet working toward the Santa Claras. He swiveled his glance to the opposite side, to the north. More men were there, crawling like torpid ants toward the hills. He could not see it, but beyond that group lay the Strickland place. He wondered, then, which group was Baldwin's and which represented Ross Meldrum's posse. It made no particular difference, but he concluded, finally, that the larger group in the south, coming from the Box K, was the marshal's. And that would be Hugh Baldwin and his Circle X crew to the north.

They were sweeping the country for him; they were methodically working toward a central point, converging, attempting to pocket him and trap him between their two forces. They knew he had headed due west when he left Gunstock and they knew, also, about how far he could have traveled since they had been close behind. They knew he was there, hiding somewhere between them, on the prairie or in the hills, and they were moving in for the kill, driving him into a squeeze, catching him between the opposing jaws of their human vise. He smiled grimly. They would be damned surprised when they found their vise empty.

For a good hour he lay watching. The sun climbed steadily, and, as is the way of the high plains country, he began to feel the bite of the lifting heat. In this land a man was a toy of the elements. At night he shivered and froze under the touch of the mountain breeze sweeping down from the peaks and ridges. In the day, the sun drove him mercilessly, sucking his body dry and cracking his lips and creating an ever-present urgency for water. He shifted to his side, letting the heat drill into his injured leg.

Insects began to clack in the brush and deer flies darted about him and settled upon him with irritating frequency. He ripped a fan of oak leaves from a nearby scrub and brushed at them to keep them moving. Five yards away in the trail a gray squirrel came to sudden attention, watching him with beady, black eyes and scolding with sharp severity. The roan ate on steadily, making loud, grinding noises with his teeth. Occasionally a stirrup became fouled in the shrubbery and he would pull impatiently away, throwing his head high, as if irritated by the obstruction.

Eventually tired of watching the slowly moving figures still far off on the prairie, hungry and becoming increasingly stiff, he crawled back to the cave. Despite his condition he was still a careful man, and he paused every few feet to wipe away the tracks he left behind with the oak leaf fan he had saved. He doubted if any of Baldwin's men or the posse members would ever find the hidden trail up the cañon's wall, but he took no chances, the old inbred caution in him having its way.

The cave, which earlier was cold and damp, was now a cool and comfortable haven from the sun. He lay back full length, unmindful of the hard, rock-studded ground. The leg was a constant ache and there was now a stiffness in his knee. But he was not too uncomfortable. Given a little more rest, some food—particularly coffee—and a decent dressing of the wound, he would be in pretty fair shape again. He had been hurt worse before. Maybe he hadn't lost quite so much blood, but there had been worse injuries than this hole through the meaty part of his leg. It was the stiffness that worried him most. Sooner or later he would have to come down off the bluffs and that would not be easy if he was unable to make good use of the leg. Walking or riding, it would be rough going.

By noon he had given up hopes of Frank Sears's coming. But that was understandable. With the prairie below crawling with men searching every square foot of it for him, Sears would take no chances of leading them to him. He would take no chances on being seen. But Sears would come eventually; Ryan was still convinced of that.

Around the middle of the afternoon he crawled back to the rim of the cliff again. The two groups had finally met and now, together, were working out the draws at the foot of the bluffs. Brush was thick in that area and it appeared to be slow work. When he saw two riders turn into the cañon from which the hidden trail curled up, he dragged his way tediously back to the cave, again wiping out his tracks. Inside, he once more settled himself against the wall, drew his gun, and began a lonely vigil.

But by dark no one had come up the trail and hunger was now an insistent factor within him. He crawled to the cave's mouth and considered his best move. Hunched there, staring into the star-studded wall beyond the bench, he heard the faint *click* of metal against stone. A moment later there was the distinctive *creak* of leather as a man shifted in the saddle. Ryan pulled back into the cave and waited, gun ready, eyes boring into the darkness.

A rider swung around the turn and came into dim view. Man and horse were briefly silhouetted against the sky and Ryan lifted his gun, ready to press off a certain shot. He thought there was something familiar about the man and his mount but he could not be sure, and of that he had to be. He waited while the rider eased in closer.

"Jim? You 'round hyar?" Frank Sears's voice called softly.

A sigh gushed from Ryan's lips. "In here, Frank," he said, and lay back against the cave's wall. It had been a long, tough day but, finally, it was about to end.

He heard Sears walk his horse back into the grove where the roan grazed and then return, his boots making small, hollow sounds on the hard surface, despite the care he was taking. The old cowpuncher came into the cave, dragging a sugar sack behind him. He holed up in a corner, squatting on his heels Indian fashion.

"Figured you'd be here. How long?"

"Since last night," Ryan answered. "Got anything to eat in that sack?"

"Sure enough," Ryan answered. "Thought you might be needin' a nip of this here firewater, too. Nothin' like firewater to heat up a man's innards."

Ryan shifted about and took the bottle. He pulled the cork and tipped down a long swallow. The liquor laced down his throat like a hot stream and had an immediate effect. He shook his head, wondering a little at the shock.

Sears said: "Reckon we better have a middlin'

194

fire in here." He moved out into the open, gathered an armload of dry wood, and returned. He cracked some of it into short lengths and laid them into a pile. "You sure got the whole dang' country out lookin' for you, son!"

Ryan grinned into the darkness. The whiskey was stirring his blood to a boil, driving the chill from his bones and muscles. His stomach, so long empty of food, was reacting quickly. "Looked like a pretty good fire there in town, judging from what I could see of it," he said.

Sears chuckled. He struck a match with a thumbnail and held it to the pile of wood. After a moment the flame caught and began to twist up through the darkness, creating a warm flare of light.

"Set there in the openin'," Sears directed. "Don't think nobody's goin' to spot the glow, but there's no use takin' any chance."

Ryan moved to comply, working his stiff leg like a pivot. When he was in the cave's mouth and settled, he glanced up and caught Sears's sharp eyes studying him.

"You hurt? They wing you?"

"In the leg. Nothing serious. Got a little stiff on me, just laying around on it."

Sears snorted. "Why the hell didn't you say somethin' about it?" He set aside the can of water he was about to place in the fire and swung about.

Ryan said: "Never mind it now. Few more minutes won't make any difference in the leg. But I don't think I can last much longer without a cup of coffee!"

Sears chuckled and turned back to the fire. He started the water, adding more fuel to the flames. From the sugar sack he produced some hard biscuits, jerked beef, dried peaches, a tin of tomatoes, and a jar of ground coffee. The water began to simmer and then boil, and he dropped a generous handful of grounds into the can and set it aside. When it boiled up, he stirred the froth down with a twig. Then, wrapping the can with his bandanna, he handed it to Ryan.

"I reckon you'll find it hot enough," he observed laconically, "and probably strong enough to peel bark off a pine tree."

Ryan sipped the scalding brew, burning his lips, the inside of his mouth, and thoroughly searing his throat. But it was good, and after two or three swallows he already felt much better. He began to eat, then, making a meal of the jerky and other items. He finished it off with a long drink from Sears's canteen of water.

"Now, let's see about that there leg," Sears said, having waited patiently for Ryan to eat. He tossed more wood on the fire. "You lay down here where I can see better."

Ryan stretched out on the cave's floor. Except for the dull aching in his leg, he felt good now. The liquor, aided and abetted by the steaming coffee and food, had poured new life into him. Now, with his belly full, things did not seem so bad, after all. He had seen worse times, very much worse, he reflected.

"Goin' to have to cut your pants leg a bit," Sears stated. "It's stuck to the place where that bullet went in."

He dumped the remainder of the coffee and refilled the can with clean water. He placed that back in the fire to heat, noting: "You sure did a right smart lot of bleedin'. A good thing, too, I'd say."

"I knew I was losing a lot of blood," Ryan answered. "Made me a little wobbly for a time." He waited a moment, then: "You been to the ranch?"

"All day."

"Meldrum and his posse stop by there?"

"Bright and early, lookin' for you. They left a couple of jaspers to watch the place. Had me a devil of a time givin' them the slip."

"What did Meldrum have to say?"

"What'd he say? Only that you shot and killed Dan Pike, after him and Baldwin cornered you, and that you knocked Hugh flat and set fire to the stable, tryin' to kill him off, too."

Ryan felt Sears working with the point of his knife around the wound, cutting free the patch of cloth that had dried hard with blood against the injury. He winced a little when Sears laid a steaming-hot pad on it.

"Not quite the way it happened," he said after a moment or two. "I dropped Pike. He forced me into a draw and I beat him to it. Baldwin and me then got into it, and, during the fight, the lantern came off the peg and started the fire. The hostler will tell you that."

Sears wagged his head. "You ain't figurin' on him standin' up for you, are you? Not against Hugh Baldwin."

He applied a freshly heated pad to Ryan's leg, stroking gently across the wound, saying: "What's this business about Tom Strickland? What happened there?"

While the old cowpuncher worked at the injury in his leg, Ryan related the incidents of the day, concluding with the fight at the stable and the brush with Reno Davis. Sears listened, clucking periodically like a mother hen tending a lone chick. When Ryan was finished, he said: "Just about what I figured. Reckon Hugh's findin' it mighty hard to swallow your pushin' his outfit around this way. There any whiskey left in that bottle?"

Ryan handed it to him.

Sears said: "You think it sure enough was Reno that bushwhacked old Tom?"

"Can't see how it could have been anybody else," Ryan replied. In that next instant he almost yelled out when Sears poured the raw whiskey into the bullet hole.

"Need us a bandage now," Sears said, tossing the bottle into a corner. "You'll be out hoppin' around good as new before long."

"I wonder," Ryan muttered. "This kind of doctoring could wind up with most any sort of results."

Sears grinned. Ryan swore softly, still feeling the fire seeping in deeper. But he knew the leg was better, despite the violence of the treatment.

"Now you wait a minute while I go fetch a blanket," Sears said. "I'll rig you a pallet here alongside the fire. You keep that leg good and warm all night and it'll be limber-like, come the mornin'."

VIII

Later, after Ryan had laid himself full length and as close to the fire as possible so the heat might soak generously into his leg, Sears said: "How long you plannin' to hole up here?"

"Not too long. Somebody will finally find this place. They'll keep on looking down below until they've checked every possible place, and, when I don't turn up, they'll start working up the sides of the hills. Could be I'll make a try for it tomorrow."

Sears wagged his head. "Too soon. Men are as thick as flies on spoilt beef, combin' out the draws and flats with a fine-tooth comb. Even saw a couple back up on the bluffs, clear on top. You better wait out tomorrow and make your move the next day. Some of the waddies'll peter out before then and go home, and you'll have a better chance. Besides, that leg of your'n needs another day's rest."

"Expect you're right," Ryan agreed after a moment. The thought of men searching along the crown of the cliffs disturbed him. "What about the riders you saw up above? There any way down to this ledge from there?"

"Never did find any," Sears answered slowly. "Only trail along this bluff I know of is the one you followed up here. And it quits about a quarter mile on. I don't think you need to be worryin' none about them seeing you. Just be careful they don't spot you when you get out on the trail."

"When I leave," Ryan said, "it will be in the dark."

Sears refilled the improvised coffee pot and set it back into the fire. "Reckon I could use a cup of coffee before I take out, seein' as how I probably won't make the ranch much before mornin'," he said. "You might leave what's left of that grub. Never know when me or you might have to come hustlin' back."

Ryan nodded. Changing the subject, he asked the question that had been bothering him. "Frank, what was the trouble between Tom Strickland and Baldwin? I'm dead certain it was more than Tom just not wanting to sell out to him."

Sears added a handful of sticks to the fire. It blazed up brightly, and, with a longer branch, he nestled the can of water deeper into the flames. "You're right. That sure wasn't all of it. There was just a lot of little things that grew into big ones."

Ryan built himself a smoke and handed the sack of makings to Sears. The tobacco was still a little damp from the rain and he had some difficulty in getting it lit. "That's the way it goes most of the time. Things that don't amount to anything, someday cause a man to slap his leather."

"Well, old Tom was a cantankerous old mossy-horn, anyway. When he was younger, he was a tough one but not much ever riled him unless'n it was rustlers and the like. Howsomever, after he got older and all stove up, he was sure somethin' to be sidin'. I worked one day for him a couple years ago in July, cuttin' and brandin' and, by granny's nose, I'd starve before I'd ever do it again! Never saw such a man! Everything I did was wrong! Didn't make any difference what I had a mind to do, he was ag'in' it. Never saw so dang' much con-tention!"

Ryan reached into the fire for a burning branch with which to light his cigarette. Outside, a light wind had risen, riffling swiftly through the brush and along the face of the cliff, setting up a soft sighing in the treetops. "How did he and Hugh get so crossways?"

Sears finished preparing the coffee and set it to

one side to settle. "Reckon that started about five, six years ago. Hugh had a pretty fair bunch of cows on that south range of his'n and it seems they drifted down into Strickland's herd. That crowded things a mite, and, when Tom found them, he had his boys drive them back up on Circle X graze and told Hugh about it. Next week or so he found that same bunch of stock down there again, right in the same place. He just rode right over to Hugh and ordered him to send some of his crew down and get them, and durn' quick! Well, Hugh did that, actin' all the time like it was a big joke and he was doin' it just to humor old Tom. But, turned out, it wasn't so funny later. Next time Tom found them critters on his land, he didn't say nothin' about it to Hugh. He gathered up his boys and they drove all Baldwin's stock they could find eighteen miles down the river and into the brakes."

Sears paused. He took up the can of coffee and drank deeply, sighing his satisfaction. For a time afterward he sat quietly, eyes staring into the fire, an old-timer remembering events that pleased him. A half smile was on his mouth, and the glow from the flickering flames touching his straggling mustache and whiskery face turned him a deep bronze.

"Baldwin do anything about that?"

"He sent his crew down after them. Took them two weeks, as I recollect, to pop them critters out of the brush and get them home. But Hugh never opened his mouth to Tom about it. Just let on like nothin' happened. But he sure didn't steal no more graze from Strickland! Then, one day, Tom and some of his crew went up to bring in the stock that had been summerin' in the high country to drive them down into the valley for winter. Well, they couldn't get within a country mile of any of them. George Cobb told me later he'd never run across such a crazy bunch of critters in all his life. And knowin' George, that's coverin' a heap of territory."

"Really spooked," Ryan murmured. "Some of Baldwin's doing?"

"Who else? George said he found out them Circle X boys had done everything from hazin' them with knotted rawhide to spittin' tobacco juice in their eyes. Ever' time they spotted a man on a horse, they'd take off like a scalded pig and they wouldn't quit runnin' till they was clean out of sight! I saw that herd after they finally got them in and I never laid eyes on such a poorly bunch of cows in all my life. An' comin' from down in south Texas, I've seen some poorly ones."

"Strickland?"

"Why, he acted just like Hugh did. Didn't say nothin'. Just went right on like it was nothin' unusual for a man to have a plumb loony herd. But the thing had really started there. From that time on they wasn't on no more than bare speakin' terms. They'd pass not more'n twenty feet apart and make out like they didn't see each other. That ended the sparkin' Hugh and Tom's gal had been doin', too."

Ryan glanced up. "Hugh and Ann? Didn't know there had ever been anything between them."

Sears's eyes twinkled. He gave Ryan an indulgent, understanding smile. "Don't reckon it ever amounted to much. Mostly Hugh's idea, I think. But that sure cooked it, anyhow."

Sears glanced at the cold cigarette butt held between his fingers and then tossed it into the fire. "The next year, I think it was, a bunch of Strickland's cows got in with a couple of Baldwin's bulls. Later, when Tom found it out, he rounded up a dozen calves at brandin' time and drove them over to where the Circle X bunch was workin'. All he said to Hugh was . . . 'Here's the calves I owe you' . . . and then rode off, proud and stiff-backed as you please. After Tom had quit his ridin', he got worse, and things between him and Baldwin really went to hell. I don't know if he thought Hugh was pullin' anything on him or not, but he sure did act like it. And when a man's settin' and wonderin' and suspectin' things and can't get around to find out nothin' for sure, either way, I guess it's the worst kind of thinkin'. Somethin' that just gnaws and chews on a man's vitals till he's dang' nigh crazy. I know old Tom was about that way."

Ryan shook his head. "Not many things worse," he murmured.

"Winterin' stock got to be more of a problem for Baldwin," Sears continued. "And he finally swallered his pride and rode over to see Tom about buyin' that north section of his ranch. Tom wouldn't even listen to him, wouldn't let him talk. He got real stirred up and accused Hugh of about everything you could think of, includin' a little rustlin'. Naturally Hugh didn't take kindly to that kind of talk and he got mad and cussed old Tom to a fare-thee-well. And that's the way it's been ridin' ever since."

Ryan shifted his position on the blanket. The fire was hot and he could detect the faintly scorched odor of cloth too near the flames. The throbbing had left his leg and it felt much better. "Not much there for one man to shoot another over, but it's been done for less."

"You don't think that's much reason? If you knew Hugh Baldwin better, you'd be wonderin' what stalled him off long as it did! Anybody gets in Hugh's way gets tromped, once he makes up his mind to do somethin'. That Circle X outfit is big, and gettin' bigger. Hugh needs more grazin' and I reckon he's decided to get it."

"What do you figure he'll do about the Strickland place now?"

"He'll get it, that's what. Sure as water's wet. It's that north section that lays along his line that he needs bad, but that won't keep him from takin' it all if it works out that way. Could be, if he got that strip, it'll pacify him, but I sure wouldn't take no bets on it. It's like Hugh, now that he's made his move, to go whole hog and pull up only after he's got everythin' that's took his fancy. He'll figure he's settin' in a game with a pat hand now, since there's only Strickland's gal left at the S-Bar."

"You think he'll just try and move right in on her and take over the place?"

Sears shook his head. "Not this time, not where the gal is concerned. He'll first try to sweet-talk her into sellin' the place to him, and then, if she won't see it that way, things will start happenin' around the ranch. And they won't be good things. Sooner or later, she'll have to sell."

"You seen her?"

Sears leveled a glance across the fire's glow. "Nope. But from what I been hearin' around the posse, she ain't thinkin' any kindly thoughts about you. Hugh's got her sold that you killed her pa."

"She knows better than that," Ryan murmured.

"Well, if she does, she sure ain't actin' like it."

"Somebody ought to warn her about Baldwin."

"Way Hugh's got it fixed, I don't think she'd do much listenin', 'specially from you."

"Well, she may have to before this is done."

Sears remained silent for a time, having his own thoughts about the matter. "Reckon I'd better be moseyin' along. Man can't afford to push his luck too far."

He crawled to the cave's opening. He stopped

there, thinking of something, and turned around. "Now, I don't want you worryin' none about your place. Me and the boys will take care of the old Box K. And stay off that leg for another day."

Ryan nodded. "My thanks for coming, Frank. And watch yourself going back. No use of you getting caught up in my troubles."

The old cowpuncher snorted. "I can take care of myself, don't fret none about that. As for Hugh Baldwin, I'd miss a meal of fried chicken and a woman's biscuits to aggravate that man a little."

Ryan watched him squeeze through the opening and disappear into the darkness of the night. Minutes later he heard him pass by, leading his pony, as he headed down the trail.

IX

Sometime around midnight Ryan awakened. The fire was down to feebly glowing embers and it was bitterly cold inside the cave. He scratched around and found a few sticks of the wood Sears had brought in and tossed them into the coals. After a bit of fanning with his hat, he brought the flames to life. Pulling the blanket up over his shoulders, he built himself a smoke and sat there, a hunched, somber shape gathering in the scant warmness the fire was throwing out.

He was thinking of Frank Sears's words, and the more he considered them, the more disturbed he became. Hugh Baldwin, in true form and character, was now established in his mind and he had him, at last, pegged for what he was—an utterly ruthless, wholly selfish egotist. Ryan's past experiences with men of his caliber recognized that fact. A man gets big, and the feeling of power possesses him and takes over his life, and from then on it is like a runaway fever, never letting him rest, never letting him call a halt. He tries his hand and comes out on top and from that moment on he is lost. Everything he sets his will to get, he does, by one way or another, the kinds of ways never mattering much. And those who happen to fall in the line of action suffer the consequences.

But eventually somebody comes along that does not frighten so easily, that fails to back down when things get rough. A little man, perhaps, a man that's lost everything and doesn't give a hoot because there's nothing more to lose and not much further to go. Or possibly a drifter with an urge to right the wrongs of the world and become a hero in a land where heroes are short-lived. Or maybe a man who was just plain sick of seeing big men push little men around, of seeing the Hugh Baldwins rush in like wolves when the gates are open and the lambs unprotected. *Like me,* Ryan thought, startled by the realization.

For a time he let that mull about in his mind. It bothered him and he tried to shake it off, but it remained there, firmly anchored, and his thoughts were suddenly desperate. *Maybe I am that man. But I don't want any of it. I don't want any of this fight. I've had all the gunsmoke I want in this lifetime and I'm through with it for good.* He shrugged and tossed the burned-down cigarette into the fire. Something became clear to him and a deep sigh moved gustily through his long lips as he recognized another truth. *I'll never be through with it now if I stay here. I'll never find that peace I'm looking for on the Cuchillo Plains. Hugh Baldwin's put his mark on me, and now it's fight or run . . . and I'm through with fighting. I got into this thing by accident. I'll get out of it the best way I can, and the quickest.*

He felt of his leg, rubbing it carefully and testing its sensitivity by gentle prods and squeezes. It was still sore but not as stiff as it had been. Frank Sears's treatment and the fire's warmth had done wonders for it.

Still thinking of Baldwin, he left the cave, remembering Sears's instructions not to put his weight on the injured leg just yet, and crawled to the edge of the bench. The sky was a dark, star-studded bowl overhead, and the prairie a silvery-sprinkled mist far below. Tiny spots of orange fire marked the camps of the posse members and the Circle X men posted at intervals, like a sparkling band across the sloping base of the Santa Claras.

They were waiting for him. They knew he was there, hiding somewhere in the maze of draws and cañons and brush piles. And when morning came with its bright, revealing light, they would again begin their search. And eventually they would find him. No man could hide forever.

Seeing the winking campfires brought the old days washing back through Ryan like a rushing flash flood. Men on the hunt. Men on the dodge. It was always like that, and there was never any end to it. When one stopped, another began, and a man could spend his life in the doing of it, if, somewhere along the line, he did not call a halt to it. And Jim Ryan had called that halt one bloody day in the dusty street of Tascosa. But now it could begin all over again.

He came to a standing position, gingerly trying his weight on the weakened leg. It began to ache immediately and he paused, waiting to see if it would become worse, the pain more intense. When it did not, but remained merely a dull throb, he took a few tentative steps, and, finding those not too bad, he walked back the distance to the cave. By the time he reached there, he had reached a decision. He would not wait out another day; he would not hang on until the next night to leave the hills. He would go now, while the blackness of the night still held. If Frank Sears could get by the posse and Baldwin's men, so, also, could he.

Before putting out the fire in the cave, he tore the blanket Sears had brought into narrow strips. Lopping them over one arm, he took up the canteen of water and walked to the roan. He moved slowly and carefully, placing no undue strain on his bad leg, endeavoring to avoid any objects in his path that might cause him to trip or stumble. Sears had removed the roan's bridle and loosened the saddle cinch and put the horse on picket. He remained quiet while Ryan got him ready for riding.

Sears had not mentioned it, but he had not believed any of the posse would be camped within the cañon. More than likely they were out in the open where they could more easily watch the brush along the foothills and see a man if he tried to break out onto the prairie. Gambling on this being a fact, Ryan tucked the strips of wool into his saddlebags and swung, stiff-legged, onto the roan. It required several minutes to find a comfortable position, but he finally managed it. He turned then toward the trail.

It was slow going but not too difficult. Star shine made the narrow trail fairly distinct, and the roan was a sure-footed animal that took his own sweet time when the going was tough. The only bad moments in the entire descent came when they were along the narrowest part, and the roan, hugging the cliff's wall, dragged Ryan's leg against the solid, rough surface. It swept his breath away when the pain stabbed through him, and he knew the bleeding undoubtedly had started again. But there was nothing he could do about it.

At the bottom, he halted in the deep shadows, well off the trail. If he had been heard coming down, there would be someone along to investigate shortly. He drew his gun and waited quietly, but after thirty minutes had dragged by, he came to the conclusion that the occasional clink of the roan's shoes against stone and the scraping noises his infrequent contact with the cliff's face had made had passed unnoticed.

Now was the time for care. He took the strips of blanket from his saddlebags and bound the roan's hoofs, folding the wool several times to deaden completely all sound. The roan did not like it much, but after a few experimental steps he decided it was all right, and forgot about it. Ryan, gun in hand, swung back to the saddle and began the long, slow ride out of the cañon.

It seemed better to follow the trail. It was open and no brush dragged against him, setting up that loud, cracking noise. There were no sounds from the roan's hooded hoofs and Ryan strained to keep the creak of leather to a minimum by doing no shifting about and maintaining a slow, regular pace. In the pale, eerie light, they drifted silently along like ghostly shadows.

Ryan saw the glow of the campfire before he reached the end of the draw. It was a good fifty yards out. Two figures lay near the smoldering coals, heads pillowed upon saddles, sleeping restlessly in the night's chill. A third man hunched close by, arms doubled across his knees, head resting face down. They were evidently alternating at watch and this one was finding the long, quiet hours hard to fight.

Just within the shadows, Ryan studied the situation. To his left, 100 yards or so away, another fire flickered in the darkness. The same distance to the left lay a similar camp. In each, a guard was visible against the low flare of light. Others, if there were others, were lying beyond the fire's range and were not to be seen. Far back on the ridge, a coyote suddenly threw his challenge, shrill and lonely, into the night, setting up a string of faint echoes that laughed through the cañons and hollows. The man on watch stirred uncomfortably, but he did not lift his head.

Ryan waited out a long five minutes. Then, touching the roan lightly, he moved gently left, following out the sandy bed on the narrow draw. He struck a course that would take him approximately halfway between the two camps, a strip that was somewhat darker and more shadowed than any other and where any noises made by the roan would be the least likely heard.

He was well out in the open country when the guard woke. Ryan, realizing instantly that motion, even in the solid blackness, could be detected, pulled to a quick halt. His nerves pinching a little, he watched the man as he got to his feet, stretched and yawned noisily. He spent a few moments rubbing his face and neck and ears, endeavoring apparently to drive the sharp chill from them. Afterward, he bent down and gathered up an armful of wood and tossed it onto the fire. At first there was only an answering billow of smoke, but he poked around for a time and finally a burst of flames broke into the night. Satisfied, he then drew a sack of tobacco from his shirt pocket and leisurely built himself a cigarette, taking great pains in doing so. This finished, he glanced around the camp, throwing his eyes into the encircling night, but the fire lay between Ryan and the guard, and he knew the man could not see him.

It was a long ten minutes. Holding entirely still in the saddle, keeping the roan from making any sound-lifting movements were nerve-wracking chores. And, despite the coolness, beads of sweat formed on Ryan's brow. He was ready, his plans laid, if the man discovered him. At the first sign, he would place two or three bullets not at the guard, but into the fire. This would create no little confusion and give him time to get the roan under way at top speed. It would be tough on the bad leg, but he would just have to weather that. And whether he could lose the posse and Baldwin's men, who would come storming in at the first shots, was problematical. But at least he would have a good chance.

The coyote *yipped* his wailing lament again into the night, and the guard listened, cocking his head to one side. But eventually he settled back down, having had his smoke and stretch. The fire once more was burning strong and its spread of warmth was lulling him into a state of drowsiness. Ryan breathed deeper. He waited until he was sure the guard would not rouse again, and then put the roan back into his slow walk. His leg was bothering him some now; perhaps it was the strain of the tension, or it could be the after-effects of having been dragged roughly against the cliff when they came down the trail, but he ignored it. He knew the bleeding had stopped, and that reassurance helped.

He maintained the slow pace for a full mile until the campfires were but tiny spots in the far night. The roan was anxious to be let out, to run in the sharp coolness, but Ryan kept him in check, taking no chances. When they reached a shallow bowl that dropped below the plane of the prairie, he pulled up and came slowly from the saddle. Taking his knife, he cut the strips of wool from the roan's hoofs. They would not be needed now and they would hamper the roan's speed if left on.

Once again in the saddle he swung due south, and just before dawn spread long fingers of light out from the east, he halted in the tangle of cedars that edged out from the hills bordering his ranch. The ride had been a cold one and had brought a steady throb in his leg. He sat, half cocked around in the saddle, resting the wounded leg in an awkward, stiff position.

From where he rested, he could see the back of the buildings that made up the Box K. In the gray half light, they seemed to be forlorn and deserted.

X

Ryan came off the roan stiffly, settling his weight slowly upon his good leg. Sears had been right; he should not be using it, should be giving it more time to heal. To have waited another day would have been better. But a great urgency was driving Jim Ryan. He wanted out of this country and its quarrel. He knew only too well the chain of action and reaction that would come now as a result of Hugh Baldwin's moves. He had tasted his share of that way of life before and he wanted no more of it. He wanted to get away from it before it pulled him any deeper into the blood-soaked mire.

Something was wrong. It was too quiet, too empty-looking around the place. No smoke was coming from the kitchen flue, and this was far from being right. The cook should be preparing breakfast for Sears and the crew long before this hour. And there were other things that did not appear just right—no horses were in the corral, except Sears's little pony, when there should have been several all saddled and bridled, ready for the day's work. No sounds were coming from the barn, no talk, no laughter, no creak of leather or heavy noises from livestock moving about.

Dark suspicion closed in upon Ryan. He glanced sharply at the bunkhouse, a short distance to his left, while a river of tension and worry began to flow through him. If any of the crew was around, most likely they would be in there. Sears had said two guards had been posted on the ranch but he could see no sign of them. However, they could be in the main house and their horses tied to the rail in front of that building. From where he stood he could not see that point.

Ryan looped the roan's reins through a short cedar. Doubling back for a short distance, he limped silently across the open yard at its narrowest, keeping a close watch on the closed doors and drawn shades of the main house. He reached the bunkhouse, noting the back window was open. Removing his wide hat, he stepped up close and laid a cautious glance into the room. It appeared empty. The usual piles of gear were missing from the corners, the coat and hat pegs stripped.

The odor of tobacco smoke struck his nostrils, and he swiveled his search to the bunks lining the near wall. Frank Sears was lying flat on his back in one of the lower beds. His fingers were laced across his belly, and he was watching smoke drift upward from the cigarette clamped between his lips, strike the slats overhead, and curl back in small, boiling clouds. Ryan checked the room once more. Sears was alone.

In a loud whisper he called: "Frank!"

Sears rolled swiftly to his feet and faced the window. He threw one startled look at Ryan and waved him toward the door. "Hurry it up! Them jaspers'll see you!"

Ryan moved as fast as possible to the front of the building. Sears held back the door and he brushed through, favoring the leg by bracing himself against the wall with his left hand. Sears closed the door and dropped the bar across it.

He said: "They spot your hide-out?"

Ryan settled himself on the edge of a bunk. He shook his head. "No point in staying there. What's wrong here? Where's the crew?"

Sears ignored the questions. "You know, you ain't showin' much sense runnin' around on that leg while it's still pretty raw. You ought to stay off it another day."

"It'll be all right. I said, where's the crew?"

Sears met his gaze straight on. "Gone. Ever' danged one of them. Run like skeered rabbits."

Ryan was not too surprised. No man could be blamed for refusing to set in a game where the odds were piled up like they were here. He said: "Baldwin come here?"

"Not that I know of, but them two rannies are still in the house waitin' for you to come back. I understand they did some pretty strong convincin' with the crew. They had all gone when I got back."

Ryan moved to the window and looked toward the main house. It was still closed and silent. He could see the two horses now, waiting hipshot at the rail.

In a wondering tone Sears asked: "You figure they really expect you to come back here? That you'd be that crazy a dang' fool?"

Ryan half smiled. "I'm here. Looks like maybe they're right." He shrugged. "Hugh covers all the possibilities." He came back to the bunk and sat down. "How come you didn't pull out?"

"Me? I don't scare so easy. Figure I got just as much sand as they got. I've spit in the eye of better men than them two sleepin' over there on your bed. They took my gun and told me to stay put here in the bunkhouse. They're tryin' to make a cook out of me," the old cowpuncher added with a show of distaste.

He walked then to the window, as Ryan had done, and for a time let his glance rest upon the yard. Turning about after a moment, he said: "They's a lot of places you could have gone to hide out. Why the hell did you come here? I told you they was watchin'."

Ryan shook his head. "They're watching everywhere, Frank." He lifted his gaze to the old cowpuncher. "Doesn't make any difference, anyway. I'm getting out. I want none of this fight."

Sears stared at him. A long, falling—*"Ahhh."*—slipped from his lips.

"I'm in this thing deeper now than I thought I would ever again let myself get. I know this kind of trouble and I'm sick of it. I came here to get away from it, not get right back in the middle of more of it. I'll not be dragged into it any deeper. They can have it 'cause I'm pulling out now!"

"Knowin' you, I can believe your reasons," Sears observed slowly, "but I don't figure that's goin' to satisfy the others and what they'll be thinkin'."

"A long time ago," Ryan answered, "I quit worrying about what other people think. Man has to live with himself and that's who he's got to stay right with."

Sears nodded his understanding. "But what you goin' to do about this place? You got every dime you had sunk into it. You just ain't goin' to walk off and leave it, are you?"

Ryan shook his head. "No, that's one of the reasons I came here. I want to ask a favor of you. Killibrew at the bank told me he'd buy any time I wanted to sell. I'd like for you to see him and tell him that the time has come. Tell him I'll take that standing offer of his and just to handle the sale and hold the money for me. I'll get in touch with him later."

"You can figure on Killibrew doin' you right," Sears murmured absently. "Howsomever, there's goin' to be a right smart lot of people around here sorry to hear about this."

"How do you figure that?"

"Good many thought somebody'd finally moved into this country with enough backbone to stand up against Hugh Baldwin and his Circle X bunch. Reckon they're goin' to be plumb disappointed now."

"They are the ones that let Baldwin and Circle X get big," Ryan said, a little stiffness riding his voice. "He wasn't always the big shucks he is now. When he started showing the signs, that's when they should have pulled him down to size."

"You're sure right," Sears agreed readily, "but fact is gunpowder needs a spark to set it off. That's what they been needin' all this time, somebody to be the spark."

Ryan let his gaze run through the open window to the slowly lightening day outside. "I'm not that man," he said wearily. "I've had my time at that. Let them get somebody else. There's plenty of men around."

"What about Meldrum? He's still got you pegged for killin' Tom Strickland and Dan Pike. When you turn up missin', he's goin' to spread the word in all directions."

"He'll find out who did it," Ryan said. "Reno Davis got Tom and Pike was killed in a fair and even draw. The hostler will testify to that."

Sears snorted. "Supposin' Meldrum ain't got the

sense to figure all that out. Or the hostler won't speak up. Then what?"

Ryan shrugged. "I'll be a long way from here, Frank."

Sears wagged his head. "Well, I can see you're set on driftin' along. Maybe you're right. I don't know. Smart men don't mix in other people's fights. I was sort of figurin' it the other way, though, like this is your fight and not somebody else's. But you ought to be knowin' best about that. Now, what about that stuff of yours there in the house? You want to go in now and get it? I suspect you and me could handle them two waddies in there without much work."

Ryan grinned. "I suspect we could," he said, the old rider's belligerent confidence bristling all over him. "But there's nothing in there I need. Anything Killibrew doesn't want in the sale is yours."

"Nothin' in there I'd want," Sears said, "unless, maybe, I could have them shirts."

"Shirts?"

"Them fancy duds you got over at San Antone that time and then didn't like."

Ryan said: "I told you a long time ago they were yours, if you wanted them. I thought you had them by now."

"Just never got around to it, I reckon," Sears murmured. "I'm obliged to you. When you plannin' to leave?"

"Now. One thing I've got to do first, though. I

owe it to Tom Strickland to see Ann and warn her about Baldwin. And I'd like to talk to her and convince her I had nothing to do with Tom's shooting."

"You got yourself a right big chore," Sears said, pulling at his mustache. "How you goin' to get there without bein' spotted? 'Specially in broad daylight. These hills and flats are crawlin' with men."

"Figured to drop down to the river and ride up through the brakes. Don't think they're looking for me down there yet."

"Been one or two along there," Sears said. "But most of them are still back along the bluffs. You might get through, if you keep your eyes peeled and your ears open." He walked to the window and glanced to the main house. "First, we got to get you away from here without bein' seen."

Ryan came to his feet. "Somebody out there?"

Sears said: "No, but they're inside, and up and movin' around by now. Here's what you do. I'll go in and stir them up a mess of breakfast. When they set down to eat it, I'll give you a high sign and you get out of here quick. Savvy?"

Ryan nodded. "I'll swing down through the lower meadow. They can't see that from the house."

Sears moved for the door. Reaching there, he paused and half turned. "You sure you want it this way? You're throwin' away somethin' mighty nice and you stick around, I figure there'll be a lot of good men line up with you to see this thing through. And you can count on me, all the way."

Ryan said: "Frank, there's no place worth what this is all going to finally cost." He smiled and extended his hand to the old cowpuncher. "Thanks for saying that, anyway. I'll wait for your sign."

Sears grasped Ryan's hand. "All right, son," he said. "Good luck."

XI

In the willows and dogwood along the river, it was shaded and cool. Ryan, needing rest from the saddle even after so brief a ride, pulled the roan to a halt and came gently off the roan's wide back. He rested himself against a young cottonwood and let the big horse have his drink of the cold and clear water. Afterward, he led him into a stand of tall brush and there, perfectly screened, he turned him to graze and stretched out full length on the damp grass.

He had laid there but a short time when his ears caught the muted *tunk-tunk* of a walking horse. He realized immediately that he was being followed. The roan paused in his cropping and lifted his head toward the back trail expectantly, but after a brief time he resumed his eating. Ryan cautiously pulled himself to a sitting position. The sound of the approaching horse grew louder. Ryan, gun now in hand, calmly waited out the long moments.

It was Turk Paulson, one of Baldwin's riders. He was a huge beast of a man—powerful, dull-witted, and with a single-purpose mind that resolved itself into one straight and narrow groove—to hate anything not Hugh Baldwin's.

Ryan saw him come in close to a thick stand of willows, saw him throw his hard, suspicious glance in a wide, reaching circle. The man knew Ryan was somewhere near, but not seeing him checked him, brought him to a halt. He had little reasoning power, this Turk Paulson, and now, faced with something he could not see or touch, he was at a standstill.

Knowing this, Ryan kept entirely still, obeying that first law of nature that not to move is not to be seen. He watched Turk's shaggy head pivot slowly on its bull-like neck, searching through the shadows and other likely places where a man might hide. When his eyes came to the willows where Ryan and the horse were, they halted. Ryan prayed the roan would not choose that moment to move.

But the big blue roan moved. He lifted his head, ears cocked forward, and stared expectantly at Paulson's horse. Paulson emitted a triumphant snort. There was a *creak* of leather as the man shifted hurriedly in the saddle. There came a *crash* of brush and Ryan knew the Circle X rider was rushing him.

He came to his feet, pain wrenching through the wounded leg as it took more than its share of the sudden motion. Disregarding it, he stepped into the saddle and spun the roan about to face Paulson's charge. His gun was in his hand but he was reluctant to use it unless it became an absolute necessity. Paulson would not be alone. There would be others working along the river and a gunshot would bring them piling down upon him.

He sent the roan out of the willow stand in a broad leap, almost colliding head on with Paulson. The big man yelled—"Hey! What the hell you doin'?"—in a startled, surprised voice and jerked his horse savagely away.

The roan hit the ground and stumbled in a tangle of half-exposed roots. Paulson, fighting his horse, swung back and drove in close. He crowded up alongside the roan, reaching for Ryan with a huge hand of outstretched fingers. Ryan ducked and struck out with the barrel of his gun.

Paulson slid from the saddle, hitting the ground on one heel and going on over backward. A sort of amazed look lay across his dark face. But in a matter of seconds he was back up, shaking his head like some wild, furious animal and coming in again. At all costs, Ryan knew he must keep clear of those reaching hands.

The roan was with him in that thought. The threat of those outstretched arms and crooking claws was a mutual fear, and, as Paulson came crashing in, the roan backed nervously away in a tight, narrow circle.

"Whoa! Whoa!" Paulson roared.

The roan wheeled away. Ryan held the gun poised, looking for another opportunity for using it. It came almost at once. The roan, pivoting blindly, came up against a stand of brier. He recoiled from the sharp thorns and Paulson, caught suddenly and helpless to check his own forward motion, plowed into the roan's front quarters. Ryan brought the heavy six-gun down hard. It landed squarely on the top of the man's head. Paulson hesitated, his eyes clouding. A pained expression crossed his face and he began to weave a little uncertainly. Ryan brought the pistol down once more and Paulson's knees buckled. He fell away, going down like a sack of grain ripped open.

Ryan did not wait to see if the man would rise. He straightened out the yawning roan and put him forward at a fast walk, striking north. Strickland's place would be the last place they would look for him now, and they wouldn't expect him to be going in that direction. Once on S-Bar land he could feel reasonably safe.

But getting there was something else. More men must be along the river. He would have to look sharp. But he covered three miles before he saw another man. Ryan did not recognize him but he gave him a wide berth, taking no chances. He wanted no more engagements such as he had just experienced with Turk Paulson. The exertion had reopened his leg wound and he could feel it bleeding heavily again. Frank Sears's bandage was doing a good job of holding it in check, but you couldn't expect it to stop entirely under such circumstances as the last few minutes had provided.

He cursed softly. It was sheer bad luck that had put him in line with Reno Davis's snap shot. An inch more and it would have been a clean miss. On the other hand, an inch the other way and it would have been far more serious. He would not be out on the roan as he presently was. He would either be holed up, unable to get around at all, or he would be in Ross Meldrum's hands, roosting in the jail, or, finally, he would be dead.

When he came to the bridge that lay near the Strickland place, he stopped. The buildings, lying a short quarter mile away, looked remote and deserted. The shades were drawn and the doors were closed. There were no horses that he could see in the corrals and there was none standing at the rail. In front of the main house he recognized Ann's pony and buckboard.

He did not move directly across the open ground, but rode on northward for another mile, waiting for a time he would be sure he was not being followed. Then he loped the short distance to the tamarack windbreak that had sheltered Tom Strickland's killer. Again cautious, he pulled up and waited. No one was coming from any direction, it appeared, and he drifted deeper into the tamarack, working closer to the house.

He left the roan standing within the windbreak at a point close to the house and moved quickly to the front door. Trying the knob, he found it turned, pushed open the door, and stepped inside. The room was cool, dark, and empty. He crossed it, heading for another door, which led into the kitchen. It was slightly ajar. He moved silently through it, coming to a stop just inside, leaning against the frame to rest his leg. Ann was sitting quietly at the oilcloth-covered table. She was turned partly away from him, her hands folded in her lap, her eyes lost on something beyond the open window. She was thinking of her father, he knew.

Some slight noise he made caused her to turn instantly. She came up from her chair and wheeled to face him, the surprise in her eyes turning to swift anger.

"You . . . you . . . !"

"Don't be afraid," Ryan said, a slight twist of sarcasm in his voice. "I'm not here to hurt you."

He felt the close, searching scrutiny of her gaze. He saw her pause at the blood-spotted area on his breeches and at the bandage showing through the hole Sears had cut. "You've been hurt!"

Ryan smiled. "Nothing serious."

"They said you were hiding in the hills. What are you doing down here? What do you want?"

She was cool now, in perfect control of herself

and her emotions. She seemed drawn, a bit pale, the last few days having taken much out of her. Ryan said: "Two things. I want you to understand and believe that I had nothing to do with the death of your father. I'm truly sorry about it, Ann."

She met his gaze steadily, her face a pale, serious oval beneath the wealth of dark hair. "You said two reasons."

"You can't stay here alone, now."

The expression on her face did not alter. "You expect me to believe anything you tell me? I saw you there, on your horse, your gun still in your hand. Reno Davis saw you shoot. Why should I doubt what I saw myself?"

"Because that's not the way it happened. It was just the way I told it to Meldrum." He paused. Then: "Ann, look at me. You know I couldn't do a thing like that. I couldn't pull a gun on your father, much less shoot him down."

She faltered momentarily. "I . . . I didn't think you . . . ," she said, breaking a little, but immediately she regained her composure. "The marshal says the proof is all there, that there's no question about it."

"The marshal is an easy man to convince, particularly if Baldwin's got anything to do with it." Ryan shifted his weight, leaning more heavily against the door frame.

"What else was it you wanted?" she asked then. "It was something about me not being safe here."

Ryan nodded. "Hugh Baldwin's on the move now to take over this range for himself. He won't stop at anything. You can't stay here, Ann. Not until it's all over. It will be too dangerous."

"What makes you think Hugh is going to do this? Did he tell you?"

Ryan said: "Of course not. But I know his kind . . . I've been up against them before. I know how the Hugh Baldwins do things in this world once they get the fever. Believe me, Ann, you can't stay here and try to stand against him."

"Believe you?" she echoed, her voice lifting. "Why should I believe anything from you? A gunman, a killer that shot down one man and tried to kill another. A man that maybe killed my own father!"

Ryan came up straight, his face going still and cold. He said: "Ann, do you believe all those things you are saying?"

She half turned from him, tears all at once flooding her eyes. "What else can I believe? There's so much proof! You say Hugh wants to take over this ranch . . . this whole country, and that it was his man that killed my father. He says the same of you. That you plan to control the Cuchillo Plains by the power of your gun. Your first move was to get my father out of the way so you could take over the S-Bar. And now you will try to do the same with the Circle X, only your attempt to kill Hugh failed."

Jim Ryan waited patiently, hearing it out to the last word. It was the old pattern, the old divide-and-conquer theme, ageless as time itself. When he made his reply, his voice was low. "If that is what you believe, there's little use of me saying more. Only for your own sake, be careful of Hugh. Don't trust him or any of those around him."

"Who then can I trust? Everything is so mixed up, so confused. I don't know who to trust any more."

"Only one man I'm sure of," Ryan said, "and that's Frank Sears. I'll send him to you tonight. Listen to him and do what he says."

In silence she nodded to him. Ryan touched her face with one last look and turned to leave. She halted him with: "Where are you going now?"

A measure of the deep bitterness in the man rose to the surface. "On, just on. Would you like for me to tell you exactly so you could send Baldwin or Ross Meldrum after me?"

The stricken look that crossed her face shamed him in that same moment. He said, more kindly: "Forget that. I'll send Frank over after dark. If there's one man in this country that is on the level and that you can trust, it is him."

He moved again to depart, steadying himself as he pivoted, against the door.

"Will you be back?" she asked in a small voice.

He gave her a short, tight smile over his shoulder. "Not likely. Good bye, Ann."

XII

It was near the end of the afternoon when Ryan, having followed a devious route back along the river, rounded a sharp bend in the green band of willows and other growth and came into view of the Box K. He stopped within the last extreme outthrusting of brush and let his gaze rove over the premises with deliberate thoroughness. It was still deserted; more so now for only Frank Sears's pony was to be seen. The horses of the two guards left by the posse were gone.

They had tired of their fruitless waiting and had moved on, probably joining up with the others still somewhere along the bluffs. But Ryan, ever cautious, waited a time until he was convinced before he crossed the open ground and came in to the buildings from their blind side. He reached the main house, drifting quietly in from the yard's southern tip, and paused there at the corner, listening for voices, for any sounds. But the ranch seemed still as death. He wheeled the roan around and crossed by the front door, which was standing open, and pointed for the bunkhouse. Sears would most likely be there.

He came to a sudden stop. There, halfway out, lay the body of Frank Sears. A wide, ugly stain covered his back, starting just below the shoulders and spreading down to his hips. Ryan spun quickly toward the house and leaped from the roan. Gun in hand, he ducked into the kitchen doorway. From that shelter, he checked the rest of the ranch, the edging brush, the low hills to the west. But he could find nothing that appeared to be a hidden man. The thought came to him then that the killer, or killers, might possibly still be in the house.

He moved silently into the kitchen. A scatter of dirty dishes was on the table. The coffee pot was on the range and Ryan moved to that, laying his hand on the stove lids. They were cold. There had been no fire in the range for hours.

He turned to the other rooms, treading softly down the hallway; anger was a suppressed flame beginning to burn hotly within him. The rooms were all empty and in each he found nothing but destruction: furniture smashed, walls kicked in, glass broken. The bedding had been ripped to shreds, the mattresses slashed, and the stuffings strewn about. In the parlor, where he kept his desk and which he used as a sort of office, the desk was broken open and all his papers and records had been piled in the center of the room. A match had been set to them. The floor was burned almost through and the smell of that still hung about the walls.

Satisfied, finally, that no one was hidden in the house, he made a check of the bunkhouse, the barn, and all the lesser sheds and structures, finding nothing. His face a grim mask, he returned to where Sears's body lay in the yard. A rumble of thunder sounded somewhere, off to the east.

The old cowpuncher lay face down, arms pinned beneath him. There were two bullet wounds in his back. Death had struck solidly as he apparently had been walking across the yard, going from the main building to the bunkhouse. Ryan, the roar of anger rising steadily within him, turned the body over gently.

Folded over one arm were the three fancy woolen shirts Ryan had given him. He remembered how Sears had always admired them. He had planned several times to put them in the hands of the man, but somehow he always forgot. He was glad he had made it plain, earlier in the day, that they were actually his and that he was to get them. Three fancy shirts—that was all the old rider had asked for his loyalty to the Box K before it passed on to someone else.

Ignoring his agonizing leg, Ryan slipped his arms under Sears's frail body and carried it into the bunkhouse. He laid it on the bed, straightened out the stiffening legs, and folded the arms over the chest. The shirts he placed nearby, and over it all he drew a blanket.

In the hot closeness he stood there, thinking deeply. His gaze reached out through the window to the sun-swept prairie, to the Santa Claras lifting their rugged bulks beyond. Men were still searching for him out there, men ready to shoot and kill him the moment they saw him. That was the chance any man took when things shaped up in that order. A man stood against his own enemies and took his chances with them, just as they did with him. But brutally to murder Frank Sears! A harmless old man! To shoot him in the back as he walked, unarmed, across an open yard was another matter. They had nothing against him, nothing other than he was a friend of Ryan's. And that was little cause.

Anger was a brittle, moving force through Ryan, not a wild, furious blaze, but a deadly sort of cold determination. It pulled down the corners of his lips and made livid the area around his mouth. His eyes narrowed to a straight, dark line. Turning to look again at Sears, the thought moved through him: *There's no leaving this thing now. There's no way out of it. A man can't turn his back on a mad dog or walk around a poisonous snake and sleep easy. Whether I want it or not, I'm in this thing because, in some way or another, it affects me. No matter where a man turns, I guess, there's a Hugh Baldwin knocking down a Frank Sears.*

He left the bunkhouse, the growling thunder to the east rolling across the hot, afternoon sky again. He went to the kitchen and rustled himself a fair amount of food from the shelves in the storeroom, selecting the kind that would not require any amount of cooking. He tossed this into a flour sack and to it added coffee and a small lard bucket to brew it in. He moved swiftly but methodically, wasting no motions, knowing it was dangerous to remain there for long. At any time Baldwin or some of his men or Ross Meldrum and members of the posse might return and he was not ready just yet to meet them.

Completing his stores, he started for the yard, and then remembered the canteen. He filled this from a bucket of water, brought in by Sears probably earlier in the day, and once again started to leave. Outside, he glanced to his gun belt. It was less than half filled. He placed the sack of grub and the canteen on the ground and reëntered the house, this time going to the front room, hoping Baldwin's men had passed up the closet.

They had not entirely, as the clothing tossed to the floor proved. But the shelf was still up and they had not found the two boxes of cartridges stashed in one corner. He thrust the boxes into his pocket and went back into the sunlight.

The roan had drifted to the water trough. Ryan crossed that distance with his load, limping heavily. He wished there was something he could do to ease the wound, but there seemed to be nothing more except to stay off of it. And that, of course, was out of the question now.

He crammed the sack of grub into one saddlebag, the canteen in the other, making sure no sounds of metal would arise when the roan moved. He filled his empty cartridge belt to capacity from one box of shells, folding those left over into a handkerchief and tucking them into a shirt pocket. The remaining box he also put in the saddlebag.

Ready at last, he swung to the saddle, settling his injured leg slowly into the stirrup. He glanced to the west—at least two hours remained before sundown. Time enough to get back within the shelter along the river before it became fully dark. There he would eat a little and after that he would travel, heading north for Circle X and Hugh Baldwin.

XIII

Ryan delayed until night had fully settled before starting upriver. Deep in the tangle of willows and brier, he ate from the food he had brought, denying himself, however, the strength and comfort of coffee. A fire's glare or its plume of smoke, no matter how small, might be seen and lead searchers to his camp. Physically he was feeling fairly strong again. The man's immense vitality, that hard, stringy core of strength that came from a life of rugged, outdoor living under all conditions, was making its own repairs and recoveries. He required little help from outside measures for healing.

When he swung up on the roan, he had almost forgotten the wound in his leg, but the sharp pain that shot through him when he came too solidly against the leather was a pointed reminder that it was still tender and weak. Nevertheless, it was greatly improved over the previous night. There was still some stiffness and the soreness was to be expected. By another sunset, he realized, the leg would be in good condition if he could keep it from becoming overtaxed and the wound broken open again.

Ryan, however, was wasting little thought upon it. In his mind there now existed a single, solitary purpose—get Hugh Baldwin, bring him in to face up for his actions. He was the match that started the flames of range fire; he was the power behind the killing of Tom Strickland and now of Frank Sears. And there would be many more if he was left to go on. Pull down Baldwin now! That was the only answer. To break up his empire before it became an entrenched, towering reality blighting the Cuchillo Plains—that was the need of the hour.

It was because Hugh Baldwin was already so strong, so powerful a figure, that made the doing difficult. The threat of him and his ruthless Circle X riders had laid a firm grasp upon the minds of most all who lived in the shadows of the Santa Claras. Tom Strickland had bucked against that yoke and now he was dead. This they all already knew, and that knowledge would make them careful, turn them fearful.

Ryan concluded then that it likely would have been he who next would have been likely to fall. The way things happened served only to simplify and bring him into the picture sooner. Had he not been at Strickland's that day and thus walked conveniently into Baldwin's plans and a charge of murder, Baldwin would have gotten around to him later. In a way it was all to the good. Now he was forewarned, and the advantage of surprise was lost to Hugh Baldwin. Actually it now lay with Ryan. And Jim Ryan, wise to the ways of men like Baldwin, knew well how to use such a weapon.

He met no riders on his steady journey up the river. When he came to the Strickland bridge, he paused as he had done earlier in the day, an impulse to see Ann pulling at him. For a time he studied the squares of yellow light scattered among the buildings, and then, reaching a decision, he put the roan to a soft trot toward the windbreak. Reaching the cover of the tamarack, he advanced more slowly until he was close to the main house.

The shade was drawn upon the window closest to him. Ignoring the possible danger, he drifted across the front of the house and down the side to where the kitchen lay. That window was still open and he pulled up outside it, just beyond its gush of light. Ann was there at the table, reading a thick, black-bound book.

Lamplight lay across her serene face. Her lips were set in soft, curving lines, and, when she moved slightly, the blackness of her hair reflected the light and glinted brightly. Every man has his own conception of personal paradise in which all ideals have come to pass and all desires are fulfilled. Ryan knew then, in that moment, Ann Strickland constituted a major factor in his idea of paradise. And he had the realization in that same moment that such was not now likely to be his or ever to be.

He was a man alone, one of the friendless. The last of those few he might call friend lay dead in his own bunkhouse. He was completely and utterly alone, with all the country turned against him, or else fearing to help. And he was undertaking a mission from which he might never return. But even if it came to that, there might be some satisfaction in the knowledge that he had eliminated Hugh Baldwin from the land.

A door slammed, somewhere off to the left. He let his glance rest upon Ann for another run of seconds, and then wheeled the blue toward the tamarack.

A voice broke the stillness: "Who's that? Who's out there?"

Ryan touched the roan with spurs and the blue leaped away.

"What's goin' on out there?" George Cobb's voice took up the challenge.

Ryan reached the windbreak and dropped quickly into its tangled depths. The roan had to move more slowly now but so would any pursuers,

if there were to be any. He came out on the opposite side and waited there, listening into the night.
He heard the distant drumbeats of thunder, farther
away than it had been earlier and heard, also, the
slam of a door. And that was all. Whoever had seen
him had not been sure, and the other men in the S-
Bar bunkhouse likely were having their joke with
him at that moment.

Circle X lay deeply in the bottom of a grassy bowl.
A few trees ringed the place, and along the back,
where a spring bubbled from the rocks, there was
a stand of bayberry and thick-growing willows.
Ryan directed the roan into that. He had been to
Circle X only once before, attending a meeting of
cattle growers when there was a shipping problem
to be ironed out. He sat there now in the full darkness, trying to remember all he knew about the
spread.

It was laid out much like his own Box K, which
was a fairly common plan of arrangement in that
part of the west. The main house, a long, rambling
structure, was on the right, facing east. The
bunkhouse stood across a hard-packed yard and
behind it lay a scatter of smaller buildings, corrals,
pens, and sheds. Finishing it all off was the barn.
Baldwin would be in the main house at this hour.
Supper would be over, and the crew either in their
bunks or gathered there, shooting the breeze about
the events of the day. The question was, would

Baldwin be alone or would some of the men be with him?

Ryan drifted the roan out of the willows and reached the extreme rear of the main house. Pausing there to listen, he heard nothing and pressed on once more until he had reached the front. Here he dismounted and left the roan standing just out of sight in deep shadows, reins looped over a stunted juniper.

He took three steps forward and then froze against the wall of the house, hearing the sudden, rapid approach of riders. They rushed into the yard, four of them cutting away toward the bunkhouse, while two pulled up at the rail in front, not fifteen feet from where Ryan stood. They stepped down, and, in the splash of light coming from the open door, he recognized Reno Davis and the huge bulk of Turk Paulson. A blunt, red welt lay across Paulson's face, running from temple to cheek bone, showing where Ryan's gun had laid its mark.

"Hugh!" Davis sang out his greeting and came up on the narrow porch. He did not pull open the door and enter, but waited for Baldwin's invitation. Turk Paulson thumped up behind him, rubbing at his neck in a reflective sort of fashion.

"Hey, Hugh!"

"All right, all right," Baldwin's voice came from the center of the house. "Come in and set. I'll be with you in a minute."

Davis and Paulson entered, the big man letting the screen door bang loudly behind him. Ryan heard Davis swear softly at that and then caught Paulson's rumbling reply. He moved around to where he could hear better. The window shade was pulled down tight and he could see nothing. But he was content with his position; to move farther out where he might see better would be too risky.

Baldwin came into the room. Ryan heard the chair creak under his weight and his deep-throated voice say: "Well? You get him?"

"Not yet," Reno Davis answered. "Turk, here, saw him."

"Saw him?" Baldwin echoed. "How come you didn't nail him?"

"Never had no chance," Paulson grumbled. "He tried to run me down with that big horse of his and then beat my head in with a gun barrel."

"And what the hell were you doing all that time? Where was your horse? What were you doing off him?"

The dull wits of Turk Paulson could not match the speed of the questions. "I reckon I fell off, Mister Baldwin," he stammered out slowly. "I was tryin'. . . ."

"Fell off!" Hugh Baldwin's words exploded from his lips. "The only man to see Ryan in two days and *he* falls off his damn' horse! What kind of men you got working for me, Reno?"

"Somebody else will find him," Davis said

soothingly. "He's bound to show up soon. He can't hole up much longer with a bullet in his hide."

"Who's watching his place?"

"Pete Santee and Al Thompson. They drilled old Sears."

"Sears? Why?"

"Don't know for sure. Turk and me found him layin' out there in the yard. Pete and Al was arguin' about takin' out."

"Running out, eh. What's got into them?"

"Reckon old Sears was the first man they'd ever cut down. Reckon their feet was gettin' a little cold."

"You change their minds?"

Davis laughed. "We sure did! They changed their minds all right, after me and Turk got done talkin' to them."

"What about Sears?"

"Left him layin' there."

"Good, good thinking, Reno," Baldwin said. "That'll put the fear in some of these weak-kneed ones and maybe change the minds of any others who may have ideas. How many of the boys still on the job?"

"Five, and the marshal's still got some of his posse workin'. They're beginnin' to peter out, though. We better catch this Ryan by tomorrow night or I figure we'll be doin' this all alone."

"We'll have him by then," Baldwin stated, assuming some of Davis's earlier confidence.

"One more night with a bullet hole in his guts will make a lot of difference. I figure he'll show up tomorrow crying for help."

"Maybe you're right," Davis said, now seemingly unsure of Ryan's inevitable capture. "But the workin' over he give Turk here don't look to me like a man about ready to cash in."

"Strength of a desperate man," Baldwin said. "Probably put everything he had left into it. Now, first thing in the morning you take Turk and a couple of the boys and go back to where Turk saw him . . . to where Turk fell off his horse," he added with heavy sarcasm. Ryan heard the big man grumble and shift about on his feet. Baldwin continued: "Work the brush over close. My guess is you'll find him crawled in under a bush, dead."

"Could be," Reno Davis murmured.

Ryan heard the scrape of chairs upon the floor as the men got up. The ponderous bulk of Turk Paulson blocked the door briefly, and then moved out onto the porch. Davis followed.

"I'll ride down first thing I can and see what you've found!" Baldwin called after them. "Now, get down there early."

"Sure, early, Hugh," Davis replied, and crossed the porch. Paulson let the door bang shut again, and Davis expressed his feelings once more in a single, withering word. Together they thumped across the hard pack. Ryan waited until they had entered the bunkhouse and then, drawing his gun, he covered the porch's width in a half dozen long, stealthy strides.

Baldwin sat, deep in a cushioned chair, relaxed, studying the backs of his broad hands. Ryan stepped inside the room like a swift shadow. Baldwin looked up, surprise breaking through his eyes and blanking his expression.

Ryan said: "Get up, Hugh, we're riding to town."

XIV

For a short, breathless space of time Hugh Baldwin made no sound. Somewhere in the depths of the house, a clock ticked loudly. Outside, at the hitching rail, one of the horses blew and stamped wearily. Gradually the look of incredulity faded from Baldwin's face and his gaze firmed up and locked with that of Jim Ryan.

"That's a mighty big order," he said.

"Not with you helping," Ryan answered coolly.

Baldwin smiled, the old cocksure confidence once again threading through his voice. "Just how far do you think you'll get, walking across that yard with a gun in my back?"

"Guess again," Ryan said softly. "We're not crossing any yard. You're going to get up and go quietly out the door and mount one of those horses standing there at the rail."

"And then?"

"My horse is around at the side. We'll get him and go into town."

"What for? I don't understand what you want me in town for."

Ryan said harshly: "The hell you don't, Hugh! Cut out the stalling. It's late. And you know as well as I do that nobody's going to be coming over here before daylight."

Baldwin shook his head. "Still don't know what you want me in town for."

"Several things. Mainly I'm going to fit you into place so everybody can see who and what you really are in this country. Then you're going to explain why you had Tom Strickland and Frank Sears killed."

Baldwin said—"Frank Sears?"—in a wondering way.

Ryan shrugged impatiently. "Don't give me that, Hugh. Reno and Turk just told you all about it. I heard everything they had to say." Ryan paused, the glitter in his eyes hardened, and the lines around his mouth became deep, rigid cuts. "Sears was a friend of mine," he said. "One of the few honest men I've ever known. If I didn't have any other reason in the world to want to see you swing, I'd drop everything for that one."

Baldwin sighed. His eyes gave Ryan a close, hard scrutiny. "I didn't know about Sears until it was over," he said. Then: "Ryan, I wish you'd think about this thing. I'd give a pretty penny to have a man like you working for me. I need a man of your cut . . . somebody that's got some sense and can think for himself."

"For what you're trying to do, you need a lot of men, a lot of things," Ryan said dryly.

"What makes you so sure Sears is dead? Reno didn't say that. He said he'd been shot."

"I was there," Ryan answered. "I found him in the yard, two bullets in the back. I carried him into the bunkhouse. He's dead, Hugh."

"And you did all this and my boys didn't see you?"

"Your boys had run. Left you flat."

A change of expression moved fleetingly across the cattleman's face, first of surprise, and then of slight worry. It was as if he were seeing the first crack in a wall he had thought impregnable. "Gone?"

"Gone," Ryan echoed. "They'd had all they wanted of this deal. Maybe they saw what was sure to come and they didn't want to be on hand when it got here."

"Coming? Nothing's coming," Baldwin declared flatly. "They were just yellow. Things got a little rough and they didn't have the guts for it. Good men are hard to come by nowadays."

Ryan shook his head. "Maybe, the kind you want. But good men are plentiful. And they'll have a few things to say when they stand you up before them. Get up, Hugh, we're going out of here now."

Baldwin rose to his feet. Small beads of sweat on his brow betrayed the calmness on his face and his hands trembled slightly. He nodded to the gun held ready by Ryan.

"You're not horsing me any, Ryan. If I make a break, you wouldn't dare pull that trigger. One shot and you'd have a dozen men down on your head."

"Something you wouldn't live to see, Hugh," Ryan said with a tight smile. "You'd be a dead man long before that first half minute was up. Let's go." Ryan stepped aside and motioned to Baldwin. The cattleman moved toward the door. "Walk slow. Go out to the rail and take one of those horses. Don't make any unnecessary noise doing it. I'll be three feet behind you, my gun pointed at your backbone. Make a quick move in the wrong direction or try and sing out and you'll never know what hit you."

Baldwin was sweating freely and some of his confidence had fled. "You'll never get away with this," he said, but it was more to assure himself than deter Ryan.

"We'll see," Ryan murmured softly. "Move."

Baldwin crossed before Ryan, dragging his steps. He pushed back the screen door and walked onto the porch. He was in his stocking feet and he made no sound other than his deep, labored breathing. Ryan caught the door and closed it gently.

"Hold it, Hugh," he said in a quick, low voice.

For a minute he stood there, a rigid, square black

shape, listening into the darkness. The yard was stone quiet, almost too quiet, it seemed to him. He said: "Take the reins of that first horse. Don't mount up. Lead him around to the side of the house. I can watch you better while you're walking."

"Not my horse," Baldwin said in a mild, protesting way as he moved to comply.

In the quiet Ryan smiled grimly at the workings of the man's mind. "Makes no difference now," he said. "Whoever owns him will get him back."

"Reno's horse," Baldwin grumbled. He pulled the leathers free of the rail and turned to Ryan. "Now what?"

"You know what I said . . . lead him around to the side. And do it slow. I'm right behind you."

Ryan pulled back to let Baldwin pass by. The night was crackling with tension and the stillness was solid enough to feel. Ryan kept his gun close to the cattleman; he was not sure of him, not certain if he would follow orders or would make a break for it. He did not want the man dead and he was hoping Baldwin would come along without trouble. But he was prepared to shoot, if necessary.

Baldwin moved slowly by leading the pony. He cast a sidelong glance at Ryan, and in the faint light Ryan could see the heavy shine upon his forehead and cheeks and across his upper lip. "Walk slow, Hugh," he warned in a dead, level voice.

Whatever qualities Hugh Baldwin lacked, one of

them was not courage. In the complete stillness of the night, he made his desperate move. Ryan saw him lunge at the horse, a shadowy outline in the gloom. He saw the horse's head go down as Baldwin wrenched at the reins. The animal, startled, pivoted wildly, its hindquarters swinging at Ryan. Ryan stepped back hurriedly, forgetting his weak leg. He half fell.

"Reno!" Baldwin yelled.

The summons rocked through the yard and echoed against the buildings. The back door flung open and Davis and three or four other men pounded into the open.

"Hugh? That you yellin'? What's up?" Davis's voice lifted into the night.

Ryan, back on his feet like a cat, moved in against Baldwin. He jammed the barrel of his gun into the man's ribs. "Answer him, quick. Tell him everything's all right. Quick, damn you."

Davis came trotting across the yard. He stopped in front of the house, uncertain. Ryan saw him throw a glance at the rail and note the missing horse. But he seemed a little in doubt. "What's wrong, Hugh?"

"Nothing, nothing," Baldwin replied in a rasping voice. "Everything's all right, Reno."

"Who's that out there with you?"

Ryan dug the gun barrel deeper. Baldwin winced. "A friend, Reno. That's all. Just a friend."

"Little late for a social call," Davis murmured

into the night. The others had turned and were drifting to the bunkhouse. Davis hung on. "Anything you want, Hugh?"

Ryan did not miss the hard note of suspicion coloring the cowpuncher's tone. He was not convinced, not fooled one minute. But Baldwin's answers had him pinned down. He was at a loss as to what he should do.

Baldwin said: "Never mind, Reno. Go on back to bed."

Davis turned slowly about to follow the others. Ryan watched him closely as he crossed the dimly lit hard pack and entered the bunkhouse. He saw the door close, and almost in the same instant the light went out. Something wasn't right. He could feel it even though he could not put his finger exactly on it. To Baldwin he said: "Now, Hugh, we'll move on. That was your last false move. This is a one-time deal and the next time you try anything, I won't bother to wait."

Baldwin made no reply. He gathered up the reins of the horse and moved around the corner of the house. Ryan watched him narrowly, the flags of danger still waving in his mind. He again had that strong feeling that something was not exactly right but he was still unable to pin it down. For one thing, he had no way of knowing how many men had come from the bunkhouse in response to Baldwin's summons, and he did not know if they had all returned. It was possible they could have split and some circled the house and were now waiting ahead in the deep blackness where the roan stood.

Ryan shrugged. Little matter now. He was this far and there could be no turning back these last few minutes. If they did jump him, Baldwin was due to get his first bullet. He would do the Cuchillo Plains that favor before they cut him down.

Ahead, Baldwin stumbled in the darkness, cursing softly. Ryan said: "Slow, Hugh. Take it slow. No hurry now."

It seemed far longer to the point where he had left the roan. Baldwin stopped there and Ryan slipped by him, keeping his gun leveled at the Circle X owner's breast. "When I get in the saddle, you mount up," he said. "And do it slow and easy-like."

Reno Davis's voice cracked suddenly through the darkness. "Nobody's mountin' up! 'Specially you, Ryan!"

Ryan squeezed the trigger of his gun. The report shattered the night and the orange flare up was a brief, vivid, and blinding flash. But Baldwin had lunged away into the brush, keeping the horse between himself and Ryan. The bullet went wild. Davis fired in the next breath and Ryan felt the heat of the lead scorch his cheek. He ducked away, wheeling toward that man.

Davis's bantering voice said: "Come on, Ryan! Come on in close! You're an easy target! Where'd you like to have it? In the head? In the belly?"

Baldwin's strong voice broke in from the shadows on the right. "Hold it up, Reno. I want that jasper alive. Where the hell's that light?"

Several Circle X men closed in, one bearing a lantern. Ryan realized he was pretty well surrounded. Baldwin came into the group.

"You were a long time getting here," he said sourly to Davis.

"When there's shootin' to be done, I like to pick my own time and place," Davis replied coolly.

Baldwin swung to Ryan. He reached over and wrenched the gun from his hand. "Out front, friend. And don't you make any false moves. There's a dozen guns looking at you. You wouldn't have the luck I had."

Ryan headed for the yard, hearing the others fall in behind him. Near the center of the hard pack, Baldwin said—"Hold it!"—and he stopped. "Turn around!"

Ryan pivoted slowly on his good leg. The roan was being led over to the corral and tied up. Nine men, he ticked them off methodically, stood in a half circle with Baldwin, enclosing him. Eleven in all, counting the rider looking after the roan. This must be the entire crew. The gunshots would have brought everybody out.

Baldwin said: "Well, Ryan, like I tried to tell you, you cut yourself a big piece of pie. Too big to chew. I told you that you'd never get away with it."

Ryan shrugged. "Not over yet, Hugh."

"For you, yes. I've got all I need now. I'll keep you under cover for a couple more days to give me time to finish up a few things. That way Meldrum and his posse will keep out from underfoot. When I'm ready, I'll take you in. You just dealt yourself a hand in a game 'way too big for you."

Ryan said: "No, you're wrong there. It's the other way around. You dealt me in when you tried to frame me for Strickland's murder."

Baldwin chuckled. "Can't see that it makes much difference since we're playing my game." He turned to Reno Davis. "Put him in that old shed next to the bunkhouse. And keep a watch over him. He's a smart one."

Davis said: "Turk, here's your playmate. You hear what Mister Baldwin said?"

Paulson shuffled out into the fan of light where Ryan waited. His mouth was split into a wicked, happy grin. His big hands swung like huge hams at his sides. "I heard."

"I want him alive," Baldwin said, eyeing the big man sharply. "Watch yourself now, Turk."

"Yes, sir, I heard," Paulson said, and swung his balled fist like a club.

Ryan tried to duck but the blow caught him fully on the ear. Lights flashed through the darkness and the sound of laughter rushed loudly in, and then faded swiftly away into a void. And that was all he remembered.

XV

Sometime near midnight, Ryan came back to his senses. He remained quiet, feeling the solid throb of his head and the steady, dull ache in his leg. The dry crustiness there told him the wound had burst open, bled, and now was again closed.

Hearing no sound but the rasping of his own breath, he sat up. The rush of pain behind his eyes almost turned him sick and he sat there, motionless, holding his face between his hands while the nausea passed. After a few minutes he felt somewhat better. He glanced about the small room. It was only dimly lit, there being no other light save feeble star shine. He was alone and the room was barren except for the hard cot upon which he sat.

Back toward the Santa Claras a gunshot sounded, distant and empty. And somewhere on Circle X premises a dog began to bark. Ryan settled down on the cot, too tired to listen, too tired to look further, and too sick to think much about the things that had happened. His throat was dry and he wished he had a drink of water, but there was none to be had in the shed and he knew it would be useless to call out.

When he again opened his eyes, he felt much better. The blinding headache, memento of Turk Paulson's punishing roundhouse blow, had dwindled to minor proportions, and there was only a thin string of pain running through his leg to remind him of that injury. Warm sunlight streamed through the streaky glass of the single window, flooding the cell-like quarters, and he was already aware that the stuffy closeness was beginning to grow. He got unsteadily to his feet and crossed to the window. It was down, shut tight, and he slammed the lower half open.

Instantly Turk Paulson was there. He came from the front where, apparently, he had been keeping guard at the door. His pig eyes sparked their suspicion and he had a gun in his big fist.

Ryan grinned at him. "Hot in here." He moved back to the cot.

Paulson grumbled something inaudible and returned to his post. Ryan gave him five minutes to settle down and moved softly back to the window. He laid a sharp glance over the yard, the corral, and the main house. Men were moving about, doing their daily chores. In front of the barn, fresh horses were being saddled for the day's use. The cook came out of a side door near the end of the building and rapped on a triangular gong with a claw hammer and returned quickly inside.

Riders began to drift toward the kitchen. Ryan counted them off. Seven, Paulson at the door of the shed made eight; Baldwin, inside, would raise it to nine. Two missing from last night's count. They showed up at that moment, coming from the depths of the barn where they had been working.

Ryan returned to the cot but checked himself when he heard the pound of hoofs. Four men rode into the yard. They pulled up before the corral, slapped their horses through the gate, and disappeared immediately into the house. The rest of the crew, Ryan guessed, but he could not be sure. Circle X was a large spread and fourteen hands could be right or it could be considerably short. Men of Baldwin's stripe like plenty of help. It could be that this was only the floating crew. There might be several more men out working the range.

For the first time Ryan thought back over the night's events. He questioned himself as to his wisdom in attempting to take Baldwin in. In the cold brutal light of failure it seemed to him now there must have been some other, better way to accomplish what he had tried. But, even at this point, he could not think of what it would be. He was a man of direct, simple action, prone to move on straightforward lines when necessity dictated. As a result, he seldom indulged in regrets for something gone awry. The gain, to his way of thinking, far outweighed the risk at times such as this, and that was the important thing to be considered.

He heard the screen door bang at the kitchen and then the sound of boot heels rapping across the hard pack. Glancing out, he saw Reno Davis approaching and he moved back to the cot and sat down.

The door kicked back and Davis said: "Grub. In the kitchen."

He ducked his head toward the main house and stepped back, watching Ryan with a surly intentness. Outside, Paulson waited in dumb silence. Ryan walked into the open, moving stiffly and with some difficulty.

"Come on, come on," Davis said testily. "Ain't got the whole day. You eat, too, Turk."

Ryan started across the yard, followed closely by Davis and Paulson. Men were coming out of the kitchen, pausing along the step to roll their cigarettes, or pick their teeth and watch. Ryan halted near the door and placed his gaze on one of the riders.

"I'd appreciate your feeding and watering my horse," he said. "He's been standing there at that fence all night."

The man eyed Ryan carefully. With a half smile he said: "Why? You figurin' on goin' somewheres?"

Several of the others laughed, and Ryan moved on. But when he glanced back, he saw the man starting for the roan to carry out his request.

There was no one in the kitchen when they entered. Ryan sat down at a clean plate and Paulson took a chair almost directly opposite. Reno Davis made a stand near the door, never removing his sulky gaze from Ryan's form. The cook entered, bringing two platters heaped with eggs and fried meat. He left these to return shortly with a pan of hot biscuits and a pot of steaming coffee.

Ryan drank a cup of the scalding brew almost without pausing. It seared his throat and warmed his belly and immediately, it seemed, he felt much better. He refilled the cup. The loosening of the tightness in his muscles was a most welcome sensation. He glanced at Paulson who wolfed his food in great gulps.

Davis said: "Better eat, friend. You may be a long time gettin' the next meal."

Ryan turned to the eggs and meat. He was hungry and he ate steadily, washing the food down with more of the strong black coffee. When he was finished, he leaned back from the table. Paulson continued to eat.

Ryan looked to Davis. "Any chance for a smoke?"

Davis tossed him a sack of makings. Ryan rolled a deft cigarette and started to get up. Davis stopped him. "Never mind that. Just throw it."

Ryan shrugged and settled back. Outside, the crew was bringing up the horses. Baldwin was there. Ryan heard his voice overriding all other sounds.

"Tip, you take six of the boys and get back to Meldrum and the posse. Keep them looking for Ryan. Say you heard he was farther back on the ridge. I want the marshal and his bunch out of the way for a couple more days."

Ryan heard the men mount up and rush out of the yard. The door opened and Baldwin thrust his head inside. "You about through in there, Reno?"

"Waitin' on Turk," Davis grumbled. "Man eats like a horse."

"Well, hurry it up. Get Ryan back in that shed. Time we were moving."

"You heard him," Davis said, throwing a glance at Ryan and motioning him to the door. To Paulson he said: "Come on, Turk. You'll have another chance at it tonight."

Ryan stepped into the yard. Baldwin awaited him with sly humor in his eyes. The others of the crew stood by in expectant silence.

"Pretty tame this morning," Baldwin said. "Not the ring-tailed cat you were last night."

Ryan pulled up in front of the cattleman and faced him. He reached the cigarette from his lips and flicked it straight at Baldwin. Baldwin swore and stepped quickly back, brushing ashes and tobacco from his shirt while the color in his neck flushed red.

Davis crowded in at once, dragging at his gun, but Baldwin stopped him. "Never mind, Reno. Not time for that now." He turned to Ryan. "Too bad you can't see it my way. I like a man with guts. We'd make a good team."

Ryan shrugged. "Wrong team, Hugh. Your kind never runs far enough. And never fast enough to get away."

Baldwin considered that for a moment. He smiled. "We'll see," he said. "Tuck him away, Reno."

Ryan started for his cell. He heard Davis say: "You want Turk to stay with him again?"

And Baldwin's reply: "No, let Turk get some sleep. Put Halverson there."

That man, a squat, powerful rider built much along the same lines as Reno Davis, came off his horse and followed along to the shed. Ryan entered and heard the door snap shut behind.

Davis's voice said: "If he makes a break for it, cut him down. Hugh says keep him alive, but I don't hold with that. He's too damn' cute to take a chance with, and, far as I'm concerned, you can do anything you want. Just don't let him get out of here alive."

Halverson grunted some sort of reply and Davis thumped away. In a moment he was back, coming to the window. "Ryan, thought maybe you'd like to know where we're headed . . . to your place. When we get back, you'll be ownin' a nice pile of ashes."

Davis wheeled away and Ryan, standing at the window, watched him mount up and wait with the others for Baldwin. After a few minutes the cattleman came out, dressed in some sort of fine, gray material and wearing a broad white hat. His boots glistened blackly in the sunlight as he stepped to the saddle. They rode out in a body, striking south.

Ryan settled down on the cot and the morning

dragged on, hour trailing hour. The shed grew hotter with its trapped heat and Ryan finally went to the door and swung it open. Halverson was alert at once, his gun boring straight at Ryan's breastbone.

Ryan said calmly: "Plenty hot in here. Like to leave this open for a spell."

Halverson wagged his head. "Close it. And don't make no more sudden moves like that if you want to keep livin'."

Ryan kicked the door shut and turned to the window. At least the roan was getting fed and watered and was in out of the sun. He tried to see where they had taken his horse, but the roan was not in sight. Likely in the barn. Ryan tried then to gauge his chances for escape. Halverson, of course, was the big obstacle, waiting there outside the door.

Turk Paulson would be in the bunkhouse asleep. He wished Baldwin had left the big man on guard, but Baldwin was too smart for that. He had realized Ryan probably would try and trick the slow-witted giant and he was taking no chances on it working. The cook was somewhere in the main house. A thought came to him then and he remembered the four men who had come in later. Where were they? He swiveled his glance to the corral; their horses were still there, saddled and waiting. Apparently, like Turk Paulson, they were catching up on a little sleep.

If only he could figure out a way to get by Halverson and not kick up a row that would awaken the sleeping men. It would be easy, after that. But how to get by Halverson? That was the big problem.

He was still threshing it around in his mind, casting in all directions for some answer when the crew returned. It must have been around two o'clock. Looking through the open window, he saw Hugh Baldwin was not with them, and he had his own quick guess as to where that man had gone, dressed as he was. Reno Davis rode straight to the shed and, leaning from the saddle, called to Ryan.

"Like I promised, you own a mighty nice pile of ashes, cowboy. Made a right pretty fire."

"My stock?" Ryan asked.

"We're lookin' after them. We're letting them run with some good Circle X stuff."

Ryan waited a moment. Then: "Frank Sears's body was in the bunkhouse. You bury him before you burned the place?"

Davis grinned. "He went up in smoke just like all the rest of it. What's the difference? One way's as good as another. He didn't know nothin' about it, anyway."

Ryan pulled back from the window, disgusted and a little sick at what he had heard. Any man deserved a decent burial and he particularly would have liked for Sears to have had one. The deep, glowing anger for Hugh Baldwin increased its intensity.

He heard Halverson, near the corner of the building, say: "Didn't the boss come back. What happened to him?"

"Stopped off at that Strickland gal's place," Davis answered, turning away. "Reckon we'll be payin' her a call tonight if she don't see things his way."

Ryan settled down on the cot, his mind now racing desperately with his problem. There had to be a way out, a means for getting by Halverson. He had to think of something, and think of it soon.

XVI

Baldwin rode in sometime later. He pulled up in front of the main house, tied his horse there, and, pausing, shouted—"Reno!"—then went inside.

Davis went trotting across from the bunkhouse and entered through the kitchen. Darkness was falling early. Masses of heavy, full-bellied clouds again piled up over the peaks and ridges of the Santa Claras and hung low above the prairie. The heat was holding, a stuffy sort of heat with the threat of rain riding with it. Examining the sky, Ryan saw the first streak of lightning stab through the overcast. The slow rumble of thunder was a distant, hushed sound.

A few hours earlier and it might have saved my

place, Ryan thought, watching the storm gather. Davis came from the kitchen, the slam of the door overly loud in the pre-storm calmness. He headed directly for the bunkhouse, and, when he came out again, the others were close on his heels. Some, heeding the grumbling, overhead warnings, were carrying their yellow slickers. Others were not bothering.

Davis detoured toward the shed. Ryan heard him say to Halverson: "We're movin' in on Strickland's."

"The gal wouldn't listen, eh?"

"I don't know. Reckon not. Anyway, she must have said a few things that stuck in his craw. He's in no humor to talk about it."

"I got to stay here and watch this jasper?" Halverson asked after that.

"Somebody's got to. Might as well be you."

"Why can't Turk do it? He likes it."

"Uhn-uh," Davis said at once. "Baldwin's scared to leave him here alone. That bird would have him talked into ridin' into town before we got out of sight. Turk ain't got all he's supposed to upstairs."

"But it's goin' to rain!" Halverson protested. "What'll I do about that? I can't set out here in the wet."

"Then get inside with him. Only, watch him. Don't give him a chance to jump you."

"Don't worry about that. He won't get even half a chance," Halverson said.

Davis said: "Don't pay to be too sure about anything when you're foolin' with that one."

"What can he do? He's crippled up and there ain't nothin' in there he could jump a man with. What you so worried about?"

"Just don't give him any chances," Davis said, and turned away.

Ryan smiled tightly and glanced through the window at the blackening sky. Rain had helped him once—that night when he had escaped into the hills. Maybe it would be that way again. Maybe his luck would run good once more. He pivoted slowly, making another careful search of the room, of the walls, of everything in it. He needed something with which to fight. A weapon of some sort, anything, anything at all that might be used. But the room was barren as a slab of granite.

He heard then the clatter of horses in the yard. This was followed by a low run of voices and grunts as the men swung up to the saddle. From the window, he watched Hugh Baldwin come out, dressed now in rough working clothes, and take his horse from Davis. He could not see too well in the rapidly dwindling light, but he counted the riders. He took a deep breath. They were all there, ready to leave, except for Halverson.

The first drops of rain began to pelt down, rapping loudly on the shed's thin roof. Two of the crew made a hurried break for the bunkhouse, deciding they would need their slickers after all.

Davis dismounted and hurried to fetch Baldwin's. Halverson grumbled his discomfort from beyond the door.

Ryan, watching the crew assemble, suddenly had his answer. He glanced down to the heavy gun belt still around his waist. They had taken his gun from him the night before in the yard, but they had not bothered to strip him of his cartridge belt. Unbuckling it, he slipped the holster off and tucked it under the cot. Doubling the belt, to form a sort of club, he sat down on the cot and made a few tentative slaps at his open palm. The weight of the brass shells, concentrated as they were in the folded leather, made an excellent weapon.

The clatter of raindrops increased, and water began to slide down the walls where time and the sun's drying rays had warped loose the roof joists. A screech of metal against metal came from Halverson, and he knew the man was lighting a lantern against the closing darkness.

Reno Davis's voice lifted above the tumult and Ryan heard the Circle X crew move out, turning south out of the yard. He remained seated, figuring Halverson would soon come. And he was now ready. He had a weapon with which to fight. It would be a gamble, long odds, but considering what lay ahead of him when Hugh Baldwin was through, it was worth it. He hoped Halverson would not wait too long; he didn't want Baldwin and his riders to get too good a start on him.

"Hey . . . you in there . . . Ryan!"

Halverson's voice came through the door. Ryan waited a time before answering. Then: "Yeah? What do you want?"

"Where you at?"

"On the cot, trying to catch some sleep. Sure could use a blanket."

"Stay there," Halverson directed. "I'm comin' in out of this rain. I've got a gun in my hand. Don't make any false moves!"

"Come ahead," Ryan answered, and set himself for sudden, desperate action.

Halverson kicked back the door and entered. He carried the lantern in his left hand, leveled gun in the other. Water ran down his face and dropped on his chest and plastered his shirt against his barrel-like body. A small rivulet trickled off his hat and fell to the floor. He booted the door shut.

"You look pretty wet," Ryan remarked.

Halverson said sourly—"Stay right where you are."—and set the lantern in the corner.

"Sure," Ryan murmured agreeably, and lunged to his feet. He struck with the folded gun belt, all in one single motion, aiming at Halverson's head.

Pain roared through Ryan as he came down on his injured leg. It gave under his sudden weight, and, in so doing, it saved his life. Halverson's gun shattered the quiet, deafening them both within the narrow confines of the small room. The bullet whistled past Ryan as he went down and *thunked* dully into the floor. The belt missed Halverson's head, but it caught him across the neck and arms and knocked the gun away. The gun went skating across the floor, with Halverson clawing frantically after it.

Ryan caught the man by the foot and brought him hurtling down. Halverson struck out at him as he fell, but Ryan rolled away, taking the blow on his shoulder. He lashed out with both fists at the same time, using them like a club. Halverson grunted as Ryan kneed him in the belly. He lashed out for Ryan's face, searching for his eyes with probing fingers, but Ryan twisted around, getting free. Halverson's fingers caught his hair and began to pull back his head. In that same moment, he felt the Circle X rider's throat and clamped down. They pulled together and began to roll, locked together like that, around the floor.

They crashed full tilt against the cot, Ryan wincing as his bad leg took the brunt of impact. He heaved and they broke apart, Halverson coming out on top, breathing hard. Ryan felt the man digging again at his throat. He struggled to throw off the heavy, solid weight pressing him down but he was lying at an angle and could not get the necessary leverage. He flailed out with both hands, trying to strike Halverson's face but his efforts fell short.

The man's powerful fingers were closing him off, shutting out the drumming of the rain, the quick rasping of his own strained breathing. He threw his arms wide across the floor, fighting now for wind, for that leverage that would allow him to roll out from under the man and break free. His fingers touched the gun belt, lying partly under the cot, and a surge of hope rocked through him. He gathered the belt in a tight grip and lashed out at the indistinct shape looming over him.

He heard the dull, chinking sound the heavy buckle made as it struck Halverson's head. The fingers at his throat relaxed and dropped away. The dark shape over him sagged. Ryan, gasping for breath, shoved with his last remaining strength, and Halverson tipped stiffly sideways and went out of his line of vision, thudding dully to the floor.

Ryan crawled across the room to where the gun lay, his head clearing with each deep draft of air. He retrieved the holster and strapped the belt back on, dropping Halverson's gun into place. He moved slowly and painfully to the man's side and peered closely at him in the dimness. The raw imprint of the buckle's edge was a livid mark across his temple. Ryan felt for his pulse. The man was not dead but he likely would be quiet for some time.

Wasting no more time, he moved to the door and slid stealthily into the open. Rain drove into his face and he took a moment to get Halverson's hat. His own was gone, lost somewhere after Turk Paulson had knocked him out the night before.

There was a dim light burning in the kitchen at the main house, and, watching it intently for a moment or two, he saw the dumpy figure of the cook pass before the window and back again, doing his chores. Either he had not heard the explosion of Halverson's gun or else just assumed it to be a clap of thunder. Keeping close to the fence, he limped to the barn and entered. Here again he hesitated, certain no one was in the huge, gloomy building, but taking no chances. Satisfied after a minute's listening, he passed along the stalls until, at last, he came to the roan. He heaved a sigh. The roan was still saddled, only the bridle having been removed to make it easier for him to eat.

Ryan had him ready in short time. He mounted up in the stable, taking a moment to check the caliber of Halverson's gun. It was the same common size as his own and for this he was grateful. He refilled the spent cartridge from his belt and rode out into the yard.

Rain was coming down much harder. Pools were beginning to form in the yard, making dark mirrors in the night. He started for the road, when a flash of lightning brought everything into quick, brilliant relief. Two figures stood near the kitchen door. Halverson, weaving uncertainly on his feet, and the cook, an old double-barreled shotgun clutched in his hands. While he was bridling the roan, Halverson had revived sufficiently, at least, to make his way to the kitchen and summon the cook.

Ryan drew his gun and laid a shot at their feet. Halverson staggered back and fell against the side of the house, mud and water splattering over him. The cook yelled and the shotgun boomed into the darkness, lead pellets whistling off, high overhead. Ryan touched the roan with his spurs and they raced by the pair. When he drew abreast, he snapped another bullet toward them, digging more mud from beneath their feet. The cook dropped the gun and ducked inside the kitchen door. Halverson sat weakly back, his mouth working with curses.

That would hold them. He swung the roan due south toward the Strickland place.

XVII

The roan's pace was a fast and reckless one. The going was slippery over the wet prairie and through the draws, and Ryan knew he was taking short odds on the roan's falling. But he had to reach Strickland's; he had to get there as soon as possible. He realized he could not overtake Hugh Baldwin and his crew, but, with a little good luck, he might arrive before they had done much damage.

Rain was a steady punishment upon his face and neck, the cold drops sharp and stinging when they struck. Lightning flashed regularly, broad sheets that flooded the landscape with blue-white brilliance. Some of the draws were beginning to run with foaming brown water rushing downhill. By morning the river would be glutted and out of its low banks. It was one of those rare, hard rains that came to the Cuchillo Plains country, often doing far more damage than they did good.

He came into the S-Bar property at the far, northwest corner. The roan was breathing heavily from his labors, but he had stayed upright, slipping only once or twice on the long run and never entirely going to his knees. Ryan kept him pointed due south until he was parallel with the tamarack windbreak, and then cut back eastward. He thus approached the buildings of the Strickland spread from the blind side and, therefore, could not be so readily seen by any of Hugh Baldwin's crew that were on guard. That seemed unlikely to Ryan, however. Baldwin had little fear of intervention from any quarter, particularly where Ryan was concerned. Indeed, Baldwin had reached a point where, in the overwhelming certainty of his own power, he frankly ignored all possibilities of danger.

There was no light in the front of the house when Ryan halted the roan in the depths of the tamarack. The thick growth was some protection from the drizzle, and, after he had stepped from the saddle, he stood for a time, listening and considering his best move. The S-Bar lay in deep quiet, only the steady rain setting up a drumming noise. Under the vivid flashes of lightning he could see the wet, glistening buildings silhouetted blackly against the sky, its few trees and fences. The pools of water deepened in the low places of the yard, reflecting these trees and fences.

He wondered if he could have overtaken and passed Hugh Baldwin, if they could have stopped, waiting for the rain to let up, before they moved in on the S-Bar. But where would they hole up? There was no place in between unless they chose to swing far westward where there was one of the line shacks. That didn't sound like an idea Baldwin would have. He was not the sort to countenance any delays once he had gotten under way, and he doubted if he had overtaken them. With the start they had, even before he had tangled with Halverson, it would have been a near impossibility. No, they were there, hiding probably in one of the structures on the place, preparing to strike.

Ryan left the roan and crossed the porch of the main house. The door was closed but not locked, just as he had found it previously. He pushed it open softly and stepped inside. There was a low drone of voices coming from the kitchen, and he paused, trying to isolate and identify them. It was possible Baldwin was there, endeavoring to swing Ann Strickland to his way of thinking. But if he was, Ryan could not distinguish Baldwin's deep tones.

It was difficult to tell who it was. The rain maintained its steady rattle on the roof and against the glass of the windows. He listened intently and came finally to the conclusion that it was only two people, Ann and someone else—George Cobb, perhaps, or it could be some neighbor come to pay his respects and express his condolences for the death of Tom Strickland. But it was more logical to believe it was the S-Bar foreman. He moved silently across the room, opened the connecting door, and stepped into the kitchen.

George Cobb sat at the table, his back to Ryan. Ann, standing near the big range, was in the act of pouring each a cup of coffee. When Ryan came into the room, she lifted her glance to him, and he saw her eyes spread wide into circles of surprise.

"You!"

George Cobb came around in his chair. His dark brows snapped down into an angry line and he clawed at the gun at his side.

Ryan said—"Don't do it!"—in a sharp, crackling sort of way. His hand had dropped to where it hovered lightly over the curving handle of his pistol. His face had a cold, empty sort of look.

Cobb relaxed gently, letting his arms fall slowly forward.

Ryan said: "I've got no quarrel with you, George. Let's don't begin one now."

Ann Strickland met his gaze. "Who is your quarrel with, then?"

"Nobody in here," Ryan answered. Then: "Baldwin been here since dark?"

He was wet to the skin. Water dripped from his soaked clothing and was forming small puddles on the floor around him. He removed his hat—Halverson's hat—and held it at his side.

"Not tonight," Cobb said. "Why?"

"I'm looking for him," Ryan answered.

Cobb laughed. "Not the way we heard it. Understand Meldrum's posse has orders to shoot you on sight. Since you murdered Frank Sears, you got a mighty big price on your head."

Ryan heard the words and felt their shocking impact. This was more of Hugh Baldwin's work; he should have expected it. He should have known the cattleman would pass a tale such as that on to the marshal. "So, I murdered Frank Sears. Is that what you've been told?"

"That's what they say. You shot him when he flat quit your outfit. He wouldn't go along with what you're doin', and you nailed him to keep him from talkin'."

"This was Hugh Baldwin, telling you all this?"

Cobb nodded. "He was by here, lookin' for the marshal. You sayin' it ain't so? That Frank ain't dead?"

"Frank's dead," Ryan replied, "but not by my gun. Two of Baldwin's crew did it."

Cobb shrugged his thin shoulders. "Seems to me like you always got a different story than everybody else. They're always wrong, but you're always right, to hear you tell it."

"That's exactly right," Ryan said in a close, tight voice. "Everybody else *is* wrong. I'm telling you that straight and you'd better start believing me if you expect to come out of this mess with a whole skin!"

Ann Strickland, quiet during this interchange between Ryan and the S-Bar foreman, suddenly spoke: "Believe you? A gunman, a killer who thinks nothing of shooting a man down in cold blood! Why should anybody ever believe a man like you against one like Hugh Baldwin or the marshal? Or even Reno Davis! You can't deny any of what's been said about you."

Ryan met her gaze, seeing the uncertainty lying there in her eyes, the alarm and disturbance his presence in the room was creating. He shook his head in a weary fashion. "No, I'll not deny what has been said about my time with the gun. You've said some things that aren't true, but that's neither here nor there. The main thing is that you are dead wrong about Hugh Baldwin. And that's why I'm here now."

Rain battered against the walls of the house and a rising wind rattled the windows and doors. Somewhere outside, an unfastened gate slapped steadily against its post.

"This morning Baldwin and his crew burned down my place. He brought them here to do the same for you tonight."

George Cobb snorted. "That'll be a little hard to do in all this wet."

"It won't stop him," Ryan answered. "Not now."

Cobb paused, looking squarely at Ryan in a perplexed way. "Now, just why would Hugh want to do that? You give me one good reason."

"He was by here today, wasn't he? Wanted you to sell out?"

Ann said: "Yes, he was. But he's offered to do that before."

Ryan shook his head. "I can't make you people understand what you're up against. Hugh Baldwin is a dangerous man. He's out to take over this country, even if it means wiping out every outfit in it. I've seen his kind before. Once they've had a taste of what force can do for them, they go wild. And Hugh's had his taste."

Cobb stirred in his chair. Ann glanced toward the rain-covered window. Cobb said: "You don't make much sense, mister. If Hugh's gone loco like you say, why would he be blamin' it on you? You're a newcomer to this country. There's a dozen others he could have pointed to."

"It's you that's not making sense. Being a newcomer made me the best bet. And I happened to be handy that day Tom Strickland was shot. Now, if he burns down this place tonight, I'll get credit for it just like I did for Reno Davis's bullet when it cut down Tom, just like I did for the bullets that went into Frank Sears's back."

"You sure wouldn't be burnin' down your own place," Cobb admitted thoughtfully.

Ryan shook his head. "I don't know how Baldwin will explain that," Ryan said then. "Unless he gives them a yarn that he did it so I'd have no place to headquarter from. It would have to be a thin story, but people would believe Hugh. They have so far," he added with a note of bitterness, looking at Ann.

She said: "You told me you were leaving here. What made you come back?"

Ryan shrugged. "I don't know for sure." Purpose and cause was all confused in his mind—Ann or Frank Sears or the thought of men like Hugh Baldwin running loose and roughshod over the land. He could not separate any of the reasons; they all seemed to interlock and hinge, one upon the other. He said: "Finding Frank Sears there, shot in the back, I suppose. He was a fine old man who never hurt anyone. I guess that's my reason. Anyway, it will do."

"I see," Ann murmured in an odd, falling voice.

"Still don't any of it make much sense to me," Cobb grumbled. "I've known Hugh a right smart lot of time. He's tough, and I reckon he keeps what's his, but I don't see him pullin' all these things you've been talkin' about. Sure, we've had trouble with Hugh, but that's to be expected. Everybody has some trouble, now and then. Seems like nowadays you can hardly move without rilin' some jasper. Nope, Ryan, I just can't swallow your tale, not after considerin' your reputation as a gunman and killer."

Anger brushed swiftly through Jim Ryan. "You keep mentioning the past. Well, that's just what it is . . . the dead past, so leave it there. Now, I want to tell *you* something. If it was just you and the S-Bar alone in this, I'd forget about it and walk out that door. I'd leave you to Hugh Baldwin and his Circle X crowd. But there's others involved. He gets my place, then the S-Bar. Next time it will be some other rancher or homesteader. Nothing's going to stop him if we don't stand together and fight him. If you can't see it that way, then it will be me and my gun alone, but I'll not quit now."

"That's your answer to all things," Ann broke in quietly. "Always a gun, a bullet."

Ryan shook his head. "No, I would not say that is true. But a man fights fire with fire. Men like Hugh Baldwin follow no rule books and you do the best you can with what you have when you're bucking them."

Cobb said: "What made you think Hugh was comin' here tonight?"

"I was there, at Circle X. They had me penned up with a guard, a man named Halverson. I overheard

Reno telling him they were coming here. Later I got away and came here."

"Baldwin caught you, eh? Why didn't he turn you over to Ross? Him and that posse's still huntin' the hills."

Ryan remembered Baldwin's instructions to the men who worked with the posse—keep the marshal busy, keep him working the hills and out of the way for a couple of days. He repeated this to Ann and George Cobb.

The old foreman stroked his chin. "Makes some sense, part of it," he admitted. "Some don't. But there could be a reason for it. I just can't figure Hugh would do a thing like that and. . . ."

Ryan's patience finally snapped. "All right," he snapped. "Have it your own way. Believe what you want, believe Baldwin or Reno Davis or anybody else! I'll handle this alone, in my way, and, if you get hurt in the doing of it, remember it was of your own making!"

He wheeled to go back through the front room. Halfway across the parlor he pulled up short. Ann's stricken voice had cried out: "Look! Fire in the barn!"

XVIII

Ryan spun around, pain from his injured leg jabbing through him. George Cobb came off his chair in a long leap and wrenched open the door. Rain was still falling in a steady sheet and thunder pulsed a low crescendo through the blackness. Through the barn doors and the loft windows Ryan could see the bright flare of reaching flames as they raced through the interior of the structure.

Cobb yelled: "I'll get out the crew! Got to get that stock out of there!"

Ryan jumped to intercept the foreman, but Cobb was outside and running hard for the bunkhouse. Sudden lightning shattered the blackness. Ryan saw the shape of Reno Davis astride his horse, waiting somewhere near the center of the yard. Davis's gun roared as the lightning died. In the succeeding flash, a split second later, George Cobb was a writhing, long shape in the mud. A small cry escaped Ann Strickland's lips.

"Douse that lamp!" Ryan said, and dropped to his knees. Gun in hand, he crawled his way to the still open doorway.

The room plunged at once into darkness. Ryan waited for the next eerie spread of light, the spot where Reno Davis had been, fixed in his mind. The shot had roused the crew and the windows of the bunkhouse were now yellow squares. The door flung back and a man, clad only in his underwear, stood framed there. The vicious crack of a gun coming from over near the flaming barn drove him stumbling back inside. Immediately the bunkhouse lamp went out. Lightning came again, but Davis was no longer in sight. There was only the crumpled frame of George Cobb, lying face down in the shallow pool.

"There a rifle in here?" Ryan asked in a low voice.

Ann said: "Yes. Mine."

"Get it. Stay in here where you can watch the yard. Shoot anybody that tries to get close to the house. *Anybody,* understand?"

"Yes," Ann replied in a small voice.

He heard her moving about the room. "Better lock that front door," he said, remembering he had twice found it open.

In a few minutes she was back. He caught the faint shine of light on the rifle metal. "Now, remember, shoot first and we'll look afterward. Don't trust anybody."

"Except you," she said. "I know that now, Jim."

His tone relented a little. "Sometimes things are hard to believe. The people you least suspect are your worst enemies. Are you all set?"

"Yes. What are you going to do?"

"Go out there. I want to look at George. He might still be alive. And I want you to get your crew together and see if we can stop Baldwin before this gets worse."

Gunshots suddenly began to racket near the barn, the reports mixing with the screaming of the trapped horses. Despite the rain's steady fall, the fire was beginning to push along the building and through to the outside. New flames were darting within several of the smaller sheds where Baldwin's men had thrown torches. Lightning ripped the night again and again, and Ryan, crouched within the doorway, saw the bunkhouse was deserted. Ann's crew was out there somewhere in the yard, starting to fight back. This at once created a new problem for him; they could easily mistake him for Circle X. But he would have to take that chance.

Ryan moved to leave, keeping well down. He felt Ann's fingers touch him lightly. She said: "Be careful, Jim. After this night I'll have nothing, only you."

Ryan made no reply for a long moment, considering her words. He said then—"I'll be back, don't worry."—and darted out into the sopping darkness.

He moved quickly away from the doorway, staying as close as possible to the house itself so as to offer very little target to any Circle X man. Reaching the corner of the building, he laid full length in the mud and water, waiting to cross the open yard to the corral. Getting set, still favoring the bad leg, he crouched. It was cold, bitterly cold in the rain, but this, like the restricting leg, he tried to ignore. He wanted only to meet with Reno Davis and Hugh Baldwin. After them would come the two who had cut down Frank Sears.

Lightning came, a great, blinding sheet that lit up the yard in bluish-white brightness. It held for a long moment and closed off. Ryan, taking a deep breath, leaped to his feet and sprinted across the open ground. He came dangerously near to falling when his feet skidded on the slick mud, but he caught himself and finally reached the corral fence. No shots came lacing through the night after him and he concluded he had not been seen. Keeping low again, he trotted along the fence until he was but a few feet from Cobb's prostrate form. Lightning flashed and he had his full look at the foreman and knew at once that he was dead. Davis's bullet had struck squarely in the forehead. Likely he went down without ever knowing what had happened.

Ryan moved on toward the bunkhouse. The shooting had almost ceased, only a report coming, now and then, when a man saw movement he knew was not a friend. Ryan could hear the crackling of flames, rising above the drumming raindrops. The horses had stopped their screaming, all dead by this time. Ryan waited, his eyes probing the darkness ahead. In the next quick explosion of light he saw a man crouched behind one of the feed wagons, his face turned toward the barn.

Ryan crept in close. "Don't shoot. I'm behind you."

"Who is it?"

"Ryan. Where's the rest of the crew?"

Surprise rode the man's tone. "Ryan? Whose side you on? Who's that out there?"

"Baldwin and his crowd. Circle X."

There was silence for a moment. "I thought I saw Reno Davis out there! By God! Them scurvy sidewinders! Only today they was here, makin' out like they was our best friends. They get George?"

"Straight through the head. Reno got him when he started across the yard after you and the rest of the men."

"Reno," the cowpuncher murmured in a low, remembering sort of way, "ain't he the one claimed you killed old Tom?"

Ryan answered: "Yes, but he did it himself. Couldn't have been anybody else." Several shots broke out then in that area between the barn and the feed house. Ryan got to his feet. "Looks like that's where we ought to be."

"Let's go," the cowpuncher said, and started along the scatter of discarded wheels, crippled, unused vehicles, and other old equipment strung along the bunkhouse. They picked up another S-Bar man and the three of them reached the wagon shed just as a flash of lightning silhouetted a man riding across the yard. It was Hugh Baldwin.

"My meat," the first cowpuncher declared and slammed a quick shot at the cattleman.

Ryan said quickly—"Scatter!"—and lunged away. Immediately a dozen bullets laced the spot where they had crouched. Ryan pulled up against the overturned bed of a wagon. "All right?" he called softly.

"All right," a voice came back.

"Me, too," came the other. "By jeemies, that was close! You hit Baldwin, Tod?"

"Don't know. Too dark to see much."

Ryan took advantage of the following lull to cross the calf yard and work in closer to the barn. The far side of the doomed building was visible to him from there, and, when the next flash of light blanketed the place, he saw Baldwin for the second time, along with several of his crew. They were milling about, glistening yellow shapes in the lurid glow. The fire within the barn was beginning to die down, only the naked outer shell remaining upright. Most of the roof was gone in spite of the rain.

"Get up there and get a fire going in the main house!" Baldwin's voice shouted.

"How about the girl? She's still in there, ain't she?"

"She'll come out, once you get a blaze going!" Baldwin yelled back. "Rest of you boys, work on those sheds! And that feed house! I don't want anything left here but ashes when we're through!"

"Somebody over there, hiding along the bunkhouse!" a voice spoke up. "Watch it!"

Ryan strained his eyes to locate the man delegated the job of firing the main house. But in the blackness he could pick out no movements, and the noise of the rain and hissing of embers drowned out all sound. He waited tensely for a flash of lightning. It came suddenly. Immediately he heard the crack of Ann's rifle, twice in rapid succession.

In a moment the Circle X rider was back, coming into the pale flare of light behind the barn. Ryan heard him swear and say: "Can't get close enough! She's got a rifle there, just waitin' for a man to come up!"

Reno Davis's voice called across the yard—"I'll take care of it, Hugh!"—in his drawling, confident way.

Ryan came quickly to his feet and hurried toward the house. He was gambling on the lightning—or the darkness again, that there would be no revealing flash until he reached a point where he could intercept Davis. Luck was with him. He reached that point and waited, hearing the man coming. The horse was walking slowly through the puddles and deeper pools, its hoofs making wet, mushy sounds in the mud.

Ryan remained silent until the horse was a short ten feet distant. Then: "Reno . . . right here."

Davis fired at the sound of Ryan's voice. But Ryan had spoken and stepped away. He fired then, aiming at the orange bloom of Davis's gun. He heard the bullet strike dully and drive the wind out of the man in a great explosion of breath. The horse shied away, slipping badly on the wet ground, and Davis came out of the saddle in a heap. Waiting patiently, Ryan saw him lying prone, face turned upward, when lightning came again.

Bedlam had broken out. A welter of shots crackled behind the barn. Baldwin's crew began to answer. A man shouted—"Hey, Reno!"—and then was drowned out by another flurry of gunshots.

Ryan, keeping close to the ground, doubled back. The Strickland crew had collected near the feed house and was pouring a merciless fire into Baldwin's men. Ryan stumbled over a dead body, and fell flat. In the next break of light he saw Baldwin and three or four of his riders, lined up in an irregular sort of formation, returning the fire. He recognized the huge bulk of Turk Paulson, down to his knees, hat gone, sinking slowly to the sodden ground as a half dozen bullets caught up with him.

He laid his own shots at Baldwin, thus placing the cattleman and his crew in a wicked crossfire. A yell went up at once. A horse screamed in agony and another voice cried out: "They got some help!"

Ryan ran to the corner of the barn that was still hissing loudly as cold water continued to fall upon glowing embers. In the uncertain, dim light of one of the sheds he could vaguely see Baldwin and the men who were still mounted. Two of them wheeled suddenly and charged off into the night. Another, close by Baldwin, sagged as a bullet struck him, and slid from the saddle.

"Hugh!"

Ryan sent his call out through the rain-soaked darkness and stepped away from the barn.

Baldwin fired wildly and spurred his horse away, beyond the pale flare of flames. Ryan withheld his shot, trying for a better position from which to shoot. A Circle X rider crossed in front of him, his face white and glistening from the rain. He threw a glance at Ryan, visibly startled by what he saw. He snapped a hurried shot but it was yards wide. Ryan laid his answer through the darkness and had an indefinite vision of the man reeling and grabbing at his shoulder, and then fading from sight.

At the end of the barn Ryan hesitated, standing as close to it as the heat from the smoldering wood allowed. He was watching that point of darkness into which Baldwin had plunged. He knew the cattleman would not be there now, that he likely would appear some distance away. But the flash of lightning might catch him, still moving. The broad sheet of light came and held a long while as it flickered strongly. The yard and its surroundings came out sharply—the huddled shapes of Turk Paulson and two others, a drowned horse. But Baldwin was not to be seen.

"S-Bar!" Ryan called.

Strickland's crew came from their various

points. Four men. They gathered soberly around him. The cowpuncher, Tod, who he had first met near the bunkhouse, was not among them.

Ryan said: "Any of you see where Baldwin went?"

There was a murmur of negatives. One said: "I saw him take a shot, at you I reckon, and then dive back out of sight. Ain't seen him since."

Baldwin had got away. Seeing his crew melt before his eyes, he had turned tail and fled, fearing the death he so ruthlessly meted out to others.

"You men clean up this mess best you can," Ryan said then. "Do it now, before daylight. Get George Cobb's body and these others out of the yard before Ann sees them. One of you better start out and find the marshal."

"Where you goin'?"

"After Baldwin," Ryan said. "This thing's not finished until we get him."

"I'm goin' with you," one of the cowpunchers said at once.

Ryan said—"No."—in a short, terse way. "I'll take care of Baldwin."

XIX

Ryan swung away from the men and struck out across the yard, heading for the windbreak and the roan. He stayed purposely clear of the house. Knowing Ann was safe and that he had little time if Baldwin had it in mind to leave, he wanted to lose as few minutes as possible. But she saw him and came out into the open.

"Is it all over?"

"All done here," he replied, halting in stride. He bent his steps to her.

"Was it very bad?"

"Pretty bad," he said, not wanting to go into any details. He was remembering the things she had said about guns and the horror and death that rode with them.

"Did . . . was Hugh . . . ?" she began, haltingly.

Ryan shook his head. In the darkness he could not see her face clearly, but she was standing close. "No, he ran when he saw his outfit deserting and going down. Reno and Turk Paulson and a couple others. I'm going after Baldwin now. I'll find him at his place, I expect, getting ready to leave the country."

"Can't you let him go? Do you have to go after him?" she asked at once. "Why does it have to be you? It's Meldrum's job now."

"No time to wait for the marshal," Ryan explained patiently. "He could be in the next territory by the time we located Meldrum and convinced him that Baldwin was at the bottom of all this trouble. It's something I have to do myself, anyway, Ann . . . a personal matter."

"Yes," she replied in a heavy voice, "I suppose that's the way it is."

"The rain's beginning to let up," Ryan said. "You better get inside and get on some dry clothing. Then I want you to go into town. Get away from here until the crew gets things cleaned up. This is no place for you."

"Why not? It is my home, my ranch. Why shouldn't I stay here? You think I'm afraid of . . . of the death out there?"

"No," Ryan said, "I don't think that. But this isn't over yet. Trouble could come again. I want you to tell me you will do as I say . . . that you'll go into town and stay there."

"All right," she agreed in that same lost tone. "Will you come? Will I see you later?"

"Before I leave."

"You're going on when this is over?"

He said simply—"Yes."—and turned then to go.

Before he had taken a full step she had moved in close to him. She threw her arms around his neck and placed a kiss, warm and soft, upon his lips. "For everything, I'm sorry," she said. "Can you ever forgive me for not trusting you? For the terrible things I have said?"

He pulled slowly away, taking her by the shoulders. He said gently: "Think no more about it, Ann. Truth is a hard thing to recognize at times. As for mistakes, I've made my share of them."

"But can you forget it? That's important, Jim. Can you forget the things I've said and done?"

Ryan said simply and honestly: "I'm glad to be

alive. Grateful for that, I'll question nothing else."

She pulled away from him and he knew she was finding no satisfaction in his words. But he could find no other way to say it. He knew now what lay ahead, for he was a marked man and the future was an uncertain, indefinite path. The dark shadows of the past were not dead; they were here, this night, and the search would begin again, as before.

"Be careful," she said, turning toward the door. "If not for my sake, for your own."

He waited until she had entered the doorway, her slim shape vague in the gloom, and then wheeled away to the roan. For the first time since the fight had begun, he was conscious of the dull and familiar throb in his leg, but it bothered him only a little now. He drew the roan into the open and stepped to the saddle. It was cold, soaked wet, and not at all comfortable, but he was drenched to the skin anyway, and after a few moments it was not noticeable.

He cut back through the tamarack, following as direct a route as he could find. The rain had settled into a fine, cloudy mist, and in the east the clouds were breaking up, preparing for a dawn not far away.

When they broke into the open country, the roan swung into a long and easy lope. Pools of water splashed beneath him and he slid once, coming into a long-sloped draw, but he managed to stay up. Ryan did not press the big horse hard but let him choose his own pace and his own trail, and in that manner they soon were crossing the south pasture of the Circle X holdings. Unsure as to how many of the crew might still be around, Ryan swung west and approached the buildings from the spring, just as he had done the previous night.

Five horses, Baldwin's and four others, stood at the rail. Ryan studied them for a time, recognizing them finally as those used by the riders sent to work with Ross Meldrum. All, apparently, were gathered in the front room of Baldwin's house, holding a council of war or being paid off by the cattleman. While Ryan pondered his best move, the four men came out, mounted up, and rode off toward the north. They soon were out of sight, showing no indications of stopping, and Ryan concluded that, like rats leaving the doomed ship, they were getting out while there was still time.

He brought the roan in, moving alongside the house, slipping quietly from the saddle when he reached the building's corner. Anchoring the roan, he drifted softly across the porch and reached for the door handle.

Baldwin's voice said: "Come in, Ryan."

Ryan halted, momentarily caught off balance, but his gun flew into his palm at the cattleman's first word. Alert for some trick, he opened the door and stepped inside. In the center of the room Hugh Baldwin faced him. He looked much older somehow and very tired and worn, and his eyes had a dull, empty cast.

"It took you a long time to get here."

Ryan watched the cattleman closely, still wary despite the man's unarmed condition and beaten manner. This was too easy; this was not the way he had anticipated Hugh Baldwin would wind things up. "Why, you in a hurry?"

"Not any more," Baldwin said wearily. "It's all down a hole now. You saw the last of a damn' fine spread ride out of here five minutes ago, paid off and heading for new country. The whole works, the ranch, Pike, Reno Davis, and all the rest, are gone, either dead or skipping the country for fear of their necks. I'm the last of Circle X, Ryan."

"Man pays for his mistakes," Ryan said softly. "It's an old rule."

Keeping a narrow gaze upon the cattleman, he was beginning to wonder if the man wasn't really sincere, after all. It looked and it sounded genuine, yet Ryan was not fully convinced.

"Man starts out to do something, to build to the limit. He should get there. But something went wrong, just what I don't know."

"You know, Hugh," Ryan corrected dryly. "Nobody knows it better than you. Every time you stepped on a little man, you knew exactly what was going on. Nobody ever built much on that kind of a foundation. And you know that is a fact, too."

"I suppose so," Baldwin murmured, "but some-times a man gets to moving so fast, he can't see what's going by him. Well, what comes now?"

"We're going into town, like we started to do last night. I want a few things straightened out, including my name. I want that cleared with Meldrum and everybody around here. You're the one man left that can do it."

"Your name cleared?" Baldwin echoed with a half smile. "Since when did you get so touchy about your name? Pike told me all about you, Ryan, that night in the saloon. I know who you are and what you are, and everything about you."

"That was a long time back," Ryan said in a soft voice. "No point in bringing it up in this case. It has nothing to do with it. Leave it in the past."

"You figure maybe the girl won't like it, eh?"

Ryan shrugged. "I hardly think that matters, one way or another. By tomorrow I'll be out of this country."

Baldwin shook his head. "Maybe so, but I've got a little news for you. You'll have to leave without this business of having your name cleared, as you call it. I'm not going back with you, Ryan. I know where I stand and I'm smart enough to know what my chances are when all this gets out. I let you walk in here, Ryan, because that's the way I wanted it. I could have thrown a gun down on you while you were coming up from the spring. I saw you cross and turn and come up the fence and I watched you get off that roan horse. Now, we'll have it out, man to man. I figure I haven't got a show against a man of your kind when it comes to guns, but it will beat a rope and a bunch of gawking sodbusters watching me swing."

Ryan thought for a moment. "If all that's true, why didn't you leave with the others? Why didn't you head north with them?"

"Turn tail and run with them?" Baldwin shook his head as if it had not occurred to him before. "I can't answer that except maybe to say I hadn't thought of it and wouldn't have done it if I had. Maybe this is a little hard for you to understand, but I couldn't do it. Call it pride or bull-headedness or foolishness . . . I don't care which. Whatever it is, it wouldn't let me do it. That make any sense to you?"

Ryan nodded. He knew what it was, that fierce pride that rules a man and will not let him break even when necessary. And Baldwin could never drop down to a level with the men he had worked, driven so arrogantly. "I understand all right, Hugh. But we aren't going to play this your way. I won't draw on you."

"Then you'll be a dead hero. Either I go out of here feet first, or you do. Take your choice."

Ryan stared at Baldwin. The cattleman smiled back. "You think I'm afraid of a bullet . . . of dying?"

"Then why did you run out there at Strickland's?"

Baldwin shrugged. "This will make you laugh, Ryan. And laugh good. But I wanted one more look at my place before I was through. That funny to you?"

"No," Ryan answered quietly, thinking of his own desolated Box K, "it's not funny, Hugh. Not at all."

He moved suddenly across the room, his gun pressing at Baldwin. He flipped the cattleman's weapon into the corner.

A long, gusty sigh passed the man's lips. "Hell, Ryan, it's the only favor I ever asked of a man. Give me back my gun and let me try. Give me that much."

Ryan said curtly: "Forget it, Hugh. It's not my choice to make. Maybe I would welcome the chance to settle with you for Strickland and Frank Sears and a few others. But it can't be handled that way. This goes further than my own personal satisfaction."

From the doorway behind him, Ryan caught the faintest scrape of rough clothing against wood. In that same breath of time a voice barked: "Ryan! We're behind you! Drop that gun!"

He saw the smile break across Baldwin's face and a sly gleam come into his eyes. "By heaven, Marshal, you got here just in time! That was a close one!"

"Raise your hands, Ryan!" Meldrum said. "Watch him, boys."

301

The lawman brushed by Ryan and three or four posse members crowded into the room. The marshal faced Ryan. He pulled the gun from his hand and stuffed it into his waistband. "You give us a hard go of it," he said, "but I knew we'd catch up with you sooner or later."

Ryan said: "You're making a mistake. Baldwin's the man you want."

"Me?" Baldwin shouted. He laughed. "I was about to take you in when you got the drop on me. Never was much good with a gun. He's the slick one, Ross. Keep a sharp watch on him."

Ryan faced the marshal again. "You haven't been by the Strickland place?"

"No," Meldrum replied, "and I don't reckon we'd better, not while you're along. Old George Cobb's riled up enough at you to take you apart with his own hands. I expect he'd organize that crew of his into a necktie party for you if they could lay hold of you. I only got four men left, and we sure couldn't hold that bunch off for long once they made up their minds. Where's your crew, Hugh? Didn't see any of them around when we came in."

"What's not out hunting Ryan are working stock. Been pretty short-handed with all this going on and a man's got to keep his business running."

Ryan shrugged. Meldrum would believe anything Hugh Baldwin told him. He did not know about the fight at the S-Bar, that was why he still thought Ryan was suspect. And Baldwin, seeing his opportunity, was playing it for all it was worth. But he determined to try again.

"Marshal, I tell you this is a mistake. Bring Baldwin into town with me. Don't let him stay here because he sure won't be here when you come back for him. And that's just what you will have to do when you get the straight of what happened last night, and before."

One of the posse members grunted in disgust. "Never did know one of these hardcases that didn't cry like a baby when he got caught. They're all alike. Big and mean until they get caught."

Baldwin said: "Tell you what, Ross. You take him on into town. I've got to wait here until some of the crew shows up so I can tell them the hunt's over and to get back to work. Then I'll ride in. Ryan wants me in town for some reason and I'll be glad to come and tell what I know about him."

"Fair enough," Meldrum said. He turned to Ryan. "All right, let's go."

One of the posse members had found the roan and brought him around to the front. Meldrum motioned Ryan into the saddle, and then tied his hands to the horn. He swung up onto his own bay pony and rode in close. "Hate to shoot that horse," he said, ducking his head at the roan. "But that's the first thing that'll happen if you make any bad moves."

Ryan said: "Marshal, for the last time, you're

making a bad mistake. I was taking Baldwin in when you came up. He's the man you're after and I can prove it if you'll give me a chance. Main thing is not to let him get away before I can do that. Either leave a guard here with him or make him come along now."

"Didn't you hear what he said?" Meldrum asked. "He said he'd be along later, and Baldwin's word is good enough for me. He says he'll do it and he'll do it."

Ryan shrugged. "All right, Ross. We're doing it your way."

They swung out into the yard and took the road for Gunstock. Over his shoulder Ryan saw Hugh Baldwin standing in the doorway of his house. He was smiling.

XX

Ryan rode in tight-lipped silence. Ranged around him were the posse members and Ross Meldrum, forming a half circle. All were grim and haggard from the days and nights of searching, and he knew there was small hope of convincing them of the truth. But with each step he knew Hugh Baldwin was that much closer to escape. That was what the cattleman would do now. Ryan had unwittingly planted the idea and this time the cattleman would not wait. He was still slightly doubtful of Baldwin's story and his explanation,

304

but it was of no importance now; the breaks had been with the cattleman and he would not again fail to use them. It was a long ride into town, and, by the time Meldrum learned the truth, he would be far away and beyond reach.

When they rode off the prairie and dropped into the valley where the river cut its way, Ryan made a final try. They crossed the bridge, and at the turn-off for Strickland's S-Bar he twisted half around in the saddle and said to Meldrum: "Marshal, I'll say this once more. This is a bad mistake and you're making it. Take me to Strickland's and I'll prove everything I've said."

One of the posse men threw him an angry glance. "Aw, quit cryin', Ryan. You're not getting out of this and you can make up your mind to that."

Meldrum only wagged his head stubbornly and rode wearily on.

Ryan said: "We had a showdown at Strickland's last night. Baldwin's crowd and the S-Bar crew. George Cobb was killed along with Reno Davis and several others. You'll get that news when we reach town, I expect. But you can save time by cutting over to Strickland's from here."

"Sounds like it was a reg'lar war," one of the men observed. "How come we didn't hear no shootin'?"

"Why, don't you remember, Dave? There was a storm last night! Lot of thunder and lightnin'. That's how come we didn't hear any of it."

The man's obvious sarcasm brought a grin to Meldrum's face. But all he said was: "Keep going."

The sun was well out when they wheeled into Gunstock's single street. At once a crowd began to gather, forming in small groups that drifted quickly to the jail where Meldrum led his prisoner and guards.

"Stay mounted," he said to Ryan.

Meldrum swung heavily down from his horse. He stepped upon the short, raised porch fronting the building and turned to the murmuring crowd. Two of the posse members followed, taking a stand behind him.

"If you folks are hatching up any ideas, forget them. This man is my prisoner and I aim to keep him one. And alive. Move along now. I don't want trouble from any of you."

Ryan searched the fan of upturned faces for Ann, for any of the Strickland crew. She was not there and he did not recognize any of the others. Apparently none of them had yet come into town.

"Just wastin' good time!" a voice called from the crowd. "We know he shot old Tom and Frank Sears. What's the sense of waitin' for the circuit judge?"

"Sure, everybody knows he done it," another added.

Ryan shifted his gaze to Meldrum. The gathering was in an ugly mood and he could feel the undercurrent of strong resentment throbbing through it. The marshal waited in stony silence. The lines about his mouth were gashed deeply by exhaustion and his eyes reflected their weariness. In a slow, distinct tone he said: "I want every man Jack of you off this street in two minutes. Two minutes! After that, I'll take a scatter-gun and run you off!"

He ducked his head at the posse members standing near him. They wheeled together into the jail and returned a moment later, each carrying a double-barreled shotgun.

Meldrum took one of the weapons and cocked the tall, rabbit-ear hammers. The sound cracked through the hush. He said: "One minute's already gone."

Immediately a low rumble of dissent went up, but the crowd began to break apart. One man, in a far-reaching voice said—"Killer like him ain't entitled to no trial."—but the gathering continued to drift away under the marshal's steady, unrelenting gaze.

Meldrum waited until the street was clear. Then: "All right, Ryan. Get down."

Ryan moved his wrists, reminding the man he was still pinned to the saddle. He was thinking fast, seeking for an opportunity to escape and intercept Baldwin before it was too late. Otherwise, the Cuchillo Plains could forget the cattleman. As far as he was concerned, he would be a free man before too many hours had passed. Ann, backed by the remainder of her crew, would substantiate his story and prove he was guiltless and in the right. Just as soon as she came into town that would happen. But by then Baldwin would be out of reach. Ross Meldrum would be responsible for the error and the posse members would remember how Ryan had tried to persuade them all that they were making a mistake. But it would be too late then.

Somehow Ryan could find no satisfaction in that realization. Men like Baldwin, who instigate trouble for their own advantage, had no right to freedom. They were like wild, roving dogs; if left to run free, they would soon infect the whole country and turn it into a hell for all decent people. And then there was the personal matter of Tom Strickland and Frank Sears. For Ann's sake he wanted Baldwin held accountable for the death of her father. For his own, he wanted him brought to justice for Sears.

"Cut him down, Dave," Meldrum ordered.

The man came off the porch, producing a jack-knife from his pocket. He sliced through the light rope binding Ryan's wrists and stepped quickly back. Ryan swung down. As he came down on his weak leg, it gave away and he went onto the ground in a heap.

"Watch him!" Meldrum barked.

The man called Dave stared at Ryan's bloodstained breeches and the bandage around his leg. "Reckon he's been shot, Ross. Got a lot of blood on him."

"Where'd you get that?" Meldrum demanded at once. "Why didn't you say something about it, Ryan?"

Ryan shrugged. "You didn't give me much chance to say anything."

A buckboard wheeled into the far end of the street and he threw a quick glance that way. But it was not Ann. Meldrum said: "Give Dave a hand there, Ritchie. I'll hold a gun on him while you get him inside."

Behind them, in the street, the two remaining posse members shifted on their horses. "You through with us, Ross?"

Meldrum said: "Reckon so, boys. Go on home and get some sleep. Thanks for the help."

Ryan heard them turn about and trot slowly away. "You cost us all a lot of sleep," Meldrum observed. Then to the deputies: "Come on, come on, get him in a cell. I could sure use a little rest myself."

The two men helped Ryan to a standing position. One on each side, they assisted him into the small cubicle that served the marshal as both jail and office.

"Think I ought to get the doc?" the man addressed as Dave asked when Ryan was settled on the cot.

Meldrum studied Ryan's injured leg for a moment. "Well, maybe you better."

Dave half turned and Ryan, in one swift move, jerked the pistol from the man's holster and came to his feet. He moved off, out of reach, to where he could cover all three men.

Sliding the gun gently back and forth over them he said: "I don't like doing this, Marshal, but I like less the thought of Hugh Baldwin getting away free. Now all of you turn your faces to the wall and keep your hands high."

Meldrum swore under his breath in a steady stream. "I might have known this would happen."

Ryan tossed their guns onto Meldrum's desk, keeping only the one he had taken from Halverson. He slammed the cell door shut and put the keys with the guns.

"I'll be back," he said, "but likely there will be somebody along that will let you out before that."

"Where you headed?" Meldrum demanded.

Ryan gave him a short smile. "So you can follow me if you happened to get turned loose right away. Well, I guess it won't make too much difference in another thirty minutes. I'm going back to the Circle X . . . after Baldwin."

He swung about and walked onto the porch, closing the office door behind him. He climbed aboard the roan, looking neither right nor left, and cut the big roan around to the back of the jail. In this way he avoided the street, using instead the alleyway running behind the business buildings.

He kept the roan at a leisurely trot not wanting to attract attention to his passage. But when he reached the edge of town, he touched the horse with spurs and headed for Baldwin's spread at a long, ground-consuming lope. Only one thing worried him at that moment—was he already too late?

Following earlier precautions, he again came to the ranch from the blind side. Leaving the roan well hidden, and, remembering Baldwin's statement that he had watched him approach before, he came in from the opposite side of the structure. Stopping at the corner of the porch, he listened intently. Someone was inside. Whether it was Baldwin or not, he could not tell; it could be the cook or some other member of the crew collecting his belongings. He could hear the dry rattle of papers and the solid thud of a man walking about the room. Drawing his gun, he crossed the porch and, with one quick motion, jerked back the door.

Hugh Baldwin glanced up, startled. He was in the act of removing something from a lower drawer of his roll-top desk. Surprise flooded across his face. And then a slow, bitter smile cracked his heavy lips. He dropped whatever it was he had been holding and straightened up, keeping his hands open and well away from his sides.

He said: "You weren't gone long, Ryan."

"Not long," Ryan replied dryly. "And this time we'll go back together."

"I don't think so," Baldwin contradicted in the same dry way. "Look behind you, friend."

Ryan shook his head. "You know me better than that, Hugh. Nobody falls for that one."

Baldwin shrugged, the expression on his face having once again changed. "Speak up, Halverson. Tell him how big the barrel of that gun you're pointing at his backbone is."

Halverson! Ryan had forgotten that man. He had dismissed him from his mind after the fight in the shed and, later, he had just assumed he had gone with the others. He must have been in the bunkhouse when he came up. Silently he cursed himself for his own carelessness.

"Drop that gun," Halverson ordered in a level voice. "And step away from it. Be my pleasure to split you down the middle with this Forty-Four."

Ryan kept his eyes on Baldwin's face. If he did as Halverson ordered, he would live—but not for long. They would see to it that he did not remain alive to do any talking. He weighed his chances on a sudden move, studying Baldwin's eyes. He came then to a cool decision. There was small chance of coming through these next few moments, no matter what he did.

Halverson murmured: "All right, Ryan. I'm telling you no more. Get those hands up . . . *without* that gun. Drop it!"

Ryan began to lift his arms, starting first at the elbows. His hands came away from his sides.

"Drop that gun!" Halverson barked in sudden alarm.

In that same fraction of time, Ryan spun away. He remembered this time to throw his weight to his good leg. He fired as he wheeled, ducking and lunging. It was point-blank range at Halverson. The room rocked with the explosion. Smoke boiled to the ceiling and the acrid smell of gunpowder was strong. He saw Halverson stagger back, fall against the door, and go crashing through to the porch. Baldwin was then a blur, leaping for the opposite doorway, the one leading into the rear of the house.

"Hugh!" Ryan yelled his warning.

The cattleman did not pause. He was framed in the doorway when Ryan fired, aiming high. The bullet caught him in the shoulder and slammed him sideways with its force. Baldwin collided with something just inside the wall, a dresser perhaps, or a chest of drawers, and went down with a crash.

Outside, horses were pounding up. A man's voice shouted something, but Ryan paid no heed. He crossed the smoke-filled room warily, gun still in hand, and looked upon the cattleman's sprawled body. Baldwin groaned.

"Get up, Hugh," Ryan said coldly. "You're a lucky man. You could be dead like Halverson."

From the floor Baldwin groaned again. "Better that I was," he said, and pulled to a sitting position.

Ross Meldrum's voice came from the porch, brisk and business-like. "I'll take care of him now, Ryan."

He pushed into the room. Ryan stepped away, seeing Ann Strickland, standing out in the yard, waiting for him. Meldrum knew now; Ann had reached him and given him the story and the facts.

The marshal paused before Ryan. He had Hugh Baldwin on his feet and turned him over to a deputy. To Ryan he said: "Saying I'm sorry don't make for much, I guess. But a man gets off on the wrong track sometimes and it's hard to straighten out. Hope you won't feel too hard about this. I don't want you to hold it against me."

Ryan shrugged. There was short patience in him for any man that relied purely on surface values and never looked beneath the thin veneer all men wear. Too many good men were dead because of that very thing. But, already, this was the past.

He said—"Forget it, Marshal."—and, turning, moved out into the open.

XXI

They rode in silence, Ann Strickland on her little calico pony, Ryan on the roan. Last night's rain was already disappearing under the drying rays of the sun, now a high, burning disc in a field of steel blue. They mounted a long, gentle knoll and, at the top, stopped. Here the trails forked, one for S-Bar, the other for Gunstock and the roads that radiated to the west, the south, or wherever a man was inclined to ride.

He was staring off into the distance, hazy and indeterminate beyond the green-gray of the prairies and his thoughts were far-reaching and lonely.

She said then: "What will you do now?"

He did not turn his attention to her. "Anybody's guess. Another town, another place, I suppose. There'll be no more ranching. It's not for me. I know that now."

"Why not? You were doing fine. Why do you want to throw it all away now?"

"Because there's nothing left here for me, Ann. I came into this country to settle down and forget the last five years of my life. In six months I am back where I started from." Abruptly he swung to her. "Even you reminded me of that."

"I know," she replied in a miserable voice. "I don't need you to remind me of it. It's something I won't soon forget."

He stirred in the saddle, solemn-faced and serious. "It's nothing now for you to remember. Truth is truth, no matter who it hurts. But it is a thing I had hoped to forget. I wanted that time to end when I lived by a gun, actually made my living with a gun. Ann, do you know what a bounty man is? He is a gunman that goes after the outlaws other law officers leave alone. He goes after them for the reward their capture will bring. And he brings them in, dead or alive. I came here to forget that. I thought I could and I was on my way to that when Hugh Baldwin drew me into this trouble. I found then it is not possible for a man like me to become like any other."

The roan had moved slightly ahead of the pony, cropping at the sweet grass. Ann urged the calico forward until she was again next to him and could look into Ryan's set face. "And you think running away is the answer? That going to another town, even another world, will make it possible for you to forget your past?"

"It helps," he said.

"But that's all, and then for only a little while. The past is something none of us can escape, Jim. There's nothing any of us can do about it. It's not something we can just break off and throw away like the dead branch of a tree. You have to live with it, day by day, let it grow older until it isn't important any more."

He considered that for a long time, his gaze far off and deeply thoughtful. He said finally: "I never thought of it that way but I guess that's the way it could be. A man should live down the things he wants to forget. I guess that's the only real answer."

"And others forget sooner than you think."

He turned to her then, seeing her there beside him, so close, so desirable. "And you? Would you remember?"

"I would remember the good things," she replied at once, "and think of what could be ahead for us."

He smiled. She was blushing for her own boldness. He reached over and laid his broad hand on her own. "It will always be the good things for us," he said.

Center Point Publishing
600 Brooks Road ● PO Box 1
Thorndike ME 04986-0001 USA

(207) 568-3717

US & Canada:
1 800 929-9108
www.centerpointlargeprint.com